HAWKWIND

A Visual Biography

Martin Popoff

HAWKWIND

A Visual Biography

Martin Popoff

WP
WYMER
PUBLISHING
Bedford, England

First published in Great Britain in 2021
by Wymer Publishing
www.wymerpublishing.co.uk
Tel: 01234 326691
Wymer Publishing is a trading name of Wymer (UK) Ltd

ISBN: 978-1-915246-34-9

Design by Andy Bishop / Tusseheia Creative.
Printed in the UK.

A catalogue record for this book is available from the British Library.

HAWKWIND
A Visual Biography
Martin
Popoff

ROLL OF HONOUR

Wymer Publishing duly acknowledges the following people who all put their faith in this publication by pre-ordering it:

Dave Barber
Steve Barlow
Bill Bass
Tommy Blikeng
David Board
Christopher Bunnell
David Burrows
Jill Chambers
Mike Dando
Martin Douglas
Drakrats
Mark Edwards
Howard Gilbert
Vitaly Gorbash
Stuart Graham
Douglas Hext
Gerald Hughes
Alison James-Reynolds
Mark Jones
Krusher Joule
Grahame Keeping
David Kennard
David Malone
Nick McCulloch
Frank Mikos
Tim Neighbour
Simon Nixon
Ian Quick
Andrea Reaves
Mark Roberts
Phil Roe
Simon Rowley
Axel Seaton
Robert Shave
Darren Soutart
Mike Tone
Judith Walker
Aled Williams
Ian Yelton

CONTENTS

INTRODUCTION

Welcome one and all to what I hope you will agree is a psychedelic and action-packed celebration of all things Hawkwind, proudly British of pedigree, hippie free festival and anarchic in spirit, Krautrock across the aural ingredients and space-inclined by gradient.

It's hazy, but thinking back, I'm pretty sure that the first Hawkwind album I ever got was a used copy of *Space Ritual* obtained in around 1975—so I'm 12—at either Strawberry Jams or The Magic Mushroom, on one of the regular family trips to Spokane, Washington, two hours north from home over the border up into Trail, BC. I remember upon unfolding that thing that my first impression had nothing to do with the aesthetic. Rather, I thought this must've been expensive, and these guys must be important.

From that point forward it was the gradual acquisition of the previous records, usually the US issues with the thick cardboard and the odd Canadian version, and then into the early '80s, UK versions of those RCA records (the thinnest of cardboard) mixed in with all the New Wave of British Heavy Metal I was buying, usually along with a couple issues of Sounds. Eventually it was CDs and even later, once I got into the business of writing for magazines, websites, and working on rock documentaries, interviewing the guys.

Although I was into myriad bands and styles of music along the way, Hawkwind was always a constant along their own rocky path, not veering far from the original mandate all that often despite constant rock journalist narratives struggling to define unique characteristics of the latest Hawkwind album at hand versus the last one or two or three. That's one notion that I hope I can dispel over the small amount of writing included in this book, because every Hawkwind album contains a mix of the half dozen or so ingredients that make this band a singular experience unlike any other in the rock canon.

It's probably more than a half-dozen, but here's a crude checklist for survival in the silver machine that I think you can count on sustaining life until arriving at your next destination, meaning, of course, the next Hawkwind studio album.

First, look for headbanging hard rock, but single-minded of purpose, clanging along punk-like, chord changes at the minimum, buzzy bass. Next, there are lyrics that are either infinitely expansive and star-shone or microscopically internal and meditative, dark of void, and little in between. These drug-tripped mystic words might be delivered smoothly over a polite prog toward a Canterbury place, maniacally with bullhorn in a shock beat poetry session over alarm tones, or somewhere in the middle, with Dave, Robert and later folks too evoking Roger Waters—or if not Roger Waters, more like a mad flying doctor, Professor Trips explaining what was seen on the other side of his brain.

Then there are the electronics, left alone without rhythm sections, sound collages as it were, or massaged into proper songs with words. Or we might get a full-band instrumental workout, serving as a launch pad for a trip on which the reefer or the LSD or just the brainwaves left naturally humming get to write the script of the bridge, at the bridge. Synthesizers or keyboards don't begin to describe what Hawkwind did, with various noiseniks in the band harnessing and spraying electricity in new ways, each record, including the live ones, becoming a clinic on electronic music, but rarely concentrated on as such because there was always so much else going on. Because of the pioneering work done early on in the lab, later we get dance, trance, techno and industrial, signposted most dependably by electronic drums. Or, take the drums out, and ergo there goes Hawkwind making new age music.

Now head back to 1977 and 1978 and Hawkwind are participating in a post-punk realm, nudging up alongside XTC, Wire, Devo and Pere Ubu. Back up a year and outside of Hawkwind, punk proper rages. One of the cool things from that era is that Hawkwind, given their various outlaw tendencies, were considered a band that established the (un-writeable by definition) punk manifesto as much as MC5, the Stooges and the New York Dolls did. It was almost as if Hawkwind amassed their own tight fist of punk classics by 1973 or 1974, so by the time we get to *Astounding Sounds, Amazing Music*, they didn't need to say anything further and thus did not participate.

Nor did they really participate in the New Wave of British Heavy Metal. That too is a myth that needs dispelling. To be sure, some of those records feature more distortion pedal than others, but really, Hawkwind records exist within a pretty tight range of parameters, whilst enjoying immense freedom within those parameters, because of the many tools in the toolbox at their disposal.

The records we got across the mid-'90s through to the present day offer a somewhat unexpected manna from Hawk heaven, but again, they tended to check all the boxes, for good or bad, but usually with the best and clearest and most hi-fidelity productions the band had ever dared—with planning and performance to boot. Were the guys at times too responsible? Count this fan emphatically saying no, the more expensive-sounding the better, rejecting the many phoned-in things along the way, which usually, fortunately, filled up compilations, side-projects, scrubby EPs and served as bonus tracks, the latter often making a mess of a good thing.

Now, concerning the mechanics of this book, first, at the word end, what you're about to experience is a specific structure you've seen before if you've gotten any of the previous Wymer visual histories or biographies that I've constructed. This one most closely resembles the Blue Öyster Cult, the Thin Lizzy and the Van Halen, which established what we thought would be a tradition, an extensive timeline and nothing else, other than a blanket introduction along with introductions and opening band quotes by decade. Later books in the series went a couple of different ways, but there's a sense of satisfaction getting back to the core mandate of the early books.

Why I think this works particularly well here is the complicated nature of Hawkwind's release history, along with the myriad side-projects, with many of those frustratingly and even annoyingly blending into the definition of official product. For the story of Hawkwind narratively, look elsewhere. But for the story, at least to this point in time, with respect to factoid upon factoid, well, look no further.

But while you're reading along, or quite likely using this tome as a reference book over time, referring to it again and again when a refresher is needed concerning order of events, the foremost purpose of this book is to deliver pretty pictures. Like it says on the tin, this is a visual biography, the story of the band in dramatic and ethereal pictures, Hawkwind's legendary works of graphic design bestowed upon them by Barney Bubbles and others coming to life on every page, interspersed with kaleidoscopic shots of the guys themselves.

If one brain-side of this book doesn't float your boat, then the hope is that at least the other one will. But judging by the complexity and studiousness of Hawkwind fans, there's an appreciation of both the scholarly and the artistic amongst the Brock flock, and so we're confident that *Hawkwind: A Visual Biography* will find a purposeful place on your bulging Hawkshelf for years to come. And with that, supplies at the ready, let's climb aboard and make our escape from this planet gone to crap.

Martin Popoff
martinp@inforamp.net; martinpopoff.com

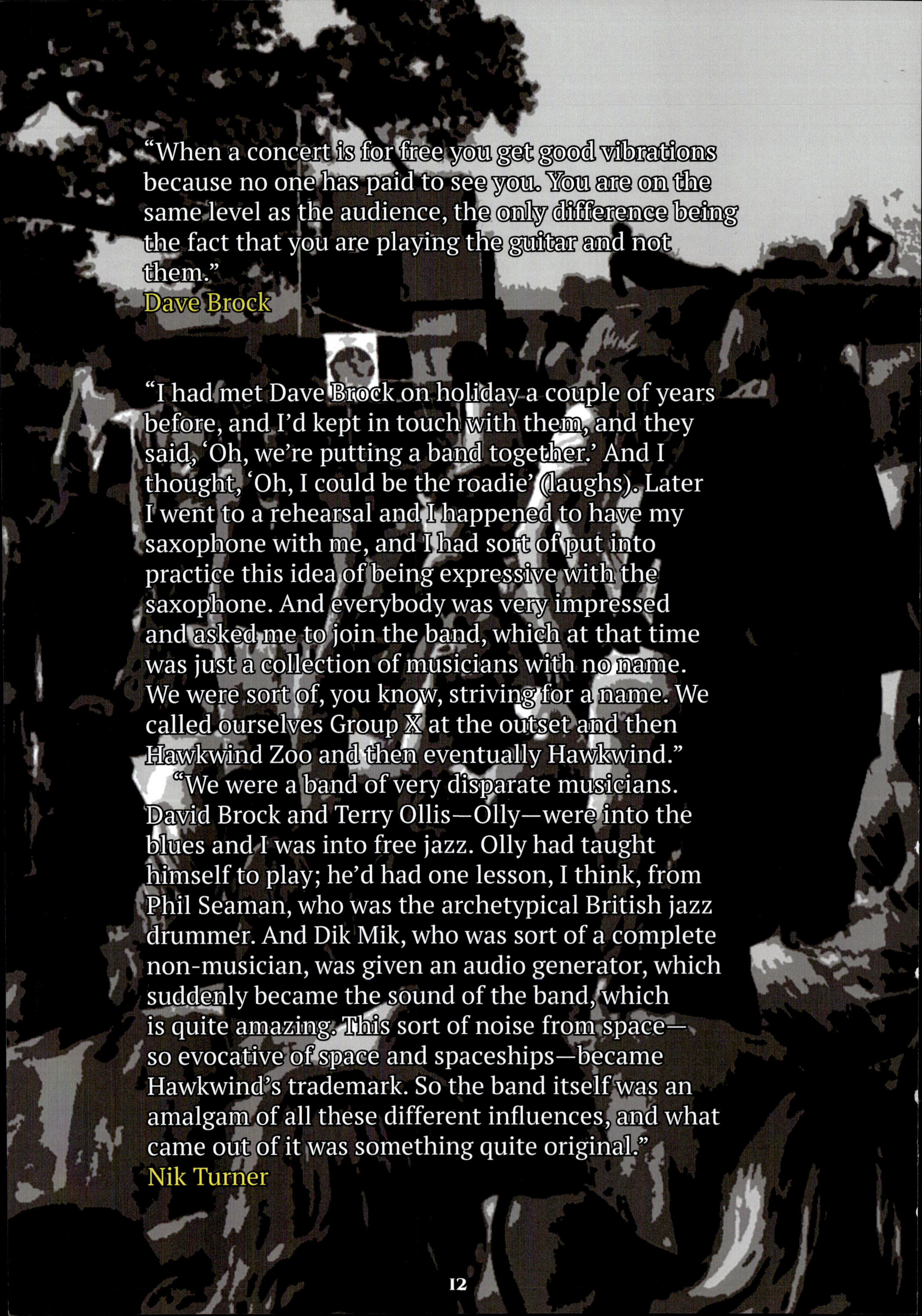

"When a concert is for free you get good vibrations because no one has paid to see you. You are on the same level as the audience, the only difference being the fact that you are playing the guitar and not them."
Dave Brock

"I had met Dave Brock on holiday a couple of years before, and I'd kept in touch with them, and they said, 'Oh, we're putting a band together.' And I thought, 'Oh, I could be the roadie' (laughs). Later I went to a rehearsal and I happened to have my saxophone with me, and I had sort of put into practice this idea of being expressive with the saxophone. And everybody was very impressed and asked me to join the band, which at that time was just a collection of musicians with no name. We were sort of, you know, striving for a name. We called ourselves Group X at the outset and then Hawkwind Zoo and then eventually Hawkwind."

"We were a band of very disparate musicians. David Brock and Terry Ollis—Olly—were into the blues and I was into free jazz. Olly had taught himself to play; he'd had one lesson, I think, from Phil Seaman, who was the archetypical British jazz drummer. And Dik Mik, who was sort of a complete non-musician, was given an audio generator, which suddenly became the sound of the band, which is quite amazing. This sort of noise from space—so evocative of space and spaceships—became Hawkwind's trademark. So the band itself was an amalgam of all these different influences, and what came out of it was something quite original."
Nik Turner

ORIGINS THROUGH 1969

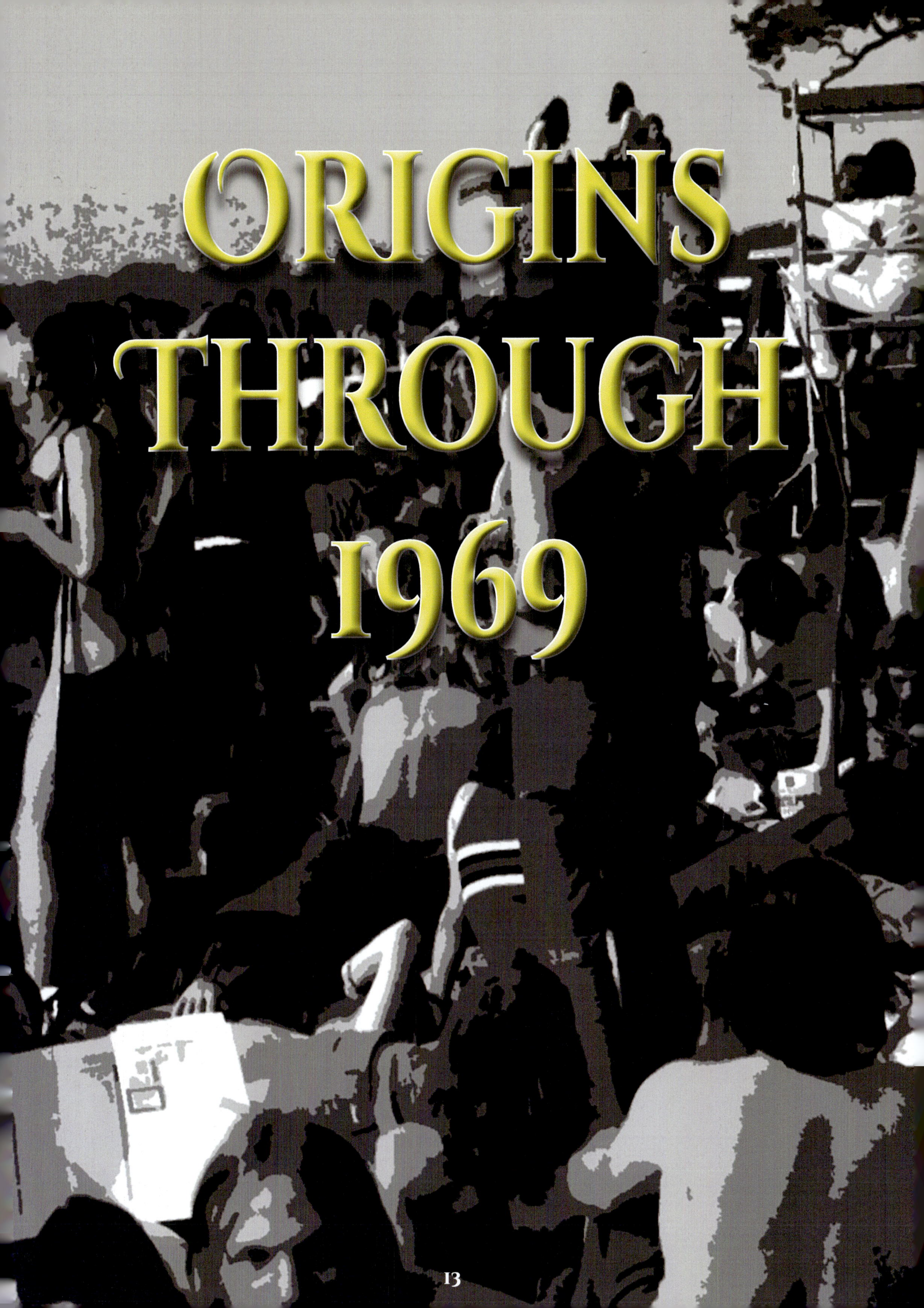

There's not much to talk about in terms of the history of Hawkwind in the '60s, given that essentially all the relevant bits happen in the latter half of 1969 with the band being birthed proper in 1970.

What is interesting, however, is how little psychedelia exists in the collective pedigree of the ragtag players that would bump into each other on a random visit to the Hawkwind Zoo. It's almost as if this particular breed of hippie time-travelled from a generation earlier, from busking, from the blues boom, from folk music, even from the pop from three or four years before, but not so much from the vaunted London psychedelic rock scene led by Pink Floyd and Soft Machine. As for beat jazz and beat poetry, well, that parachutes in even more jaggedly. Brock, Turner and Calvert were all reading Kerouac before Hawkwind ever happened, but it was only Robert who ever actually fancied himself a beat poet.

Perhaps as a metaphor for such time-travel, there's even international travel, in the case of perennial anchor to the band, Dave Brock, who seems to arrive in Hawkwind back home in the UK as an old soul, already having traversed the ages and reconsidered capitalism and its relationship to society and the arts. In any event, all of this conspires around Notting Hill, and something called space rock emerges from this disparate meeting of the minds, necessarily through multimedia dimensions when one of the minds that meets is that of Barney Bubbles.

But, more conventional, first of all, is manager Doug Smith, and talk about a calming presence, a man with all too many stories to tell (who prefers these days to garden), and most of those stories having to do with Motörhead, not Hawkwind. It is Doug who piggybacks a record deal for Hawkwind on one for Cochise, during, I must say, this intensely creativity-friendly era in the music business in which Olav Wyper and Vertigo Records had carte blanche and where every one of the big progressive rock bands was rapidly being birthed at exactly the same time. Should we count Hawkwind as one of those? It's the perennial debate, although generally Dave Brock and Co. are considered too low rent to participate, too punk, not that anybody knew what punk meant yet.

I guess, really, to address what was happening to these macro trends in 1969, psychedelic rock, in conjunction with the British blues boom, was evolving into progressive rock and heavy metal—that's the major narrative. What is less discussed is that out of what came before we got something called space rock, which, ironically, was a tiny and lonely corner of the universe practised by exactly one band—forget UFO—called Hawkwind.

1875. Edvard Grieg composes "In the Hall of the Mountain King," which Hawkwind will tap as inspiration for the title of what is arguably considered their greatest album. At least that's what Lemmy thought.

February 1899. French symbolist and pataphysicist Alfred Jarry writes an essay called *How to Construct a Time Machine*, which inspires the lyrics to Hawkwind's "Silver Machine." Jarry's most famed creation is the character Pere Ubu. Cleveland's Pere Ubu are essentially an industrial post-punk version of Hawkwind. Jarry's second most famed creation is the science of pataphysics. One might call *Space Ritual* a pataphysical treatise.

September 29, 1918. The premiere of Gustav Holst's "The Planets," which includes "Mars the Bringer of War," reinterpreted on 1977 Hawkwind instrumental "The Iron Dream."

1925. Alfred North Whitehead, in *Science and the Modern World*, states that "It is the business of the future to be dangerous, and it is among the merits of science that it equips the future for its duties."

1927. Herman Hesse sees publication of *Der Steppenwolf*, which inspires Robert Calvert's lyric for Hawkwind song (and live staple) "Steppenwolf."

December 18, 1939. Michael John Moorcock, part-time Hawkwind lyricist and declaimer thereof, is born, in London.

August 26, 1940. Early days Hawkwind saxophonist, vocalist and percussionist Nicholas Robert "Nik" Turner is born, in Oxford, England.

August 20, 1941. Hawkwind anchor, mainstay and patriarch David Anthony Brock is born, Isleworth, Middlesex, England.

May 28, 1942. Original Hawkwind bassist John A. Harrison is born.

June 24, 1942. The God of Hellfire, Arthur Brown, is born, in Whitby, England.

July 30, 1942. Colin "Barney Bubbles" Fulcher is born, in Whitton, Middlesex, England. Bubbles would be instrumental in crafting Hawkwind's celebrated early album cover images, later moving on to greater fame with his design work for punk and new wave bands.

1944. Original Hawkwind noise terrorist Richard Michael "Dik Mik" Davis is born, in Richmond, Surrey, England.

March 9, 1945. Robert Newton Calvert is born, in Pretoria, South Africa, with the Calverts moving to the UK when the future Hawkwind lyricist and lead vocalist was two years of age.

December 24, 1945. Ian Kilmister, better known as Lemmy, Hawkwind bassist and vocalist is born, in Burslem, Stoke-on-Trent, England.

January 2, 1947. Adrian Shaw, briefly Hawkwind's bassist, is born, in Hampstead, North London.

April 20, 1947. Future synthesizer and keyboardist for Hawkwind Del Dettmar is born, in Thornton Heath, Surrey, England.

June 14, 1947. Short-lived Hawkwind guitarist and Robert Calvert collaborator Paul Rudolph is born, in Vancouver, BC.

September 28, 1948. Keyboardist Simon House is born, in Nottingham, England, the milestone commemorated in the track "Spiral Galaxy 28948" from *Warrior on the Edge of Time.*

1949. Mid-'70s Hawkwind drummer Alan Powell is born, in Manchester, Lancashire.

September 24, 1949. Long-serving Hawkwind bassist Harvey Frederick Bainbridge is born, in Dorset, England.

August 12, 1950. Drummer Simon King is born, in Oxford, England.

November 6, 1950. Future Hawkwind keyboardist Keith Hale is born, in Hull, Yorkshire.

December 2, 1950. Isaac Asimov sees publication of his landmark sci-fi novel *I, Robot,* partly the inspiration for Hawkwind song "Robot," which references the "Three Laws of Robotics."

February 6, 1951. Richard Hugh "Huw" Lloyd-Langton is born, in Harlesden, London.

February 6, 1952. Keyboardist, Theremin player and "virtual lead guitarist" Timothy Blake is born, in Shepherd's Bush, London.

April 11, 1952. Original Hawkwind drummer Terry Ollis is born, in London.

November 21, 1952. Future Hawklords keyboardist Steve Swindells is born, in Ipswich, Suffolk, England.

December 26, 1952. Hawkwind dancer Stacia Blake is born, in Ireland.

1953. Dave's uncle gives him a banjo.

1953. Nik Turner's family moves to Kent, where Nik befriends Robert Calvert.

October 19, 1953. Ray Bradbury sees publication of his landmark sci-fi novel *Fahrenheit 451*. Hawkwind will include a song in homage, and with that title, on their 1982 album *Choose Your Masques*. The Hawkwind song makes use of lyrics by Robert Calvert left over from 1978.

1957. After high school, Robert Calvert joins the Air Training Corps becoming a corporal.

January 30, 1957. Future long-time Hawkwind drummer Richard Chadwick is born, in Bromley, Kent.

1959. Dave leaves school and works in metal fabrication and at an animation company, both suitable training grounds for the career that was to come. Soon he is playing low-key gigs as well as busking.

1961. Future Hawkwind collaborator Michael Moorcock sees publication of his first of a series of works on Elric of Melniboné. Hawkwind 1985 album *The Chronicle of the Black Sword* is essentially an Elric-based concept album.

February 25, 1962. Hawkwind vocalist from 1989 to 1991, Bridget Wishart is born, in Plymouth, Devon, England.

April 8, 1963. Future Hawkwind and second generation Hawklords front man Ron Tree is born, in Leeds, England.

September 11, 1963. Alan Davey is born, in Ipswich, Suffolk, England.

1964. Michael Moorcock becomes editor of sci-fi magazine New Worlds, established in 1936. Soon Robert Calvert and Moorcock would form a friendship and become collaborators, both writing for White Trash, published by Mick Farren for the White Panthers.

August 4, 1964. Jonathan "Mr. Dibs" Darbyshire is born.

1965 – 1991. Sci-fi writer Philip José Farmer writes the seven novels referred to as the *World of Tiers* series. Hawkwind would include a song called that on their 1980 album *Levitation*, in homage.

October 1966. Legendary underground magazine International Times opens for business. Soon Friends (later Frendz) will follow, with Hawkwind becoming regulars at the office. At this point, Dave was moving on from The Dharma Blues Band.

1967. Dr. West's Medicine Show and Junk Band issue as a single "The Eggplant That Ate Chicago." The song would inspire 1976 Hawkwind composition "The Aubergine That Ate Rangoon." Meanwhile Robert Calvert is performing street theatre with his troupe, Street Dada Nihilismus.

1967. Doubleday publishes a science fiction novel by Roger Zelazny called *Lord of Light*, which inspires the Hawkwind song of the same name found on *Doremi Fasol Latido*.

Mid-1967. Dave is in a band that lasts less than a year called The Famous Cure. At this point, after the departure of Pete Judd, the band consists of Dave, John Illingworth and second future Hawkwind member Mick Slattery.

Late 1967. With The Famous Cure knocked on its head, Dave returns from gigging in Holland and continues busking. The band had been offered a management and recording contract in March of 1968 by Pat Meehan of Pavion Ltd., who had been booking dates for them but they never signed it. The band at the end consisted of Slattery, Brock, Illingworth, Edward Page and Peter Fairs.

1968. Opal Butterfly issue "Beautiful Beige"/"Speak Up," the first of the act's three singles. In the band is Simon King, and at the end of their run, Lemmy.

June 1968. Dave, as part of The Dharma Blues Band, appears on *Blues Anytime Vol. 2*, doing covers of "Dealing with the Devil" and "Roll 'em Pete." According to Dave, the sessions were recorded in 1966, the year he left the band.

June 24, 1968. Hawkwind bassist from 2008 to 2017 and 2018 to the present, Niall Hone, is born, in England.

1969. Ace Books publishes a Michael Moorcock novel called *The Black Corridor*. In 1973, Bob Calvert would be featured on the *Space Ritual* album reciting a poem of the same name written by Moorcock. The theme of the book, essentially an escape into space from a world that has descended into anarchy and decay, percolates through many of Hawkwind's lyrics, whether originating with Moorcock or not, most specifically on *In Search of Space*, *Doremi Fasol Latido* and the new songs on *Space Ritual*.

1969. Skin Alley issue a self-titled debut, followed by *To Pagham & Beyond* in 1970. Co-founder Thomas Crimble, soon to be part of Hawkwind, is the band's bassist, also providing backing vocals.

1969. Putnam publishes a sci-fi novel by Roger Zelazny called *Damnation Alley*, which inspired the track of the same name on Hawkwind's *Quark, Strangeness and Charm* album from 1977.

January 1969. Sam Gopal issue their one and only album, *Escalator*. Lemmy, credited as Ian (Lemmy) Willis, is the band's lead vocalist and co-guitarist.

April – May 1969. Dave is part of the Buskers tour of the UK, on which the performers travel from gig to gig in a classic red double-decker bus.

July 1969. Hawkwind forms, when Dave and Mick are joined by bassist John A. Harrison. Next to the fold are drummer Terry Ollis, Nik Turner and Dik Mik.

August 29, 1969. A performance at the All Saints Hall in Notting Hill on this date is considered to be the first Hawkwind show, albeit still under the Group X moniker. Local shows continue through the end of the year.

October 1969. Dave appears on a compilation album issued by Columbia called *The Buskers*, doing "Bring It on Home."

October 1969. On the strength of a demo recorded as Hawkwind Zoo, the band, with the help of manager Doug Smith, secure a record deal with Liberty Records (Hawkwind are included as part of a wider agreement Smith had been putting together for the band Cochise). John Peel suggests to Smith that the band should drop the word "Zoo" from their name, calling it "too Haight-Ashbury." Guitarist Mick Slattery is replaced by Huw Lloyd-Langton. Brock knew Langton as a fellow busker as well as a clerk in a music store.

October 1969. High Tide issue their *Sea Shanties* album, uncommonly heavy and even Hawkwind-like for its day. On pioneering rock violin is future Hawkwind member Simon House.

November 1969. Quintessence issue their debut record, *In Blissful Company*. It is the first of hundreds of record sleeve designs by Barney Bubbles, soon to make his mark as serial Hawkwind jacket designer.

December 4, 1969. A show on this date at the Country Club is considered by Hawkwind expert Robert Godwin to be the band's first show ever as Hawkwind. Godwin adds that for their gig on November 28th, they were definitely still called Hawkwind Zoo.

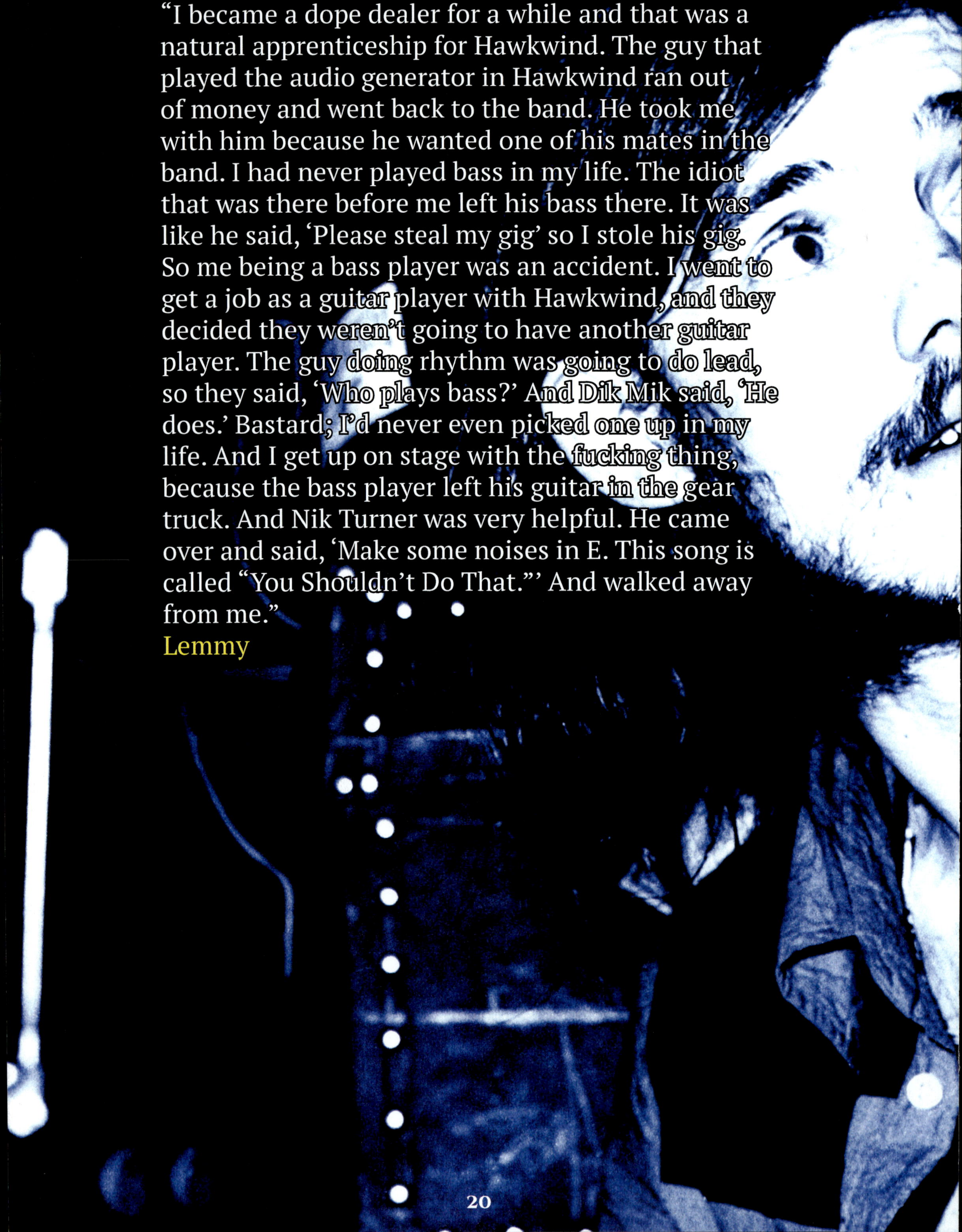

"I became a dope dealer for a while and that was a natural apprenticeship for Hawkwind. The guy that played the audio generator in Hawkwind ran out of money and went back to the band. He took me with him because he wanted one of his mates in the band. I had never played bass in my life. The idiot that was there before me left his bass there. It was like he said, 'Please steal my gig' so I stole his gig. So me being a bass player was an accident. I went to get a job as a guitar player with Hawkwind, and they decided they weren't going to have another guitar player. The guy doing rhythm was going to do lead, so they said, 'Who plays bass?' And Dik Mik said, 'He does.' Bastard; I'd never even picked one up in my life. And I get up on stage with the fucking thing, because the bass player left his guitar in the gear truck. And Nik Turner was very helpful. He came over and said, 'Make some noises in E. This song is called "You Shouldn't Do That."' And walked away from me."
Lemmy

THE 1970s

VICTIM OF SONIC ATTACK!
We flew Hawkwind poster boy, little Johnny Kaye, all the way from Los Angeles, California to London, England so he could witness a Hawkwind Space Ritual performance firsthand.
The results were positive: Permanent Brain Damage.
Now we're flying Hawkwind all the way from London, England to the U.S.A., to perform their incredible Space Ritual for you.
Be like little Johnny Kaye: A little mixed up, feeling fine.
Brain damage to go: HAWKWIND'S: A SPACE RITUAL
On United Artists Records and Tapes
UA-LA 120-H2
Hawkwind

Hell, half of the milestone moments in Hawkwind history are hard-pressed into the ten years that comprise the '70s. I'm going to try leave that story to be told through the timeline entries to follow, but the point of these decade introductions is to give you the macro story, to generalize, to slot things into compartments.

The debut album stands alone, for its plainer singing, its nods to the blues boom and its conventional production on sort of half the record, set against a very whacky other half. In essence, the Lemmy years arrive before he even gets there, on *In Search of Space*. The key records that establish Hawkwind's often annoying combination an' confluence of sounds—hard rock clashing with electronics, made worse through simplicity and the repetitive celebration thereof—begins right here with the second album, continuing drone-like through the third. It then gets blown all out of proportion with the double live *Space Ritual* album, Hawkwind's *Made in Japan* with better, less brown packaging.

This establishment of Hawkwind as outlaws, of outsiders breaking the laws of electricity both visual and aural, then continues through the two albums widely considered the band's classics, namely *In Search of Space* and *Doremi Fasol Latido*. Recap: that's two eras covered early: the outlier self-titled debut and the trademark United Artist years.

Astounding Sounds, Amazing Music stands alone, as the arty, easy-on-the-ears version of what came before, although there's more than a little eccentric Amon Düül II Krautrock to the proceedings. This record marks the emergence of Robert Calvert as creative force. As well, Lemmy has been fired for his lack of skill in not getting arrested, replaced by Paul Rudolph. New management too. This record arrives in 1976 as part of the band's new deal with Charisma, although the Charisma era doesn't really start until *Quark, Strangeness and Charm*, rolling on through the exquisite and under-rated *25 Years On* album (credited to Hawklords), en route to the troubling *PXR5*. If you recall, we imagined (Moorcock-style) Hawkwind as time-travellers. Well, *PXR5* and *25 Years On* indeed result from an acrobatic bending of time, representing the return of the Lord of Kaos to the Hawkwind saga, never again to be satisfied in his hunger for human (and alien) drama.

Is it sacrilege to reveal that the author's favourite couple of years of Hawk history are 1977 and 1978? Because it's true: there's Robert Calvert, manic, there are melodies, there's production and there's a recognition that punk has ceded to post-punk, although I really can't imagine these guys had their ears to the ground enough to make those assessments. Nik Turner sure did, because the *Pass Out* album from Inner City Unit in 1980 is as canny and deft a post-punk album as there ever was. Whatever the wokeness across both parties (later to become warring fiefdoms), I'm super-happy for the style of music everybody was making as the '70s came to a close.

Robert Calvert attacking his demons.

Promotional poster

June 1970 saw the Bath Festival of Blues and Progressive Music. The festival attracted 150,000 and included Pink Floyd and Led Zeppelin. An 'alternative festival' was staged in an adjoining field where the Pink Fairies and Hawkwind played on the back of a flatbed truck.

© Odíle Noël (Lebrecht Music & Arts / Alamy Stock Photo)

1970

January 1970. The band play a few shows this month and indeed every month, all through 1970, up and down the UK.

March – April 1970. Hawkwind work at Trident Studios in London, on tracks slated for their first album. Producer on the project is Pretty Things guitarist Dick Taylor, who also provides some guitar tracks on the record. Dave credits Taylor for bringing useful studio techniques to the sessions, such as double-tracked 12-string guitars.

April 1970. Krautrock legends Amon Düül II issue their second album, *Yeti*. It is also the second and last before bassist Dave Anderson departs for Hawkwind.

June 27 – 29, 1970. Hawkwind play outside the Bath Festival, making the acquaintance of the similarly anarchy-minded Pink Fairies, with whom they form a collaboration called Pinkwind. Most associated with the free festival scene are the likes of Hawkwind, Pink Fairies, Edgar Broughton Band, The Deviants, Skin Alley and, to a lesser extent, Brinsley Schwarz and Man.

July 1970. High Tide, featuring Simon House, issue a second album, self-titled, on Liberty. It is their last before a reunion in 1989.

August 1, 1970. "Hurry on Sundown," in edit form, is issued as a single from the first Hawkwind album, backed with "Mirror of Illusion."

August 14, 1970. Hawkwind issue their self-titled debut album, on Liberty, in gatefold sleeve. This is guitarist Huw Lloyd-Langton's only record with the band until his return for *Live Seventy Nine*. Bassist John A. Harrison leaves shortly after the recording of the album.

August 18, 1970. The band record a version of their "Hurry on Sundown" single at Maida Vale Studios as a John Peel session, which airs a month later.

1970 Isle of Wight festival.

August 26 – 31, 1970. Hawkwind continue to establish themselves as counterculture heroes, driven by the ideals of leader Dave Brock, by playing for free outside the Isle of Wight festival in protest at the cost of tickets.

September 1970. Guitarist Huw Lloyd-Langton leaves the band (due to a nervous breakdown after a bad acid trip at the Isle of Wight festival), while bassist John Harrison is replaced by Thomas Crimble, who had played with the band at Isle of Wight. The first show without Huw is at the Lyceum in London, September 6th.

1971

1971. *Hawkwind* sees belated issue in the US, on United Artists.

1971. Walker and Company publish Roger Zelazny's *Jack of Shadows* which will inspire the Hawkwind track of the same name on 1979's *PXR5* album.

May 1971. Amon Düül II's Dave Anderson replaces Thomas Crimble, who after eight months with Hawkwind, goes on to become a key member of the Glastonbury Festival staff from 1971 through 1999. Also at this time, sound man and road manager Del Dettmar replaces Dik Mik, who is sidelined by a serious traffic accident. Dik Mik subsequently rejoins four months later.

June 1971. Dancer Stacia joins the Hawkwind collective.

June 1 – June 6, 1971. The band play their first dates outside the UK, in Germany.

June 20 – 24, 1971. Hawkwind play the second Glastonbury Festival. This iteration was known as the Glastonbury Fair, the follow-up to the first fest on the site, called The Pilton Pop, Blues & Folk Festival. Organizer and ex-band member Crimble sits in with the band.

September 1971. Ian "Lemmy" Kilmister replaces Dave Anderson.

October 8, 1971. Hawkwind issue their second album, *In Search of Space*, on United Artists. The album, recorded at Olympic, with George Chkiantz producing, reaches No. 18 on the British charts and certifies gold in the UK. This is the only album featuring Dave Anderson on bass.

Promotional poster

1972, Stacia, Nik Turner, Lemmy, Del Dettmar, Dik Mik, Simon King, Dave Brock.

1972

February 1972. Robert Calvert joins Hawkwind, after a spell as "resident poet." Calvert had performed with the band as early as October 1971.

April 28, 1972. United Artists issues a multi-artist live album called *Greasy Truckers Party*, commemorating a show at the Roundhouse in London, on February 13, 1972. Hawkwind gets all of side four, performing "Master of the Universe" and "Born to Go." *Greasy Truckers Party* represents Simon King's second gig as sole drummer for Hawkwind, third overall. The band are also represented (with one track, a medley, "Silver Machine"/"Welcome to the Future" from the same show) on the triple-LP *Glastonbury Fayre* album, also issued this month, with deluxe design by Barney Bubbles.

May 19 – 24, 1972. The band conduct their second European tour.

June 9, 1972. "Silver Machine" backed with "Seven by Seven" is issued as a single, rising to No. 3 on the UK charts.

July 13, 1972. The band make their first TV appearance on BBC music show Top of the Pops, with the "Silver Machine" single more or less synched to film shot at Dunstable's Queensway Hall.

September 1972. Avon Books publishes a Hitler-based alternate history/sci-fi novel by Norman Spinrad called *The Iron Dream*. The Hawkwind song of the same name on *Quark, Strangeness and Charm* is an instrumental homage to the book.

September – October 1972. The band work at a crude early version of Rockfield Studios in Wales on tracks slated for their next album, with Dave Brock and Del Dettmar handling the production duties.

September 9 – 13, 1972. Amidst recording and the usual UK dates, the band gets to mainland Europe once again, for four shows, adding another four October 28th through November 1st.

September 28, 1972. Hawkwind's show at The Paris Theatre, London, is recorded for BBC Radio 1. The recording, featuring Stacia's only recorded appearance on its introductory countdown, will be issued officially on a number of occasions beginning in 1991.

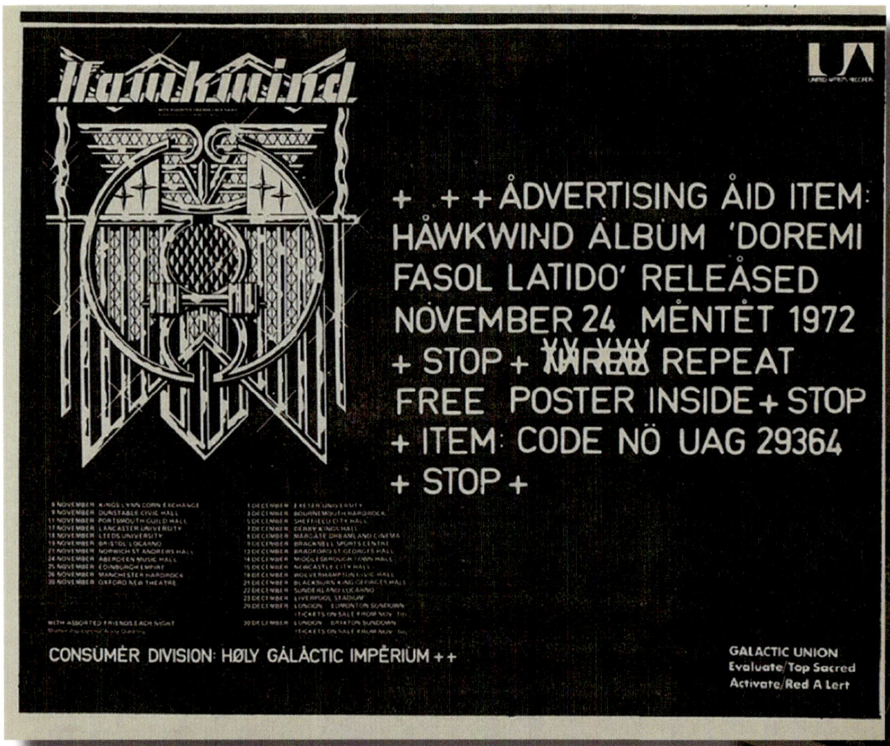
Hawkwind
+ + + ÅDVERTISING ÅID ITEM: HÅWKWIND ÅLBÜM 'DOREMI FASOL LATIDO' RELEÅSED NOVEMBER 24 MËNTËT 1972 + STOP + REPEAT FREE POSTER INSIDE + STOP + ITEM: CODE NÖ UAG 29364 + STOP +
CONSÜMËR DIVISION: HØLY GÅLÅCTIC IMPËRIUM + +
GALACTIC UNION
Evaluate/Top Sacred
Activate/Red A Lert

Hawkwind
THE SPACE RITUAL
SUNDOWN Edmonton - Friday December 29
SUNDOWN Brixton - Saturday December 30
The Faces
SUNDOWN Brixton - Saturday December 16
SUNDOWN Edmonton - Sunday December 17
SUNDOWN Edmonton - Monday December 18
ARGENT
SUNDOWN Edmonton - Friday December 1
T. REX
SUNDOWN Edmonton - Friday December 22
SUNDOWN Brixton - Saturday December 23 at 5.00 & 8.30
Osibisa
+ SILVERHEAD
SUNDOWN Brixton - Sunday December 10
SUNDOWN Edmonton - Friday December 15
STRAY
ELECTRIC LIGHT ORCHESTRA
+ VELVET UNDERGROUND
SUNDOWN Mile End - Thursday November 30
STATUS QUO + BYZANTIUM
SUNDOWN Mile End
Thursday December 21
genesis
SUNDOWN Mile End - Wednesday December 6
HOME
SUNDOWN Edmonton - Thursday December 7
SUNDOWN Brixton - Friday December 8
SUNDOWN Mile End - Wednesday December 27
Sundown

GALACTIC UNION
Evaluate/Top Sac
Activate/Red A Le
Hawkwind
WITH ASSORTED FRIENDS EACH NIGHT
+ + + ÅDVERTISING ÅID ITEM: HÅWKWIND ÅLBÜM 'DO
LATIDO' RELEÅSED NÖVEMBER 24 MËNTËT 1972 +
REPEAT FREE POSTER INSIDE + STOP + ITEM: CODE
+ STOP + CONSÜMËR DIVISION: HØLY GÅLÅCTIC IMP
CONSÜMËR DIVISION: HØLY GÅLÅCTIC IMPËRIUM + +
NOVEMBER 8th CORN EXCHANGE, KINGS LYNN
NOVEMBER 9th CIVIC HALL, DUNSTABLE
NOVEMBER 11th GUILDHALL, PORTSMOUTH
NOVEMBER 16th UNIVERSITY OF YORK
NOVEMBER 17th UNIVERSITY OF LANCASTER
NOVEMBER 18th UNIVERSITY OF LEEDS
NOVEMBER 19th LOCARNO, BRISTOL
NOVEMBER 21st ST. ANDREWS HALL, NORWICH
NOVEMBER 24th MUSIC HALL, ABERDEEN
NOVEMBER 25th EMPIRE, EDINBURGH
NOVEMBER 26th HARDROCK, MANCHESTER
NOVEMBER 30th NEW THEATRE, OXFORD

NASTY BALL
NO SISSIES
ALL NITER
A PARTY TO SUPPORT NASTY TALES DURING ITS FORTHCOMING "OBSCENITY" TRIAL
HAWKWIND. PINK FAIRIES.
BIG BOPPERS. LINDA LEWIS. SKIN ALLEY.
FOOT N DEATH MEN. SONIC 7.
STEVE TOOK.
9pm-6am. BUMPERS
COVENTRY STREET, LONDON W1 (Piccadilly tube)

Bickershaw Festival
Captain Beefheart & his Magic Band
Family
Dr. John
Hawkwind
Pacific Gas and Electric
Cheech & Chong
Sam Apple Pie
Captain Beyond
Flaming Groovies
Kinks
Grateful Dead
New Riders of the Purple Sage
Donovan
Incredible String Band
Al Stewart
Linda Lewis
Stackridge
Country Joe
Brinsley Schwarz
America
Brotherhood of Breath
Mike Westbrook
World of Oz
How to get there
Only £2.75
5,6,7 May

November 24, 1972. Hawkwind issue their third album, *Doremi Fasol Latido*, which reaches No. 14 on the UK charts. The album features a new rhythm section, in Lemmy Kilmister and Simon King. The last song on the record is "The Watcher," which constitutes the first song written by Lemmy for Hawkwind. It is the only song from the album that would not be included on *Space Ritual*, despite its lyrical congruence to the theme.

December 22, 30, 1972. Hawkwind perform live first in Liverpool Stadium, followed by Brixton Sundown, London, two shows that are recorded for the forthcoming live album.

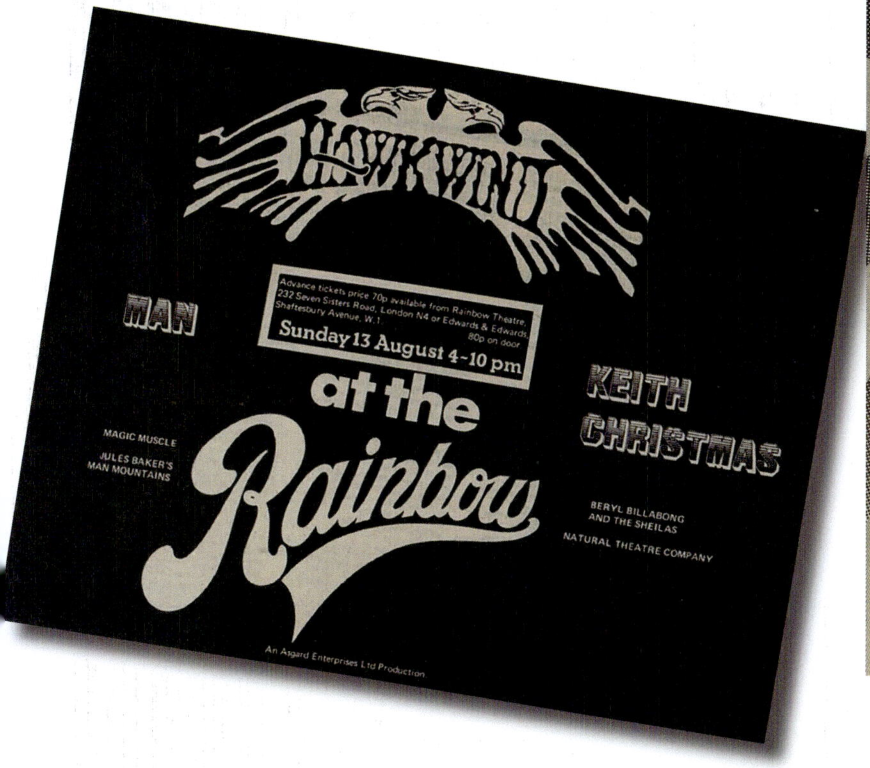

A young Lemmy with Hawkwind at the BBC studios in 1972.

© Victor de Schwanberg / Alamy Stock Photo

© Victor de Schwanberg / Alamy Stock Photo

© Victor de Schwanberg / Alamy Stock Photo

1972, Nik Turner, Simon King, Del Dettmar, Lemmy, Stacia; sitting left to right, Dik Mik and Dave Brock.

Stacia Blake photo shoot in Amsterdam, 1972.

Aldermaston Peace Festival, April 3, 1972.
Nik Turner, vocalist and sax player with the band.

Paradiso, Amsterdam, September 9, 1972.

Promotional poster

1973

1973. Sci-fi author Michael Moorcock begins his association with the band. Also this year, Robert Calvert—light duties during this era—leaves the fold. Hawkwind expert Robert Godwin contends that Moorcock had performed with the band as early as July of 1971.

March 1973– May 3, 1973. The band conduct a German tour.

April 26 – January 1974. Robert Calvert and an army of players, mostly Hawkwind folks, work on tracks for Calvert's forthcoming warplane technology concept record.

May 11, 1973. Hawkwind issue double live album *Space Ritual*, more formally known as *The Space Ritual Alive in Liverpool and London*. The album, issued in resplendent six-panel poster cover, reaches No. 9 on the UK charts and even tickles the bottom rungs of the Billboard chart, managing a No. 179 placement. New to the Hawkwind canon are "Orgone Accumulator," "Upside Down" and headbanged classic "Born to Go," the latter of which, granted, had been made available for the first time on the multi-band *Greasy Truckers Party* live album.

June 1973. An edited version of "Lord of Light," backed with an edited version of "Born to Go," is issued as a single in Germany.

August 1973. Dik Mik and Robert Calvert leave the band. Also this month, "Urban Guerilla"/"Brainbox Pollution" is issued as a single. It rises to No. 39 on the UK charts before being withdrawn due to perceived (though spurious) connections to IRA violence.

October 4, 1973. A sci-fi movie called *The Final Programme* hits theatres. The flick is based on a novel by Michael Moorcock, who gets Hawkwind into the movie—sort of: seen very, very briefly, they are more so part of the trailer and the DVD version of the film.

November 23 – December 6, 1973. Hawkwind tour the US for the first time, just after their first Scandinavian dates and a few more shows in mainland Europe.

1973
Windsor Festival

© Dave Walking

1973
Windsor Festival

© Dave Walkling

© Dave Walkling

HAWKWIND
From the frontiers of the cosmos-
88 minutes of brain damage.
The HAWKWIND Space Ritual
LIVE at Liverpool Stadium
and Brixton Sundown.
A very special double record.
SUNDAY 27th MAY 4pm ~ 10pm
HAWKWIND with their friends
EMPIRE POOL WEMBLEY
Tickets: £1·50: £1·25: £1·00: 75p
available from Empire Pool Box Office [01-902 1234],
Harlequin Record Shops and all leading ticket agencies

HAWKWIND
HAWKWIND
are back on the road
with
The Ridiculous Roadshow.
Catch them at
DECEMBER
10th MANCHESTER Free Trade Hall
11th NEWCASTLE City Hall
15th BRACKNELL Sports Centre
16th BIRMINGHAM Odeon
17th BRADFORD St Georges Hall
19th ABERDEEN Music Hall
20th PERTH City Hall
21st GLASGOW Apollo
22nd EDINBURGH Empire Theatre
JANUARY
1st BLACKBURN King Georges Hall
2nd LEICESTER De Montford Hall
3rd PORTSMOUTH Guild Hall
5th SOUTHEND Kursaal
6th OXFORD New Theatre
10th DUNSTABLE Queensway Hall
JANUARY Continued
11th CLACTON Town Hall
12th LIVERPOOL Stadium
16th NORWICH St Andrews Hall
17th CHELTENHAM Town Hall
18th DERBY Kings Hall
19th BOURNEMOUTH Winter Gardens
23rd GUILDFORD Civic Hall
25th LONDON Edmonton Sundown*
28th WOLVERHAMPTON Civic Hall
31st SWANSEA Brangwyn Theatre
FEBRUARY
1st PLYMOUTH Guild Hall
4th DUBLIN National Stadium
5th BELFAST Whitla Hall
8th LANCASTER University
9th LEEDS University
Tickets available from your usual local agencies
* Tickets for Sundown from Box Office (01-807 4649) or
Virgin Records in Oxford Street and Notting Hill Gate

Page 22—MELODY MAKER, July 28, 1973
HAWKWIND UP35566
URBAN GUERILLA
HAWKWIND URBAN GUERILLA
OUT OF NOTTING HILL GATE CAME HAWKWIND
OUT OF HAWKWIND CAME ROBERT CALVERT
OUT OF ROBERT CALVERT CAME
CAPTAIN LOCKHEED & THE STARFIGHTERS
UA
EJECTION

1974

January 1974. Brian Eno, as Eno, issues his landmark debut, *Here Come the Warm Jets*. Simon King is drummer on six tracks. Paul Rudolph also contributes, on both bass and guitar, featuring on three tracks.

March 1 – April 15, 1974. The band play a significant amount of "1999 Party" dates in the US and Canada, followed by a return to mainland Europe. Across the States, they bring the dancers, DJ Andy Dunkley and their trademark Liquid Len lightshow. Label mates Man support.

March 10, 1974. A Hawkwind show in Berkeley, CA is in support of imprisoned LSD guru Dr. Timothy Leary.

March 21, 1974. A show at the Chicago Auditorium Theatre is recorded and released in 1997 as *The 1999 Party*.

April 1974. Simon House officially joins the band, having played on the recent tour dates.

May 1974. Robert Calvert issues concept album *Captain Lockheed and the Starfighters*. Participating in the project are Hawkwind alumni Paul Rudolph, Dave Brock, Lemmy, Nik Turner, Del Dettmar and Simon King, along with Arthur Brown, Brian Eno and Twink. Producing is Roy Thomas Baker.

May – June 1974. The band record the songs slated for their next album, working at Olympic in London.

June 1974. Del Dettmar leaves Hawkwind and moves to the hippie hills above idyllic Nelson, British Columbia, Canada.

July 1974. Drummer Alan Powell joins the band.

August 1974. Issued as an advance single is "The Psychedelic Warlords"/"It's So Easy."

September 1 – November 2, 1974. The band play more dates in North America (supported in the main by Dr. Feelgood), with a hard break in September when the Indiana State Police impound their gear.

September 6, 1974. United Artists issues a fourth Hawkwind studio album, called *Hall of the Mountain Grill*. Gone are Robert Calvert and Dik Mik, with the band now consisting of Dave Brock, Del Dettmar, Simon House, Nik Turner, Lemmy and Simon King. The album reaches No. 16 on the UK charts and No. 110 in the US. The single in Europe pairs "Paradox" with "You'd Better Believe It," both being edited versions with "Paradox" being significantly remixed. There was also a four-track sampler issued as a promo in the US. Simon House is blamed in the press for softening the band's sound.

Hawkwind
Another soundsational tour with
lights by LIQUID LEN & THE LENSMEN
and sounds by ANDY DUNKLEY
PART ONE
(with DR. FEELGOOD)
Dec. 12th NEWCASTLE City Hall
13th GLASGOW Apollo
14th MANCHESTER Palace Theatre SOLD OUT
15th BIRMINGHAM Odeon
21st SOUTHEND Kursaal
PART TWO
Jan. 7th CARDIFF Capitol
8th WOLVERHAMPTON Civic
11th BOURNEMOUTH Winter Gardens
12th PAIGNTON Festival Theatre
13th WATFORD Town Hall
14th SOUTHAMPTON Gaumont
18th LIVERPOOL Stadium
19th OXFORD New Theatre
23rd DERBY Kings Hall
24th CLACTON Town Hall
25th BRACKNELL Sports Centre
Jan. 26th NORWICH Theatre Royal
30th LEICESTER De Montford
31st LANCASTER University
Feb. 2nd COVENTRY Theatre
6th MALVERN Winter Gardens
8th CAMBRIDGE Corn Exchange
9th HAMMERSMITH Odeon 01-748 4082
15th CHATHAM Central Hall
22nd FOLKESTONE Leas Cliff Hall
24th WORTHING Assembly Hall
Co-ordination by ASGARD

Hawkwind
HAWKWIND STRIKES AGAIN!
Hawkwind returns with a new musician and nine new songs in the "Hall of the Mountain Grill"—their most powerful and hypnotic recording. It's like no other 'mountain' music you've ever heard.
"HALL OF THE MOUNTAIN GRILL:"
A new Hawkwind, on United Artists Records and Tapes. Hawkwind has also returned to the U.S. for a national concert tour during September and October. Watch for the space and time near you.

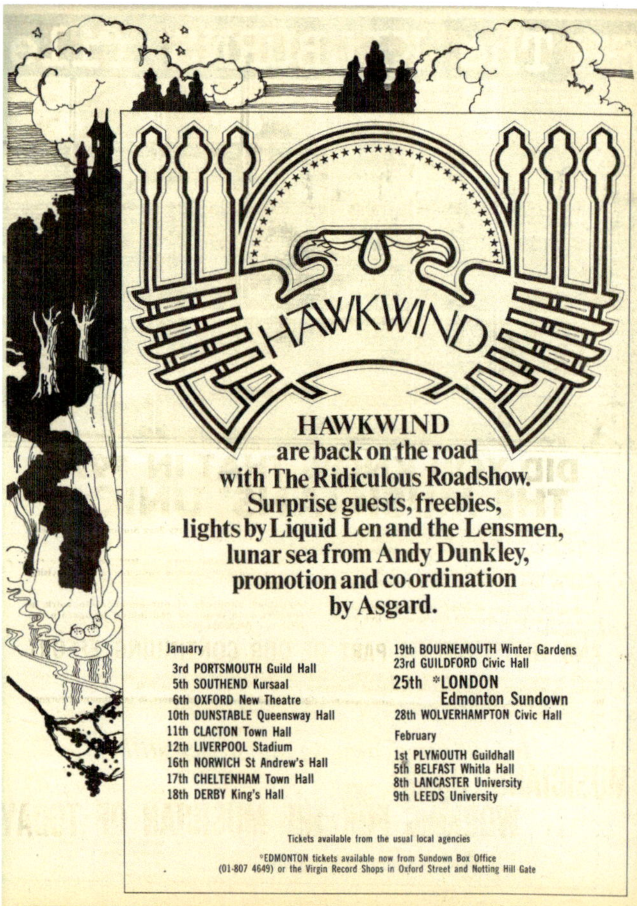
HAWKWIND
HAWKWIND
are back on the road
with The Ridiculous Roadshow.
Surprise guests, freebies,
lights by Liquid Len and the Lensmen,
lunar sea from Andy Dunkley,
promotion and co-ordination
by Asgard.
January
3rd PORTSMOUTH Guild Hall
5th SOUTHEND Kursaal
6th OXFORD New Theatre
10th DUNSTABLE Queensway Hall
11th CLACTON Town Hall
12th LIVERPOOL Stadium
16th NORWICH St Andrew's Hall
17th CHELTENHAM Town Hall
18th DERBY King's Hall
19th BOURNEMOUTH Winter Gardens
23rd GUILDFORD Civic Hall
25th *LONDON Edmonton Sundown
28th WOLVERHAMPTON Civic Hall
February
1st PLYMOUTH Guildhall
5th BELFAST Whitla Hall
8th LANCASTER University
9th LEEDS University
Tickets available from the usual local agencies
*EDMONTON tickets available now from Sundown Box Office (01-807 4649) or the Virgin Record Shops in Oxford Street and Notting Hill Gate

1975

1975. Sunset reissues the band's self-titled debut, but without the gatefold sleeve.

1975. Jonathan Cape publishes a J.G. Ballard novel called *High-Rise*, which inspires the Hawkwind track of the same name on 1979's *PXR5*.

January 5, 6, 1975. The guys enter Olympic Studios mid-tour to knock out a single, owed to UA to finish up the band's contract with the label.

March 1975. The band work at Rockfield Studios, in Monmouth, Wales, on tracks slated for their next record, with additional overdubs, vocals and mixing taking place at Olympic.

March 1975. Hawkwind's A&R guy at United Artists Andrew Lauder works out a record deal with Michael Moorcock, resulting in *New Worlds Fair*, credited to Michael Moorcock & Deep Fix, issued this month. Most of Hawkwind participate on the project, as does Snowy White, later of Thin Lizzy, Pink Floyd and Roger Waters fame. Barney Bubbles does the cover art.

March 7, 1975. "Kings of Speed"—music by Dave, lyrics by Michael Moorcock—backed with "Motorhead" is issued as a single. The non-LP B-side was the last song written for the band by Ian "Lemmy" Kilmister, who penned the track in the middle of the night at the Hyatt Hotel (a.k.a. the Riot House) in Hollywood on Roy Wood's acoustic guitar.

April 1975. Robert Calvert and assorted Hawkwind associates work at Island Studios on tracks slated for Calvert's second album.

April 12, 13, 1975. The band play Yeovil and Dunstable, in the UK as a warm-up ahead of the North American tour, testing out their newly recorded material for the first time.

April 29 – May 22, 1975. Hawkwind return to North America for Eastern and Midwest dates, followed by their most extensive mainland European tour yet. Unstated thus far in the story is the very regular gigging each and every year up and down the UK.

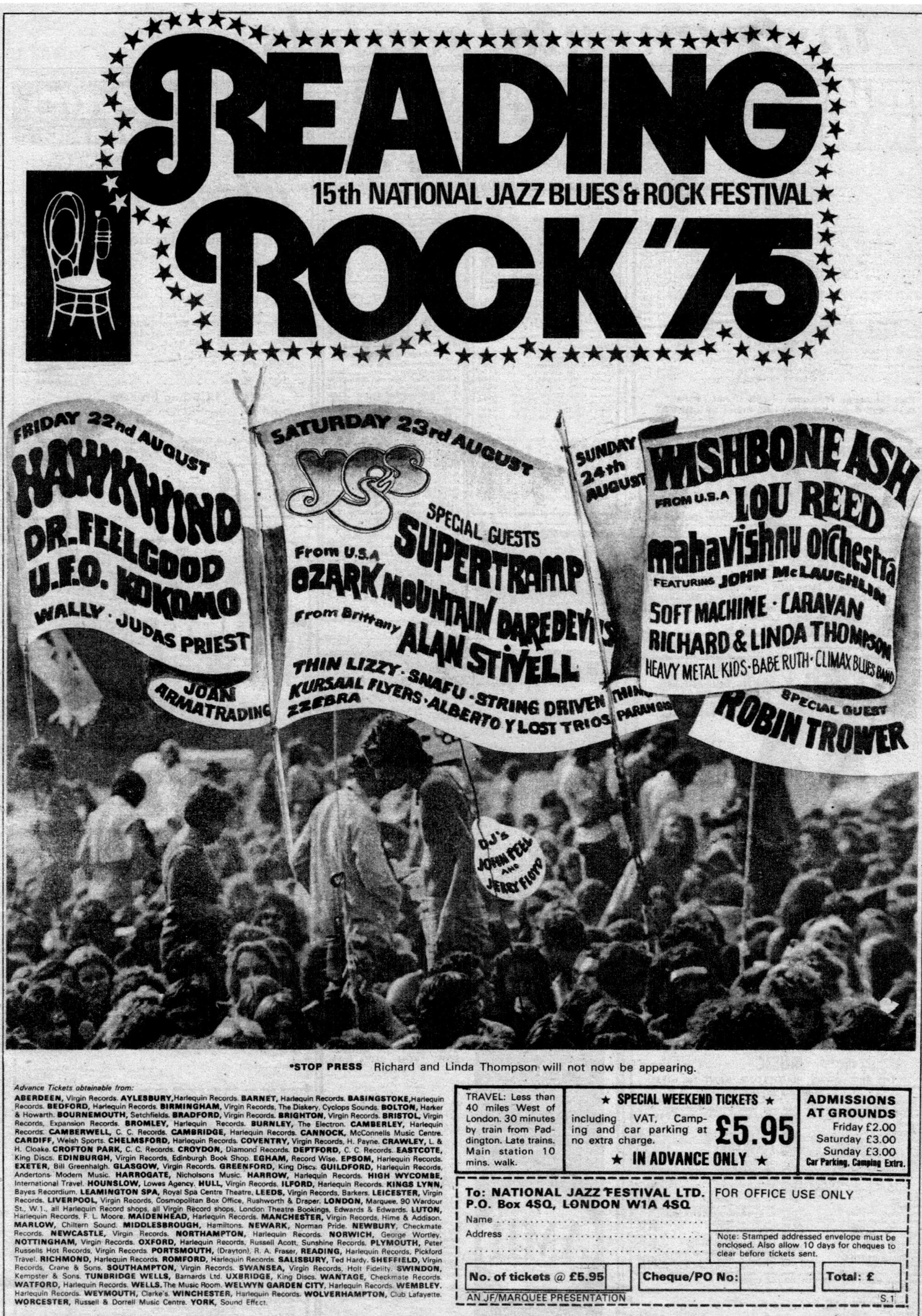

READING
15th NATIONAL JAZZ BLUES & ROCK FESTIVAL
ROCK '75
FRIDAY 22nd AUGUST
HAWKWIND
DR. FEELGOOD
U.F.O. KOKOMO
WALLY · JUDAS PRIEST
JOAN ARMATRADING
SATURDAY 23rd AUGUST
YES
SPECIAL GUESTS
SUPERTRAMP
From U.S.A OZARK MOUNTAIN DAREDEVILS
From Brittany ALAN STIVELL
THIN LIZZY · SNAFU · STRING DRIVEN THING
KURSAAL FLYERS · ALBERTO Y LOST TRIOS PARANOIAS
ZZEBRA
SUNDAY 24th AUGUST
WISHBONE ASH
FROM U.S.A LOU REED
mahavishnu orchestra
FEATURING JOHN McLAUGHLIN
SOFT MACHINE · CARAVAN
RICHARD & LINDA THOMPSON
HEAVY METAL KIDS · BABE RUTH · CLIMAX BLUES BAND
SPECIAL GUEST
ROBIN TROWER
DJ's JOHN PEEL AND JERRY FLOYD
•STOP PRESS Richard and Linda Thompson will not now be appearing.
Advance Tickets obtainable from:
ABERDEEN, Virgin Records. AYLESBURY, Harlequin Records. BARNET, Harlequin Records. BASINGSTOKE, Harlequin Records. BEDFORD, Harlequin Records. BIRMINGHAM, Virgin Records, The Diskery, Cyclops Sounds. BOLTON, Harker & Howarth. BOURNEMOUTH, Setchfields. BRADFORD, Virgin Records. BRIGHTON, Virgin Records. BRISTOL, Virgin Records, Expansion Records. BROMLEY, Harlequin Records. BURNLEY, The Electron. CAMBERLEY, Harlequin Records. CAMBERWELL, C. C. Records. CAMBRIDGE, Harlequin Records. CANNOCK, McConnells Music Centre. CARDIFF, Welsh Sports. CHELMSFORD, Harlequin Records. COVENTRY, Virgin Records, H. Payne. CRAWLEY, L. & H. Cloake. CROFTON PARK, C. C. Records. CROYDON, Diamond Records. DEPTFORD, C. C. Records. EASTCOTE, King Discs. EDINBURGH, Virgin Records, Edinburgh Book Shop. EGHAM, Record Wise. EPSOM, Harlequin Records. EXETER, Bill Greenhalgh. GLASGOW, Virgin Records. GREENFORD, King Discs. GUILDFORD, Harlequin Records, Andertons Modern Music. HARROGATE, Nicholsons Music. HARROW, Harlequin Records. HIGH WYCOMBE, International Travel. HOUNSLOW, Lowes Agency. HULL, Virgin Records. ILFORD, Harlequin Records. KINGS LYNN, Bayes Recordium. LEAMINGTON SPA, Royal Spa Centre Theatre. LEEDS, Virgin Records, Barkers. LEICESTER, Virgin Records. LIVERPOOL, Virgin Records, Cosmopolitan Box Office, Rushworth & Draper. LONDON, Marquee, 90 Wardour St., W.1., all Harlequin Record shops, all Virgin Record shops, London Theatre Bookings, Edwards & Edwards. LUTON, Harlequin Records, F. L. Moore. MAIDENHEAD, Harlequin Records. MANCHESTER, Virgin Records, Hime & Addison. MARLOW, Chiltern Sound. MIDDLESBROUGH, Hamiltons. NEWARK, Norman Pride. NEWBURY, Checkmate Records. NEWCASTLE, Virgin Records. NORTHAMPTON, Harlequin Records. NORWICH, George Wortley. NOTTINGHAM, Virgin Records. OXFORD, Harlequin Records, Russell Acott, Sunshine Records. PLYMOUTH, Peter Russells Hot Records, Virgin Records. PORTSMOUTH, (Drayton), R. A. Fraser, READING, Harlequin Records, Pickford Travel. RICHMOND, Harlequin Records. ROMFORD, Harlequin Records. SALISBURY, Ted Hardy. SHEFFIELD, Virgin Records, Crane & Sons. SOUTHAMPTON, Virgin Records. SWANSEA, Virgin Records, Holt Fidelity. SWINDON, Kempster & Sons. TUNBRIDGE WELLS, Barnards Ltd. UXBRIDGE, King Discs. WANTAGE, Checkmate Records. WATFORD, Harlequin Records. WELLS. The Music Room. WELWYN GARDEN CITY, Harlequin Records. WEMBLEY. Harlequin Records. WEYMOUTH, Clarke's. WINCHESTER, Harlequin Records. WOLVERHAMPTON, Club Lafayette. WORCESTER, Russell & Dorrell Music Centre. YORK, Sound Effect.
TRAVEL: Less than 40 miles West of London. 30 minutes by train from Paddington. Late trains. Main station 10 mins. walk.
★ SPECIAL WEEKEND TICKETS ★
including VAT, Camping and car parking at no extra charge.
£5.95
★ IN ADVANCE ONLY ★
ADMISSIONS AT GROUNDS
Friday £2.00
Saturday £3.00
Sunday £3.00
Car Parking, Camping Extra.
To: NATIONAL JAZZ FESTIVAL LTD. P.O. Box 4SQ, LONDON W1A 4SQ
Name
Address
FOR OFFICE USE ONLY
Note: Stamped addressed envelope must be enclosed. Also allow 10 days for cheques to clear before tickets sent.
No. of tickets @ £5.95
Cheque/PO No:
Total: £
AN JF/MARQUEE PRESENTATION
S.1

May 9, 1975. United Artists issues a fifth Hawkwind album, entitled *Warrior on the Edge of Time*. The album is based on a concept of Michael Moorcock's, with his novel *The Eternal Champion* being the starting off point. *Warrior on the Edge of Time* peaks at #13 on the British charts and No. 150 on Billboard—this marks the last time Hawkwind would trouble the official US chart. The album would also certify silver in the UK. *Warrior on the Edge of Time* would be the first record for the band's new American label, Atco.

May 18, 1975. Lemmy is kicked out of the band after a drug bust at the Canadian border on the 16th—he was in possession of speed, which was mistaken for cocaine. He is replaced by Paul Rudolph, ex-Pink Fairies. Ironically, Lemmy would form his next band with another Pink Fairies alumnus, namely guitarist Larry Wallis.

August 1975. Robert Calvert poem "Circle Line" wins the Capitol Radio Poetry Award. The poem is about a quick glance of connection between a man and a woman on the subway. Marillion's Fish opens his 2007 album *13th Star* with a song with a similar vibe called "Circle Line."

August 22 – 24, 1975. Hawkwind headline the Friday night (the first of three nights) of the Reading Festival, but according to some reports find themselves back on their heels following an inspired set by surprise breakout act Dr. Feelgood—Rob Godwin disagrees, paying barely any notice to Wilko Johnson's pub rock band! Also playing down the bill on the Friday are future stars UFO and Judas Priest. The show would be Stacia's last, after which the next day, she gets married. Robert Calvert guests with the band and is asked to rejoin as lead vocalist.

September 1975. Robert Calvert issues, on UA, a second concept album, entitled *Lucky Leif and the Longships*. Producing is Brian Eno, with arrangements by Robert and Paul Rudolph, who also plays guitar, bass and provides backing vocals. Also participating are Michael Moorcock, Nik Turner and Simon House.

ROUNDHOUSE CHALK FARM NW1 · SUNDAY 16 FEB · 5:30-10:30
HAWKWIND
PINK FAIRIES
SPECIAL GUESTS:
AL 'MR. SOUL' MATTHEWS
LADY JUNES
LINGUISTIC LEPROSY
LIGHTS: LIQUID LEN & THE N. KENSINGTON ALL GIRLS SPOTLIGHT TEAM
SOUNDS: ANDY 'I'M ON THE ROAD' DUNKLEY

Kennedy Street Enterprises Ltd Present

ASTOUNDING SOUNDS, AMAZING MUSIC TOUR

September
15. Sheffield — City Hall
16. Birmingham — Odeon
17. Liverpool — Empire
18. Manchester — Palace
19. Newcastle — City Hall
20. Edinburgh — Usher Hall
21. Glasgow — Apollo
22. Aberdeen — Capital
25. Oxford — New Theatre
26. Cardiff — Capitol
27. Bristol — Colston Hall
28. Guildford — Civic Hall
30. Dunstable — Queensway Hall

October
1. Southampton — Gaumont
2. Ipswich — Gaumont
4. Leicester — De Montford Hall
5. London — Hammersmith.

Other dates to be added. During late October and November, Hawkwind will be taking their ASTOUNDING SOUNDS, AMAZING MUSIC TOUR throughout Europe. Next stop will be the colonies, including the USA and Canada. Here at home watch out for XMAS SURPRISES.

The ASTOUNDING SOUNDS, AMAZING MUSIC TOUR comes to you with the help of: Lewis (Greenwich) Ltd, Projection and Display Services, Canworth Brokers, Theatre Projects, Colac Sound, C. J. Frame Up, President Tours, Button Badge Co., Ballantine Printing, Kennedy St. Enterprises, Music Center Promotions, Bron Agency Ltd., the Farmyard, Maurice Placquet, Keith Altham, EMI, Tiger, Concert Publishing, P&G Sports Souveniers, Wizard Management, Larry Smart, Liquid Len, Barney Bubbles, Tony Hyde, a cast of; a thousand road crew and humpers, and last but not least, Charisma Records (70 Old Compton St., London W1.) Any further inquiries please contact the FAMOUS CHARISMA PEOPLE. We've undoubtedly forgotten to mention someone, so if you're reading this — sorry, and Thanks!

Dave Brock — Guitar, Synthesizer, Harmonica, Vocals.
Bob Calvert — Vocals, Trumpet, Walker's rhyming dictionary.
Simon House — Violin, Keyboards: Mellotron, Piano, synthesizer.
Paul Rudolf — Guitar, Bass Guitar, vocals.
Nik Turner — Sax, flute, vocals.
Alan Powell — drums.
Simon King — drums.

Special Note: On the album, two of the writer credits are reversed. The 'City of Lagoons' is an Alan Powell track, and 'Chronoglide Skyway' belongs to Simon House.

HAWKWIND
First Hawkwind Album to Feature 'Silver Machine'
Specially Compiled and Edited by Dave Brock. Among the Many Fine Tracks on the Album are 'Urban Guerilla' and a Previously Unreleased Live Version of 'You Shouldn't Do That'
HAWKWIND
Package Includes the Famous Roadhawks Poster, Plus Vintage Hawkwind Sticker
This Compilation Chronicles the Band's Line up from Their First Album Through to 'Warrior on the Edge of Time'
ROADHAWKS
©1976 United Artists Records Ltd.
UA
UNITED ARTISTS RECORDS ®
®Trademarks owned by United Artists Music and Records Group Inc. and used by United Artists Records Ltd. under authorisation.
Album UAK 29919 Cassette TCK 29919

1976

1976. Fiction writer Michael Butterworth sees publication of *The Time of the Hawklords*, a Hawkwind-based fantasy novel. It would become the first of a trilogy, following the completion of *The Queens of Deliria* in 1977 and *Ledge of Darkness* in 1995, the latter only being produced in the *25 Years On* Hawkwind box set.

January 1976. Hawkwind leave Liberty/UA, signing with Tony Stratton-Smith's Charisma imprint.

February – March 1976. Hawkwind work at Roundhouse Studios on tracks proposed for their sixth studio album.

March 5 – December 19, 1976. Hawkwind tour up and down the UK, putting aside campaigns on the continent as well as North America for the year.

April 1976. United Artists, no longer the band's label, does the expected and issues a Hawkwind compilation, the band's first ever. *Roadhawks* reaches No. 45 on the UK charts. "Silver Machine" and "Urban Guerrilla" are previously unreleased on LP, as is the live version of "You Shouldn't Do That."

July 16, 1976. "Kerb Crawler" backed with "Honky Dorky" is issued as a single.

HAWKWIND
First Album Release on the Charisma Label
THRILLING STORIES OF SCIENCE AND FANTASY!
ASTOUNDING
SOUNDS, AMAZING MUSIC
ASTOUNDING SOUNDS, AMAZING MUSIC TOUR
SEPTEMBER
15th. City Hall SHEFFIELD
16th. Odeon BIRMINGHAM
17th. Empire LIVERPOOL
18th. Palace MANCHESTER
19th. City Hall NEWCASTLE
20th. Usher Hall EDINBURGH
21st. Apollo GLASGOW
22nd. Capital ABERDEEN
25th. New Theatre OXFORD
26th. Capital CARDIFF
27th. Colston Hall BRISTOL
OCTOBER
1st. Gaumont SOUTHAMPTON
2nd. Gaumont IPSWICH
4th. De Montford Hall LEICESTER
5th. HAMMERSMITH ODEON
More dates to be added
CHARISMA
MOORCOCK
BUTTERWORTH
Hawkwind in print
The Time of the Hawkl
Available from 23rd Septe
YOW 313

August 27, 1976. Hawkwind issue their first album for Charisma Records, entitled *Astounding Sounds, Amazing Music*. The record peaks at No. 33 on the UK charts. The title and cover art reference the old science fiction magazine, with each song conceived as a stand-alone sci-fi tale. Concurrent with the label switch is a break with manager Doug Smith, replaced by Tony Howard. As for a key lineup change, Lemmy is (long) gone, replaced by Paul Rudolph from the Pink Fairies, who is with the band for one album only. *Astounding Sounds, Amazing Music* marks the beginning of the short-lived Robert Calvert era, with Calvert providing much of the literary grist across the album, as well as lead vocals. The album sees issue in Canada but not the US, with "Reefer Madness" and "Steppenwolf" living on as the most enduring tracks from this controversial Calvert-steeped album.

Late October 1976. After tour dates in September and October, the band fires Nik Turner and second drummer Alan Powell, before entering the studio to record two new songs to be issued as a single. These tracks are recorded as a straight five-man configuration now, down from the seven members who were part and parcel of *Astounding Sounds, Amazing Music*.

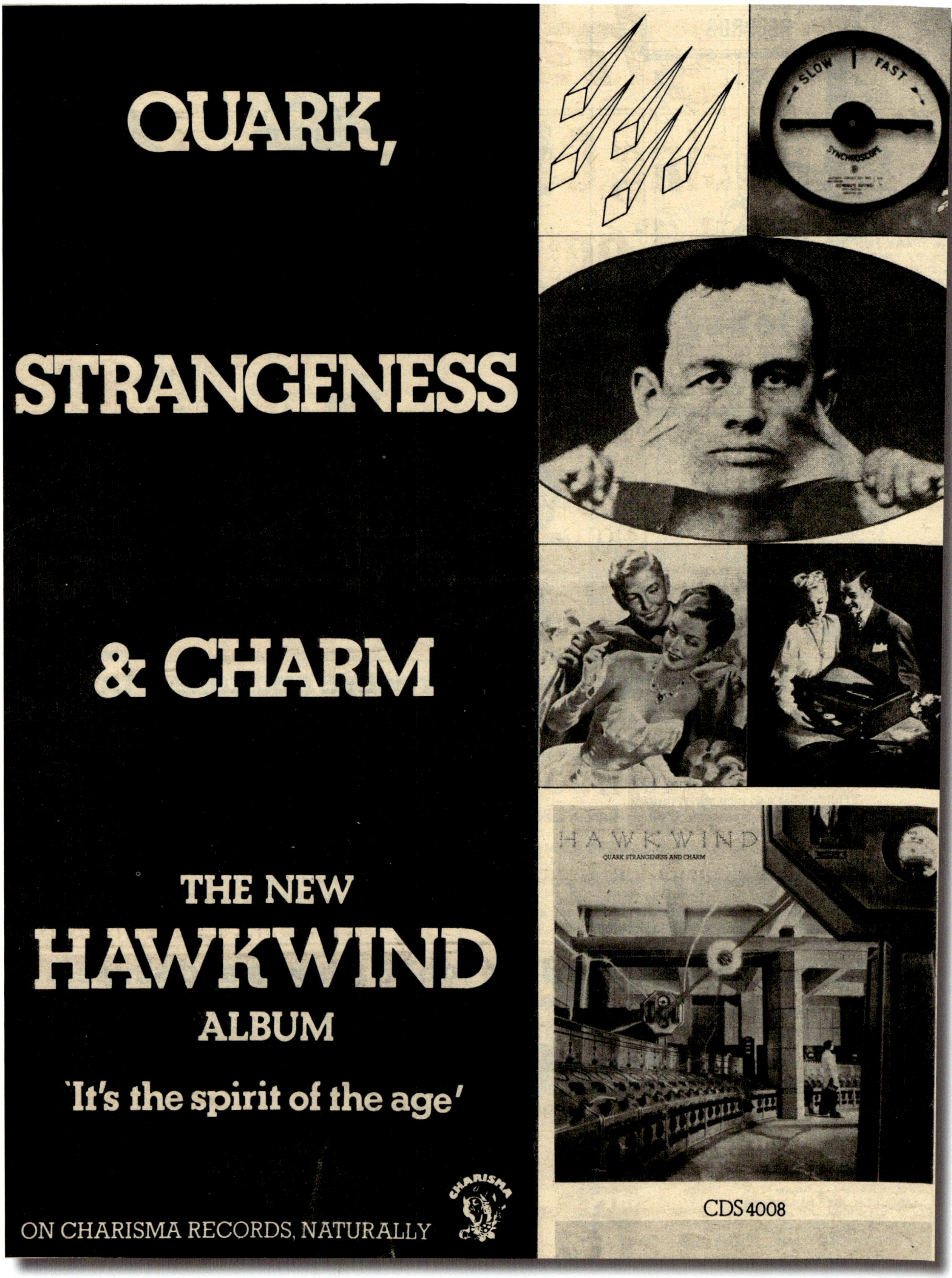
QUARK,
STRANGENESS
& CHARM
THE NEW
HAWKWIND
ALBUM
'It's the spirit of the age'
ON CHARISMA RECORDS, NATURALLY
CHARISMA
SLOW
FAST
SYNCHROSCOPE
HAWKWIND
QUARK STRANGENESS AND CHARM
CDS 4008

1977

1977. Quasar Books issues a book of Robert Calvert poetry called *Centigrade 232*, the title referring to the temperature at which paper burns, burning paper being a metaphor for destroying rough drafts of one's work. A launch event is held at the Battersea Arts Centre in London.

January – February 1977. With Paul Rudolph now gone, Adrian "Ade" Shaw joins, while the band works at Rockfield on tracks slated for their next record. Nik Turner is also gone, off to form a band called Sphynx.

January 28, 1977. The band issue "Back on the Streets" backed with "The Dream of Isis." This is new music recorded October the previous year at AIR Studios, London.

February 1977. EMI issues the second Hawkwind compilation ever, entitled *Masters of the Universe*. Only B-side "It's So Easy" is previously unreleased on LP.

March 11 – April 26, 1977. Hawkwind return to mainland Europe for an extensive run of performances.

June 17, 1977. Hawkwind issue the quite tuneful and accessible *Quark, Strangeness and Charm*, their seventh album, which reaches No. 30 on the British charts. The cover art is quintessential Hipgnosis. This second album for the band on Charisma sees wide release on that label, but also simultaneous release in the US on Sire Records. It is the only Hawkwind album that includes bassist Adrian Shaw, although Shaw would go on to a long-time association with the present-day Hawklords. Most significantly, this is the first album without Nik Turner.

July 29, 1977. "Quark, Strangeness and Charm" backed with "The Forge of Vulcan" is issued as a single; on the European mainland, the B-side is "The Iron Dream." "Hassan I Sabha," written by Bob Calvert and now ex-Hawkwind bassist Paul Rudolph, is also released as a single in mainland Europe, becoming the most famed song from the album (along with "Spirit of the Age"), due in large part to Simon House's signature violin parts.

TWO HEADS ARE
Hawkwind
Kennedy Street Enterprises present
HAWKWIND ON TOUR
September
16th Palace, MANCHESTER
17th Empire, LIVERPOOL
18th Apollo, GLASGOW
19th Usher Hall, EDINBURGH
20th City Hall, NEWCASTLE
21st City Hall, WOLVERHAMPTON
23rd City Hall, SHEFFIELD
25th Fairfield Halls, CROYDON
26th Odeon, BIRMINGHAM
27th Gaumont IPSWICH
29th De Montford Hall, LEICESTER
30th New Theatre, OXFORD
October
3rd Hippodrome, BRISTOL
4th Gaumont, SOUTHAMPTON
7th WEST RUNTON Pavilion
13th Market Hall, CARLISLE
14th LANCASTER University
5th Odeon, HAMMERSMITH
SPECIAL GUESTS
Bethnal
HAWKWIND
CHART ALBUM
QUARK, STRANGENESS & CHARM
CDS 4008
LATEST SINGLE
QUARK, STRANGENESS & CHARM
CB 305
CHARISMA
Marketed by Charisma Records Ltd.

August 21, 1977. Motörhead, led by ex-Hawkwind member Lemmy, issue their self-titled debut album. On it are versions of Hawkwind classics "The Watcher" and "Lost Johnny."

September 16, 1977. Marc Bolan dies in a car crash. Ade Shaw was about to leave Hawkwind to join T Rex. Up until his death, Bolan had hosted Marc, his own music TV show for kids. On one of the last episodes, Hawkwind (minus Dave) had made a rare appearance miming to "Quark, Strangeness and Charm."

October 1977. Keyboardist/violinist Simon House is replaced by Paul Hayles.

December 23, 1977. Various Hawkwind associates play a gig at Barnstaple Queens Hall billed as Sonic Assassins. This consortium, centred around Robert Calvert and Dave Brock, had actually spent some time as a band concept, when the two, living in Devon, had hooked up with a local band called Ark. Ark bassist Harvey Bainbridge and drummer Martin Griffin would soon join Dave in his brief post-Hawkwind band Hawklords. Portions of the set emerged over the years on various pieces of product, most substantially the Sonic Assassins EP.

Re-Issued By Demand!
Hawkwind
Silver Machine
c/w
Seven By Seven
First 15,000 copies available
in special picture bag
UP 35381

1978

1978. Robert Calvert's theatrical work *Mirror Mirror* debuts at Pentameters Theatre, reprised again in 2013 and 2019. This is Robert's second play, after 1976's *The Stars That Play with Laughing Sam's Dice*, to be followed by *The Kid from Silicon Gulch* in 1981 and *Test-Tube Baby of Mine* in 1986.

March 4 – March 28, 1978. Hawkwind return to the US for a slew of shows, after which Dave Brock quits the band! (sort of).

June 1978. Nik Turner's Sphynx issues *Xitintoday*, on Charisma. The album is produced by Steve Hillage (billed as Stiv Hillage), and includes cameos from Hawkwind alumni Tim Blake on synthesizers and Alan Powell on congas. Another connection to the old band is that the album was recorded at Rockfield.

June – August 1978. Robert Calvert, Dave Brock and Simon King from the now dormant Hawkwind, plus Ark's Harvey Bainbridge and Pilot's Steve Swindells, working as Hawklords, record tracks at Langley Farm, Devon, toward a proposed album. Amidst the sessions, King leaves the band to be replaced by Ark's Martin Griffin. Soon, however, King returns and the band has two drummers. The musical chairs experienced by the band during this period would be turned into a tale of lost-and-found astronauts soon to be told on a Hawkwind song called "PXR5."

October 6, 1978. An album from Hawklords called *25 Years On* emerges, on Charisma. After the first 25,000 copies, the title was shed, with the record essentially becoming a self-titled, although later issues have reverted to the original title. "Psi Power" backed with "Death Trap" is issued as a single with another to follow in '79. Despite the disturbing cover art, the album is almost post-punk and even more accessible than *Quark, Strangeness and Charm*, yet at the same time it feels like an evolution for the band, rather than a direction warranting a name change (which was prompted by legal squabbles more than anything).

October 6 – November 25, 1978. Hawklords conduct an intensive UK campaign, playing almost every night, with Lemmy guesting for a rendition of "Silver Machine" at the Hammersmith Odeon on October 13th. The elaborate dystopian stage set for the tour had been designed by Barney Bubbles, but had to be cut back due to budgetary constraints as the tour progressed; this caused a rift between Bubbles and Brock.

October 1978. "Silver Machine" sees re-release as a single by United Artists (backed with "Seven by Seven"), and reaches No. 34 in the charts.

an Transcendental Industries inc
Anti gravity=

1979

1979. Future Hawkwind bassist Alan Davey forms a new hard-rocking but also Hawkwind-influenced band called Gunslinger, with his cousin Nigel Potter. It's 2008 before the band issue any product.

May 18, 1979. "25 Years" backed with "(Only) The Dead Dreams of the Cold War Kid" and "PXR5" (as "P.X.R.5") is released as a single.

June 15, 1979. Charisma issues a ninth Hawkwind album, entitled *PXR5*, which reaches No. 59 in the UK charts. The album consists of studio and live tracks recorded before the US tour dates of March of 1978 and the subsequent hiatus, so before the Hawklords project. The brunt of the studio work happens in January of 1978 at Rockfield, with live tracks (subsequently overdubbed) recorded at gigs in September and October of 1977. The album was then mixed in February of '78 at Rockfield. *PXR5* is the last Hawkwind record for both Bob Calvert and Charisma Records.

September 9 – December 29, 1979. The band's only touring in 1979 takes place late in the year, and is exclusively a UK campaign.

December 8, 1979. The band's gig at the St. Albans City Hall, St. Alban's Hertfordshire, is recorded and subsequently issued as *Live Seventy Nine*.

"Barney Bubbles was one of those delicate characters, and sadly, he eventually ended his own life in 1983. Barney worked with Stiff Records after he sort of went on from us. First off, because we live in Notting Hill Gate area, that area of London, it was a bit like Haight-Ashbury. It was a cheap area to live. There were always lots of things going on there—arts centre, arts labs, interesting place—and Barney lived there as well, and so did Mike Moorcock. We all lived in that same area so we all knew each other, and we used to go down to the workmen's cafe, which inspired *Hall of the Mountain Grill*—the Mountain Grill was a café, believe it or not. It ended up being a crashed spaceship on *Hall of the Mountain Grill*—the Hawkwind spaceship had crashed (laughs)."

"We've got a wonderful new guy, who is quite ingenious with our work, and who is very similar to Barney actually, does fantastic stuff. There's a great similarity to what's going on with us now and then. But we've all got older and we're plowing on (laughs)."

"But Barney, well, what was he like? Like I say, he was a delicate character. He was about five-foot-six, had a beard, used to draw a lot, used to work for a magazine, a free magazine called Frendz. Used to work in their office doing artwork for them as well. Yeah, but in the end, poor old Barney committed suicide."

Dave Brock

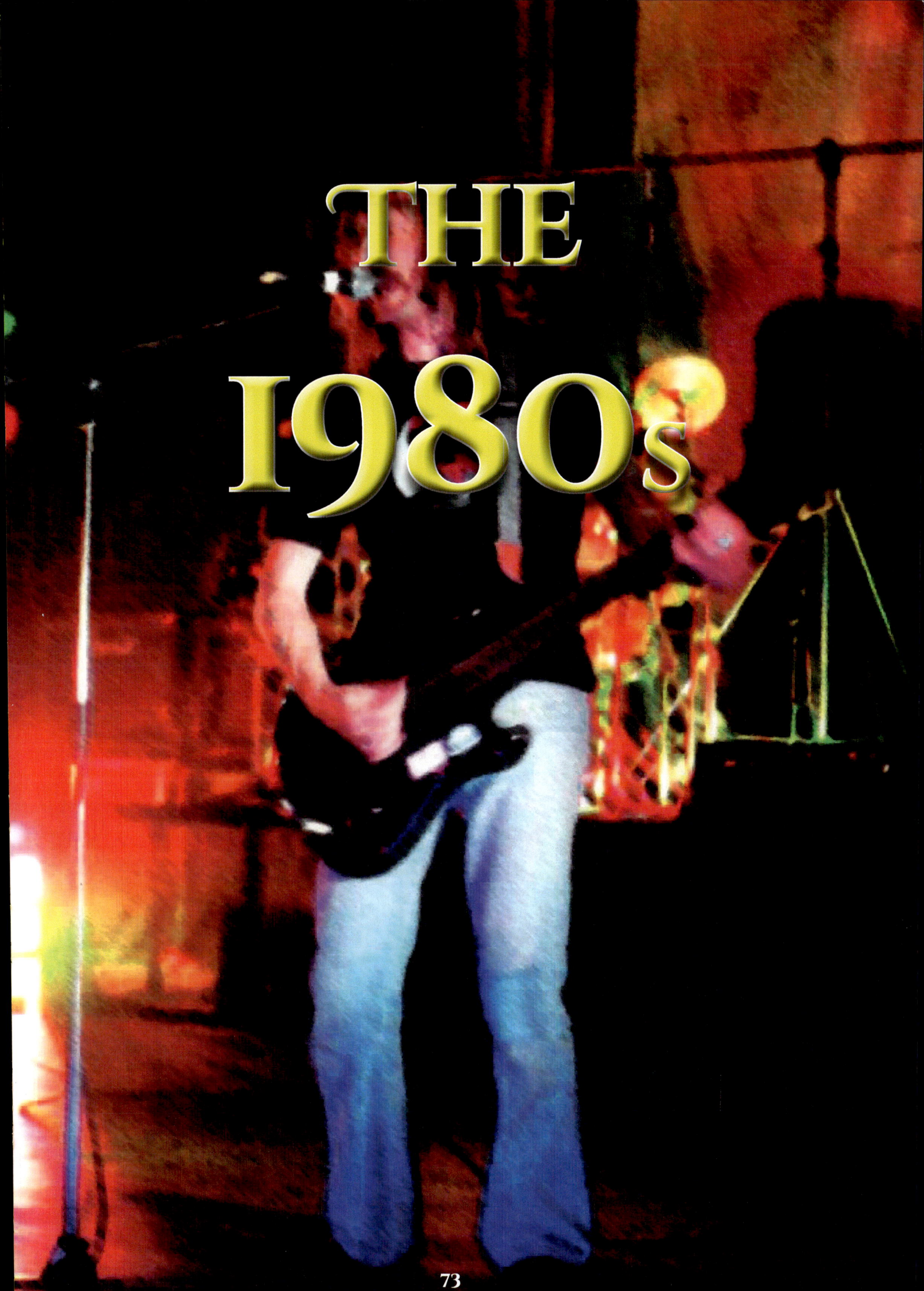

THE 1980s

© Oz Hardwick

Admirably, for a '70s band (Hawkwind made nine records in the 1970s), Dave Brock and Co. had an extremely eventful 1980s, all the while being put through the grinder of the business, through their most major label of experiences all the way down into the underground with Ficknife and GWR.

The decade starts with the inauspicious licensing of a live album to Gerry Bron and Bronze Records. Pleasantly, *Live Seventy Nine* arrives in the midst of the New Wave of British Heavy Metal, and there seem to be buyers interested in Hawkwind (a metal-looking album cover helps). This leads to a record that looks heavier than it is, *Levitation* straddling the post-punk/new wave of the Charisma years to what was about to come.

Next, the band found themselves essentially an RCA artist, with wide distribution and professional-looking records. In support and in tandem, Dave Brock was playing ball, delivering aggressive guitar, bass and drums rockers, albeit jarringly broken up by synthesizer excursions not entirely welcome in the new decade, even if synth pop was becoming a thing. The over-riding narrative is that the first record, *Sonic Attack*, and the third record, *Choose Your Masques*, are utilitarian, whereas the middle album, *Church of Hawkwind*, is a little bit too trancy and electronic. It is of no mind, because Hawkwind will lose their Active/RCA deal and they'll be left to sort out what sells on their own.

But remember, this is a band of pirate hippies who will survive and can survive. Being bumped down to Flicknife, Hawkwind deliver the more than creditable *The Chronicle of the Black Sword*, en route to the almost claustrophobic and paranoid but still tough and business-like *The Xenon Codex*, which found the band now signed to GWR.

I must digress, because obviously throughout the entries, you will see that in this decade there are all kinds of other dramas, those related to the live shows, the side-projects, and most notably personnel changes. But I can't help think that any Hawkwind fan, myself included, tries to diminish the cognitive dissonance and sense of chaos surrounding this collective by talking about the studio albums, which I figure serve as anchors and beacons in turbulent times.

It's funny: in interviewing these guys and hundreds of other rock stars, the reality of their lives revolves more so around all the shows they play year in and year out. Yet, as fans on the outside, it's the recorded works—specifically the studio albums—that form the structure of the narrative. So that's the way we will proceed, good or bad, with *The Xenon Codex* happening to be the brushstroke of reality that closes the 1980s, on a positive note, before, unfortunately, things get messy. Granted much of this is no fault of the band trying to make music: as the years grind on, it seems that more and more guys that fancy themselves label moguls claim some sort of tenuous right to some old Hawkwind live show, and the market gets polluted with Hawkwind albums of dubious quality.

But to recap, like I say, Dave did not slack this decade. We got a ton of music, with an admirable amount of blood, sweat and tears going into that music, which we can't say is always the lazy case moving forward. I mean, "Who's Gonna Win the War?," "Motorway City," "Rocky Paths," "Fall of Earth City," "Angels of Death," "Needle Gun," "Sword of the East," "Waiting for Tomorrow"... the band delivered the... blanga. Do we even use that word anymore, Eric?

St Austell, October 25, 1980.

1980

Early 1980. Nik Turner vehicle Inner City Unit issue their debut album, *Pass Out*, which sounds like a cross between Hawkwind, XTC and X-Ray Spex. Included are covers of "Brainstorm" and "Master of the Universe." The band would also issue, in fits and starts, *The Maximum Effect* (May '81), *Punkadelic* in '82, *New Anatomy* (December '84) and *The Presidents Tapes* (September '85). When Nik had temporarily been back in the band's good graces, Hawkwind played live *Pass Out* track "Watching the Grass Grow." Also part of Inner City Unit was Phil Reeves, otherwise known as Dead Fred, in Hawkwind briefly on two different occasions and, for a time, bassist Dave Anderson.

March 1980 – November 1983. Dave Brock issues, over time, eight 40-minute cassette tapes culled from his personal archive, a series known as *The Weird Tapes*.

June 27, 1980. Issued as a single from *Live Seventy Nine* is the Steve Swindells-penned "Shot Down in the Night," backed with the non-LP "Urban Guerilla" from the same gig.

July – August 1980. Hawkwind work at Roundhouse Studios in London with producer Ashley Howe, on tracks slated for their tenth album. Simon King is fired during the sessions for too much drugging and drinking and replaced by Ginger Baker, who's never had that problem (!).

July 21, 1980. Bronze issues *Live Seventy Nine*, which reaches No. 15 on the UK charts. The band in fact had no record deal and played the tapes for Gerry Bron, who signed them based partly on what he heard and partly on the fact that he had already secured offshoot band Motörhead. At this point, Hawkwind was back with original manager Doug Smith, after a troubling time during the Charisma years with Tony Howard and Jeff Dexter. *Live Seventy Nine* also marks the return of guitarist Huw Lloyd-Langton, absent since the debut, the last for drummer Simon King and the first for Tim Blake, from Gong, on keyboards.

September 1980. Charisma gets into the compilation game with their first Hawkwind set, covering 1976 through 1979. *Repeat Performance*—the title was also used for Charisma comps covering Lindisfarne and Van der Graaf Generator—includes a couple of single edits, plus the non-LP single "Back on the Streets."

St Austell, October 25, 1980.

October 1980. Steve Swindells issues his second solo album—and first since leaving Hawklords—called *Fresh Blood*, on Atco. Guitarist on the album is Huw Lloyd-Langton, with Simon King playing the drums. Swindells includes a version of his Hawkwind-issued song "Shot Down in the Night" on the record and it is also issued as a single.

October 10 – November 15, 1980. The band conduct an intensive tour of the UK and Ireland. Having joined in late '79, Tim Blake leaves after eight shows to be replaced by his tech Paul "Twink" Noble who lasts five more shows to be replaced by Keith Hale, who is in turn gone before he can participate on any of the studio records. As always, it takes the leadership acumen of Dave to hold things together and keep the ship moving forward.

October 27, 1980. Hawkwind issue a second (and last) record through the band's new deal with Bronze (granted, *Live Seventy Nine* was live and licensed to the label). *Levitation* is recorded digitally using the 3M Digital Mastering System, and represents a partial return to the band's heavy space rock sound, albeit of a highly professional disposition. Save for the switch in drummer from Simon to Ginger Baker, the rest of the band from *Live Seventy Nine* remains intact, namely Dave Brock, Huw Lloyd-Langton, Harvey Bainbridge and Tim Blake, who is nonetheless gone by the release date. The album is also distinguished by the fact that it is the first studio record of the post-Robert Calvert era.

November 7, 1980. An edited version of "Who's Gonna Win the War?" is issued as a single, backed with "Nuclear Toy."

St Austell, October 25, 1980.

HAWKWIND
SONIC ATTACK
THE ALBUM
'SONIC ATTACK'
AVAILABLE NOW
THE SONIC ATTACK TOUR CONTINUES......
DECEMBER
12th – STROUD, Leisure Centre
13th – POOLE, Arts Centre
14th – BATH, Pavillion
16th – MAIDSTONE, Mid-Kent Centre
18th – LONDON, The Rainbow
19th – DUNSTABLE, Queensway Hall
RCA
AVAILABLE ON CASSETTE

1981

February 14, 1981. The band perform "Motorway City" and "Who's Gonna Win the War?" on German TV show Musikladen.

May 1, 1981. Flicknife issues the archival 12" 45 RPM *Hawkwind Zoo* EP, featuring a live "Kings of Speed" from 1975, the original 1969 demo version of "Hurry on Sundown" and a non-LP track from those sessions called "Sweet Mistress of Pain."

June – August 1981. The band work at Rockfield studios with producer Ashley Howe on tracks slated for their next album. Gone is keyboardist Keith Hale (not replaced) and Cream legend Ginger Baker, replaced in March by a returning Martin Griffin, who gets the measles during the sessions.

September 1981. Robert Calvert sees the release of an up-tempo and synthy new wave solo album called *Hype*, based on his one and only novel of the same name. Participating are Nik Turner, Simon House and Michael Moorcock.

September 28 – October 29, 1981. Hawkwind tour the UK, supported by Irish hard rockers Mama's Boys.

October 18, 1981. Hawkwind issue their 11th album, *Sonic Attack*, through their new deal with Kingsley Ward at Active/RCA. Ward was co-owner of Rockfield studios and his label Active had a distribution deal with RCA. The album spends five weeks on the British charts, reaching a No. 19 placement. *Sonic Attack*'s relative heaviness represents a band stepping up to the challenge of the New Wave of British Heavy Metal—Welsh trio Budgie, also signed to Active/RCA, similarly toughen up their sound. This is the first album with drummer Martin Griffin.

December 1981 – February 1982. The band work at Rockfield on tracks toward a second record on Active/RCA.

December 18, 1981. Hawkwind play the Rainbow in London; guesting are Robert Calvert, Nik Turner and Michael Moorcock.

Dunstable, November 4, 1982.

© Oz Hardwick

1982

March 5, 1982. Hawkwind tour mainland Europe, supporting Krokus.

May 14, 1982. Hawkwind issue their 12th album, *Church of Hawkwind*, a relatively electronic and experimental record, produced by Dave under the alias Dr. Technical. The album reaches No. 26 on the UK charts. Virtually none of the songs from the synthesizer-heavy album are performed live. The stylistic departure comes from the fact that most of the songs were slated for a Dave Brock solo project, but were forced into a Hawk box while Martin Griffin was sidelined with the measles.

June – July 1982. The band return once again to Rockfield to record songs for a proposed new album.

October 14 – November 15, 1982. After only a handful of dates in the middle of the year, Hawkwind mount an intensive UK campaign, playing almost every night, supported by Spanish heavy metal merchants Baron Rojo. Drummer Martin Griffin leaves after the tour, not happy about his role on the new record, where he mostly supplied fills over programmed drums.

October 29, 1982. Hawkwind issue the more traditional *Choose Your Masques*, their third and last through their deal with Kingsley Ward and Active/RCA—Nik Turner guests on it. Turmoil ensues as the band goes through personnel shuffles and the odd hiatus, in conjunction with the loss of their major label deal. Given their close financial ties directly with RCA on the Ward deal, they are considered more or less an RCA artist during this period—*Choose Your Masques* would mark the last time the band would be signed to any semblance of a major label deal.

November – December 1982. The band embark on a 29-date UK tour, with Nik Turner returning to the fold.

Dunstable, 4 November 1982.

Stonehenge, 1983.

1983

February 1983. On drums, Andy Anderson replaces Martin Griffin.

March 1983. Charisma reissues 1976's *Astounding Sounds, Amazing Music*.

July 7, 1983. Flicknife issues the original 1979 Hawklords demo of "Who's Gonna Win the War?" as a single, backed with "Time of the Hawklords," also a demo from the same sessions.

September 3, 1983. "Dave Brock and Friends"—Dave, Nik and Harvey—are one of the acts at Electronica '83, performing a largely improvised set, accompanied by dancer Kris Tait, at the UK's first ever electronic music festival.

October 28, 1983. Flicknife issues *Zones*, consisting of 1981 demo recordings from Battle Studio and live material recorded in late 1980 and in 1982, when Nik Turner was back on stage with the guys singing, playing flute and saxophone (we also hear Michael Moorcock and Ginger Baker). *Zones*, the first album proper for Flicknife, reaches No. 53 on the UK charts. Also issued this year, in July, is the archival live album *The Text of Festival*, on Illuminated/Demi-Monde, a package dominated by early BBC recordings of dubious quality.

November 14, 1983. Hawkwind graphic artist—and manic depression sufferer—Barney Bubbles commits suicide.

Stonehenge, 1983.

© C. Hardwick

Electronica

Milton Keynes, 1983.

Electronica, Milton Keynes, 1983.

Electronica, Milton Keynes, 1983.

Dunstable
March 8, 1984.

© Oz Hardwick

Dunstable
March 8, 1984.

© Oz Hardwick

Brighton March 23, 1984.

© Oz Hardwick

Ramsgate May 25, 1984.

© Oz Hardwick

Ramsgate May 25, 1984.

Stonehenge, June 22, 1984.

1984

February 1984. *Hawkwind* sees reissue in the UK, in regular form plus limited edition picture disc. The album charts for the first time, entering at #75 then dropping out after a single week.

March 2, 1984. Flicknife issues a four-track EP called *The Earth Ritual Preview*, which was to be the opening salvo of an album called *Earth Ritual* and the attendant themed tour designed as a sequel to *Space Ritual*. Lemmy guests on stand-alone A-side track "Night of the Hawks." Drumming on the EP is Robert Heaton, drum tech for the band over the previous couple of years. Heaton also played live for the band (including at Stonehenge), departing in 1983 to concentrate on New Model Army. Heaton would die of pancreatic cancer in 2004 at the age of 43, also the age at which Robert Calvert would pass.

March 9, 1984. The band play an Ipswich date on their Earth Ritual Tour, the tapes of which would be used for a live video called *Night of the Hawk*.

April 23, 1984. Dave, Harvey and Huw are joined by Robert Calvert for a one-off electronics-heavy performance at the Brighton SeaCon science fiction convention.

May 1984. Dave Brock issues his debut solo album, *Earthed to the Ground*, on Flicknife. The album primarily consists of Hawkwind demos put to tape at home in Devon from 1980 through 1983.

May 28, 1984. Robert Calvert joins Hawkwind for an open-air show headlining a Ramsgate "Battle of the Bands" fundraiser. It is his last appearance with the band.

June 20, 1984. Hawkwind play the Stonehenge Free Festival, a memorable and almost milestone gig for the band. The young Alan Davey debuts for the band playing bass, with Dave moving Harvey Bainbridge over to keyboards to open up the position. Davey arrives in the spirit of Lemmy, and expresses a desire to get the band reconnected to the tough sound of the early '70s. A video of extracts from Hawkwind's two sets is released, with fans waiting until 2021 for an audio recording to accompany a DVD reissue.

November 4, 1984. Flicknife issues *This Is Hawkwind, Do Not Panic*, consisting of live material from the *Levitation* tour in 1980 along with an EP that samples from the band's 1984 stand at the Stonehenge Free Festival—the 45 RPM 12" consists of two tracks, "Stonehenge Decoded" and "Watching the Grass Grow." The album marks the debuts of both Danny Thompson and Alan Davey.

November 16, 1984 – December 1, 1985. Hawkwind mount a 13-date UK tour promoting the new live album. Support is NWOBHM act Wildfire, featuring Paul Mario Day, ex-More. A 1995 years-spanning live album called *Undisclosed Files Addendum* samples from the November 27 show at Sheffield University.

Amsterdam
July 31, 1984.

© Oz Hardwick

Dunstable November 18, 1984.

© Oz Hardwick

St Albans November 24, 1984.

© Oz Hardwick

Manchester

February 10, 1985.

1985

January 1985. Robert Calvert issues *Freq*, which features contributions from Huw Lloyd-Langton, Simon King and Lemmy.

January 1985. Demi Monde issues a rough-sounding Hawkwind archival live set from Empire Pool, Wembley, May 27, 1973, as *Bring Me the Head of Yuri Gagarin*. The album would be reissued around 15 times over the years, depending on how one counts.

February 1985. Hawkon, the first ever Hawkwind fan convention, takes place at the Manchester Exhibition Centre. Over a thousand fans attend, as does Hawkwind and assorted ex-members, several of whom get together for a jam.

April 26, 1985. The band put in a rare TV appearance, on Channel 4's ECT.

May 1985. Issued by American Phonograph is *Space Ritual Volume 2*, a restored/altered version of the second half of the original *Space Ritual* album, utilizing only the Brixton Sundown concert from December 30, 1972.

July 19, 1985. The guys record a BBC Radio 1 session.

August – September 1985. The band, at this point consisting of Dave, Huw and Harvey (now dedicated to keyboards), plus new bassist Alan Davey and new drummer Danny Thompson Jr., take residence at Rockfield in Wales to work on tracks for a new album. Producing is Dave Charles who also contributes percussion.

August 24, 1985. The band headline an anti-heroin festival at the Crystal Palace in London, at which Lemmy guests.

November 5 – December 7, 1985. The band mount an intensive UK tour promoting the new album, supported by biker-ish NWOBHM leftovers Dumpy's Rusty Nuts.

November 11, 1985. Flicknife issues Hawkwind's 14th studio album, *The Chronicle of the Black Sword*, which reaches No. 65 on the UK charts. The album is based on Michael Moorcock's Elric of Melniboné character. It emerges on CD for the first time the following year. This is the band's first studio album in three years and is generally considered the return to a heavy sound Alan Davey had hoped for.

December 3, 4, 1985. The band perform at the Hammersmith Odeon, with the tapes being used for a live album called *Live Chronicles* and a live video with the same name as the concurrent album.

Manchester

February 10, 1985.

© Oz Hardwick

Bristol

December 7, 1985.

© Oz Hardwick

1986

April 1986. Demi Monde Records issues a Robert Calvert solo album of dark synth-pop called *Test-Tube Conceived*, which is issued on CD in August of 1987, again through Thunderbolt in 1996 with the definitive reissue being the Voiceprint version from August of 2003, featuring a live version of the title track as a bonus item. This would be Calvert's fifth and last solo album. Amongst the musicians on the album is former Hawkwind bassist Dave Anderson.

August 24, 1986. Hawkwind headline on Sunday, the last night of the Reading festival. Lemmy and Dumpy Dunnell (Dumpy's Rusty Nights) guest on "Silver Machine." The set is broadcast on BBC Radio 1's Friday Rock Show, seeing release on CD in 1992.

November 1986. RCA issues the *Angels of Death* compilation, sampling from *Sonic Attack*, *Church of Hawkwind* and *Choose Your Masques*.

November 1986. GWR issues *Live Chronicles*, documenting a Moorcock-heavy show conducted December 4th the previous year. The album in effect stands as an expanded version of *The Chronicle of the Black Sword*, and is considered by many fans to be the definitive live Hawkwind album, save for *Space Ritual*.

Hammersmith Clarendon

May 16, 1986.

Hammersmith Clarendon

May 16, 1986.

Dunstable

December 7, 1986.

© Oz Hardwick

© Oz Hardwick

Dunstable

December 7, 1986.

© Oz Hardwick

1987

1987. Robert Calvert sees the publication of his second and last poetry collection, *The Earth Ritual*.

April 1987. Fairly prominent archival album *Out & Intake* sees release, through Flicknife, with Griffin reissuing the live and studio compilation in May of 1992.

1988

February – March 1988. Hawkwind work at Loco Studios in Caerleon and Rockfield in Monmouth with Guy Bidmead on tracks for their proposed next album.

April 1988. Flicknife issues *Dave Brock and the Agents of Chaos*, which sounds like Hawkwind crossed with synth pop, a logical evolution, really, from *Earthed to the Ground*.

April 21, 1988. As part of a 25-date UK tour, the band play the Hammersmith Odeon, which is recorded and broadcast by BBC Radio 1.

April 25, 1988. GWR issues a 15th studio album from Hawkwind, entitled *The Xenon Codex*, which peaks at No. 79 on the UK charts. It's the band's first album to see simultaneous CD release and also the first Hawkwind album in three years, despite, ironically, this being a rare period of stability for the band personnel-wise.

August 14, 1988. Robert Calvert dies from a heart attack, in Ramsgate, England, at the age of 43.

August 14, 1988. Having lost drummer Danny Thompson Jr. (temporarily replaced by Mick Kirton from Dumpy's Rusty Nuts), the band recruit Richard Chadwick, who plays his first gig with the band on this date, at the Aktivator Festival in Tewkesbury, Gloucestershire.

September 1988. Virgin, having acquired Charisma, issues the *Spirit of the Age* compilation celebrating Hawkwind's Charisma years, namely 1976 through 1979.

November – December 1988. The band execute a second leg of UK dates.

December 1988. Through Castle Communications, *Live Seventy Nine* gets two-CD reissue, combined with *Levitation*.

The Nik Turner´s Fantastic All Stars
Hammersmith Clarendon, November 20, 1987.

© Oz Hardwick

Camden Town and Country Club

May 30, 1988.

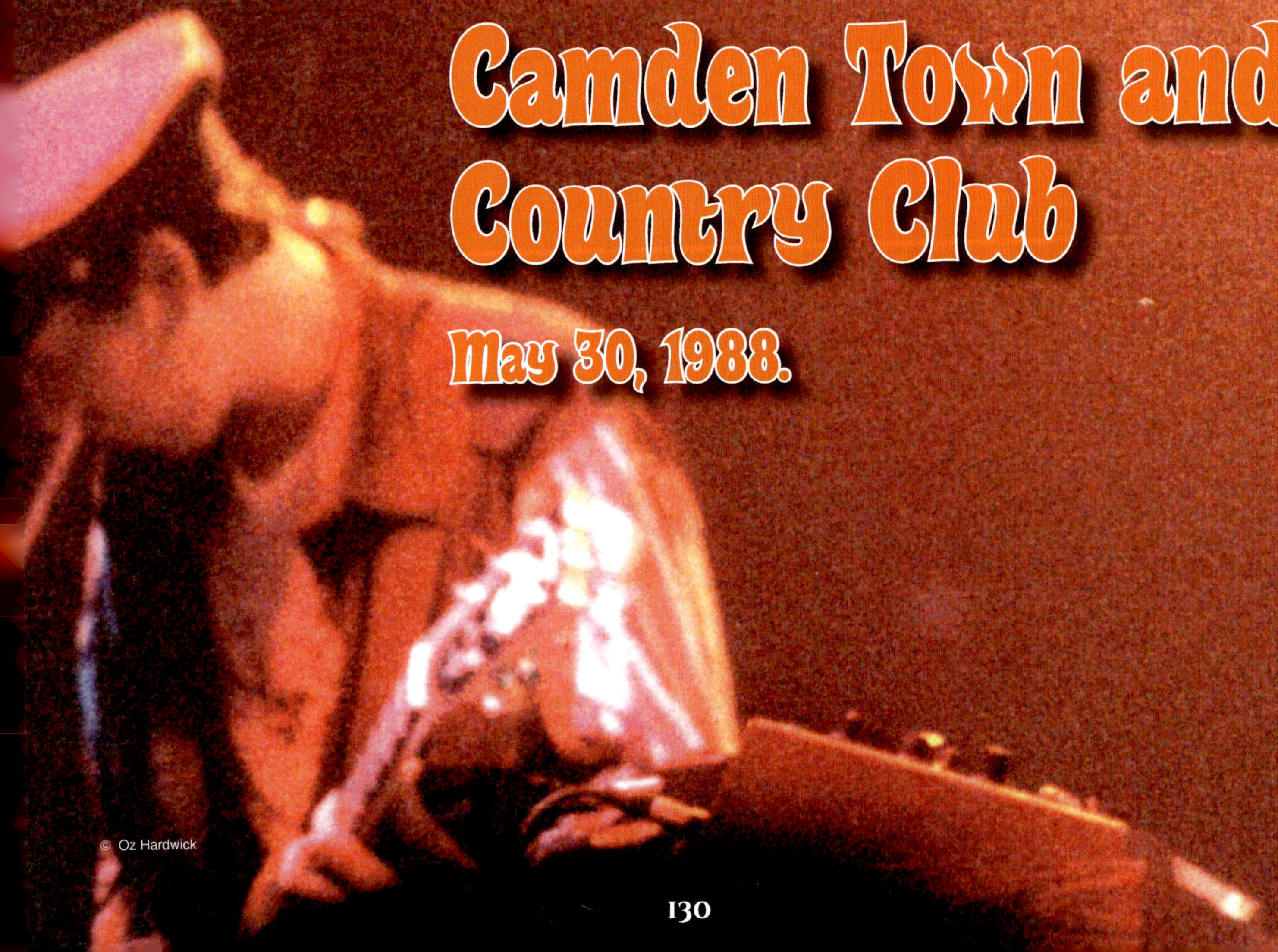

© Oz Hardwick

The Ritz, New York

September 28, 1989.

1989

1989. High Tide reforms (with two original members Simon House and Tony Hill), issuing *Interesting Times*, with more to come over the ensuing years.

1989. Krautrockers (from the UK) Amon Düül, featuring two original members of Amon Düül II, issue *Die Lösung*. On bass is Dave Anderson, with Robert Calvert co-writing most of the album and providing vocals (the album was recorded in mid 1988, with Calvert dying in August).

April 1989. *Astounding Sounds, Amazing Music*, *Quark, Strangeness and Charm*, Hawklords' *25 Years On* and *PXR5* are issued on CD for the first time, through Virgin. Griffin Music versions of the '76 and '77 Hawkwind albums for North America follow in 1995.

May 1989. *In Search of Space* and *Hall of the Mountain Grill* are issued on CD for the first time, by EMI Fame in the UK, with US releases to follow two years later, through One Way Records. Also issued at this time on CD is Dave's *Earthed to the Ground* solo album, which includes as bonus tracks, much of *Dave Brock and the Agents of Chaos*.

Mid-1989. Huw Lloyd-Langton leaves the band, sometimes replaced by Simon House. Singer Bridget Wishart joins as well, becoming the first female to provide any lead vocals.

September 24 – October 12, 1989. The band play 13 shows in North America, their first trip back in years. The October 10th date at the Palace Theatre in LA would provide the live tracks issued on the *Palace Springs* album. The October 4th show in Minneapolis would also see issue as a two-CD live package in 2008.

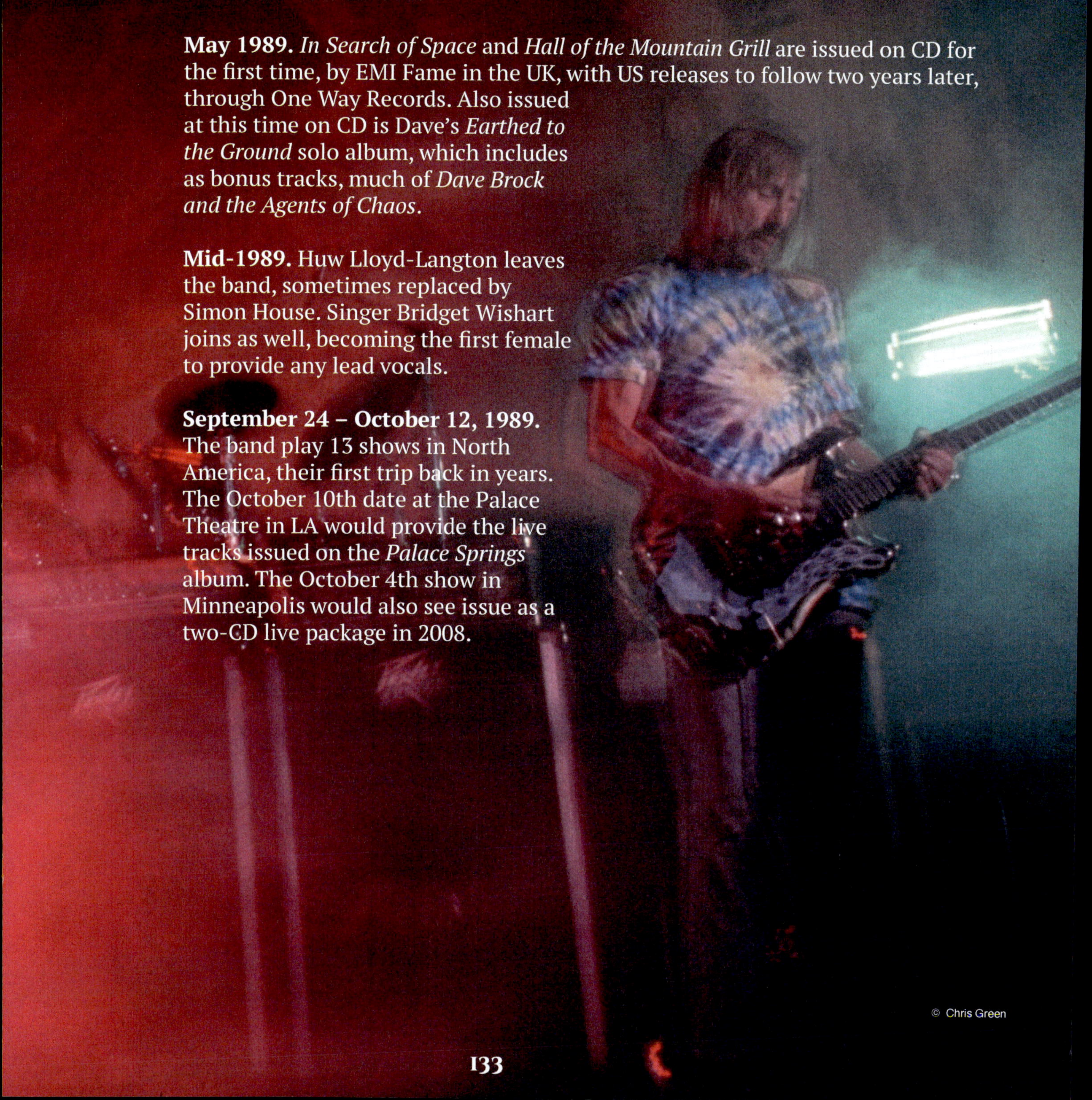

© Chris Green

Harvey Bainbridge

Alan Davey

© Chris Green

Alan Davey

Pogles running the light show.

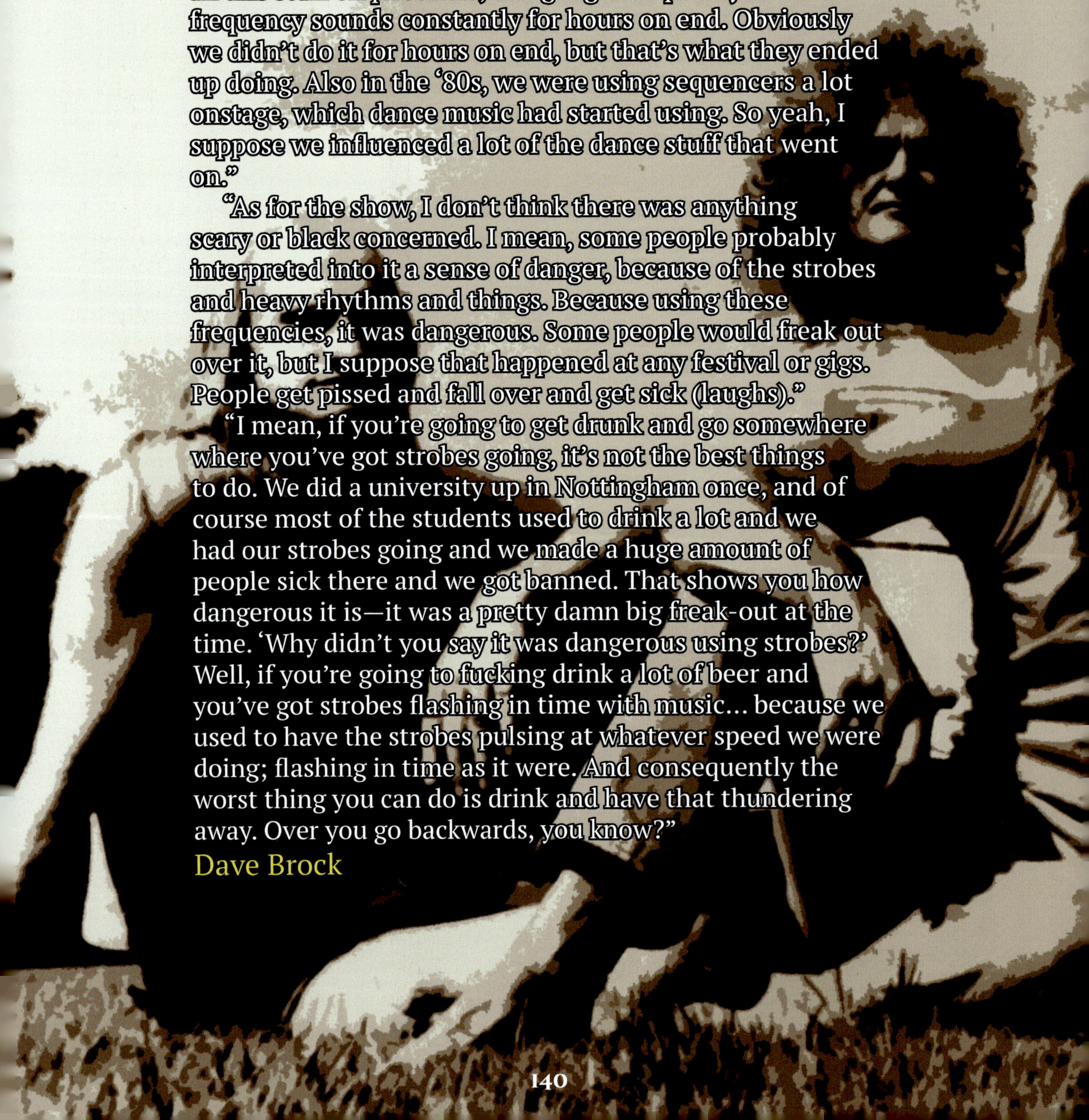

"We used to experiment a lot with high-frequency sounds, and also bottom end, low-frequency too. It's really similar to mantras, Buddhist mantras, with voices doing the same thing. 'Om'—you keep that going for a while, and you can do the same thing with electronic music, with low-frequency sounds, so they just pitch and waver around. You do people's heads in a bit (laughs). Quite dangerous, I might say. In fact the US government used to experiment with all this stuff on prisoners, using high-frequency and low-frequency sounds constantly for hours on end. Obviously we didn't do it for hours on end, but that's what they ended up doing. Also in the '80s, we were using sequencers a lot onstage, which dance music had started using. So yeah, I suppose we influenced a lot of the dance stuff that went on."

"As for the show, I don't think there was anything scary or black concerned. I mean, some people probably interpreted into it a sense of danger, because of the strobes and heavy rhythms and things. Because using these frequencies, it was dangerous. Some people would freak out over it, but I suppose that happened at any festival or gigs. People get pissed and fall over and get sick (laughs)."

"I mean, if you're going to get drunk and go somewhere where you've got strobes going, it's not the best things to do. We did a university up in Nottingham once, and of course most of the students used to drink a lot and we had our strobes going and we made a huge amount of people sick there and we got banned. That shows you how dangerous it is—it was a pretty damn big freak-out at the time. 'Why didn't you say it was dangerous using strobes?' Well, if you're going to fucking drink a lot of beer and you've got strobes flashing in time with music... because we used to have the strobes pulsing at whatever speed we were doing; flashing in time as it were. And consequently the worst thing you can do is drink and have that thundering away. Over you go backwards, you know?"

Dave Brock

THE 1990s

Hawkwind in the '90s is the story of a workmanlike band getting on with business once the fame has flown and once the hope of fame has also flown. Fortunately, however, for the intrepid explorer both new and old, there is a substantial, note-dense collection of records to keep any academic astronaut of the lysergic-inclined busy for years. *Space Bandits* and *Electric Tepee* are very much the continuation of the dark and heavy paranoid vibe displayed over the last two records of the '80s, while *It Is the Business of the Future to Be Dangerous* might be viewed as the '90s version of *Church of Hawkwind*, a slightly new age respite from the clang of the blanga.

Manager Doug Smith and the guys try something new at this juncture, setting up their own label called Emergency Broadcast System, first issuing a live album called *The Business Trip* which I recall seeing in stores all over Canada, so they must've been doing something right. They also tried to cash in on the dance 'n' trance craze with *White Zone*, issued under the name Psychedelic Warriors. But alas, rave culture is *for* the young *by* the young.

However then there's a bit of a shift, with the UFO–conceptual *Alien 4* from 1995 and *Distant Horizons* (crap album cover) from 1997 essentially sounding like the first records of the 2000s, production values brighter and cleaner, rhythm section arrangements less electronic, everything more professional but nonetheless still a mix of noisy guitar songs over repetitive four/four rhythms next to studiously constructed old-school synthesizer collages.

But as Doug has related over the years, each EBS title sold less than the one before it, and by the time we get to *Distant Horizons*, the consortium doesn't even bother to make vinyl, given that we've now entered the nadir for the format, when there was zero romance left for it, sort of seven years after the launch of CDs and another seven before anybody had wrapped their heads around the idea of downloading.

The '90s also represents an era in the band's business cycle when catalogue becomes more important, with Doug trying to figure out the best way to reissue product across a tangle of old deals in a way that doesn't upset members of the band who were on those albums but are not in the band now. Trying to work this end of the catalogue was set against a deluge of dodgy bootleg, semi-bootleg and downright pirate issues that had been showing up in shops all the time, particularly in mainland Europe and particularly given the new ease of producing CDs.

But beyond this, again, the band were good for fully five, five-and-a-half, six (depending on how you count) new complicated records on which Dave and whoever else was involved sounded like they were trying hard, for the most part eschewing rehash and reinterpretation. Particularly the likes of the well-regarded *Alien 4* represented a band that was writing fresh and anew, balancing the modern against the traditional while rising to the performance, production and mixing challenges of trying to send so many confounding signals across any given collection of Hawkwind songs.

1990/91. Alan Davey, Harvey Bainbridge, Dave Brock, Bridget Wishart, Richard Chadwick.

1990

January 25, 1990. The band play a set at a TV studio in Nottingham, for airing on ITV's Bedrock. The performance would see initial release on video as *Live Legends*, with further audio and video permutations to follow.

April 1990. EMI issues a well-appointed and nicely organized compilation called *Stasis: The U.A. Years 1971 – 1975*, which is comprised mostly of single versions and edits.

April – June 1990. The band work at Rockfield in Wales with producer Paul Cobbold on tracks slated for their next record.

September 24, 1990. GWR issues *Space Bandits*, Hawkwind's 16th studio album, which manages a No. 70 placement on the UK charts. The album continues in the dark, noisy, claustrophobic vein of *The Xenon Codex*, if even more distorted and murky, given the often electronic drum grooves. The record is also marked by significant personnel changes: *Space Bandits* is the first album for drummer Richard Chadwick (the band's ninth, by some counts), violinist Simon House is back after 12 years away, and Hawkwind have a female vocalist for the first time, in Bridget Wishart.

October – November 1990. The band conduct a 25-date UK tour, with Simon House already having left the fold again.

December 1990. The band conduct a second North American tour leg, this time playing 18 shows. The December 16th stop at the Oakland Omni Theatre is recorded and issued in 1992 as *California Brainstorm*.

Dave Brock on stage at The Wetlands, New York on December 1, 1990.

© Chris Green

1991

March 12 – April 10, 1991. The band tour Europe, after which Harvey Bainbridge leaves. Most shockingly, Dave Brock is temporarily replaced by Steve Bemand from the Demented Stoats (Bridget Wishart and Richard Chadwick were also part of this band).

June 3, 1991. GWR issues *Palace Springs*, which consists of five live tracks and two studio songs recorded with a mobile. The album represents Harvey Bainbridge's last with the band.

July 1991. *Doremi Fasol Latido* is issued on CD for the first time, through One Way Records.

September 1991. Bridget Wishart leaves the band.

October 1991. Windsong issues *BBC Radio 1 Live in Concert*, which documents the previously discussed live show from September 28, 1972, at the Paris Theatre. This is a significant Hawkwind live album due to the fact that it features the *Space Ritual* lineup, considered by many to be the definitive configuration, and that it pre-dates that definitive live album, serving as a sort of warm-up show.

1992

February 1992. Castle Communications issues *Live Seventy Nine*, *Levitation* and *Space Bandits* as a three-CD set. Castle also issues *Live Seventy Nine*, *The Xenon Codex* and *Space Bandits* separately at this time, while *Levitation* saw issue on its own back in 1987.

March 1992. Raw Fruit issues *The Friday Rock Show Sessions*, commemorating Hawkwind's headline set at the Reading festival, August 24, 1986. It's called this because the BBC had recorded it and it was subsequently broadcast on Tommy Vance's show.

April 23 - May 19, 1992. The band mount a UK tour. Supporting is Krel, from which Hawkwind years later will acquire Mr. Dibs.

May 1992. Griffin Music issues *Live*, which commemorates a Hawklords gig at Brunel University in Uxbridge, November 24, 1979, the second to last date of the extensive fall '78 tour. The set appears in the UK as well, on Dojo.

May 11, 1992. Essential issues in the UK, a 17th Hawkwind studio album, entitled *Electric Teepee*, which hits #53 on the UK charts. The title refers to the idea of a "tribal enclosure." The band at this point is down to a three-piece, consisting of Dave Brock, Alan Davey and Richard Chadwick. The album is the first one recorded in Dave's home studio. The guys absolutely rock out, bucking the given narrative that the Active/RCA period singlehandedly represents the heaviest era of Hawkwind, prompted by the adjacency to the New Wave of British Heavy Metal. *Electric Teepee* also goes to the wall of the still fairly new CD technology, clocking in at 75 minutes.

June 1992. Anagram issues a compilation called *Mighty Hawkwind Classics* that covers in their entirety the *Hawkwind Zoo* EP, the Sonic Assassins live EP (featuring Bob Calvert) and the *Night of the Hawks* EP (featuring a 1984 reunion with Lemmy). Issued by Griffin in 1995.

July 1992. Iloki in the US issues a live album called *California Brainstorm*, with Cyclops putting out the package in the UK two years later. This is a kind of sister record to *Palace Springs*, with which it would be coupled for an expanded issue in 2012.

August 1992. Dojo reissues on CD *The Chronicle of the Black Sword*, with Griffin following up for North America in May of '94, each with two bonus live tracks.

September 1992. *Hawkwind* and *Space Ritual* are issued for the first time on CD, through One Way Records.

1993

1993. Stacia graduates from the Crawford College of Art and Design in Ireland. Married with kids, Stacia's main pursuit now is the visual arts.

April 6, 1993. Monster Magnet issue their second album, *Superjudge*, which includes a cover of "Brainstorm."

May 1993. *Warrior on the Edge of Time* sees release for the first time on Dojo in the UK, in conjunction with a Griffin Music release for the US and Canada (the Dojo release is dated 1992 but it came out the same time as the Griffin issue). Griffin boss Robert Godwin brought to fruition the release when he reminded Hawkwind manager Doug Smith that the album wasn't owned by UA in America. Smith then subsequently went and read the contract and realized that the UA UK contract had expired as well, so now he could also give the record to Dojo. Smith then asked Godwin to delay the US release until the UK release was ready. The Griffin issue includes the shorter single mix of "Kings of Speed."

October 25, 1993. Essential issues a 19th Hawkwind studio album, *It Is the Business of the Future to Be Dangerous*, which reaches No. 75 on the UK charts. The album is recorded once more as a trio, at Brock's home studio in Devon called Barking Dog, with Paul Cobbold producing. Once more, Hawkwind turn in an action-packed album, heavy, proggy, nightmarish, with complicated and dense arrays of both electronic and acoustic drum tracks. It is their first album to include a cover version, featuring their take on the Rolling Stones' "Gimme Shelter," which they had released on April 12th as a charity record in an unlikely collaboration with glamour model-turned-pop star Samantha Fox.

November 1993. The band support the new album with a 21-date tour of the UK, followed by European dates into December.

1994

February 1994. The two-CD reissue of *Live Chronicles* through Griffin includes a copy of Michael Moorcock novel, *The Dreaming City*.

June 1994. Griffin issues the organized yet cacophonous *It Is the Business of the Future to Be Dangerous* in the US.

September 1994. Griffin Music issues *Live Seventy Nine* in North America.

September 19, 1994. Emergency Broadcast System issue, as their first full-length record, *The Business Trip*, a quasi-live, high-profile album credited to Hawkwind as a trio, namely Dave Brock, Alan Davey and Richard Chadwick, as no-nonsense of a lineup that there ever was. The set documents a show at the Thames Valley University but much doctoring of the tapes has taken place. EBS was set up by Doug Smith and partner Eve Carr, with Dave, Alan and Richard as shareholders.

November 1, 1994. Griffin issues the definitive Hawkwind box set. The four-CD *25 Years On* is the first and most complete set to date to sample from all eras, given Robert Godwin's careful collaboration with EMI on the project. The success of *25 Years On* in the marketplace prompted manager Doug Smith, five years later, to urge EMI to assemble and issue a similarly extensive set called *Epocheclipse*.

Late 1994. EBS issues a Simon House album called *Yassasim*.

1995

1995. Dave Brock issues *Strange Trips & Pipe Dreams*, his most electronica-heavy solo album to date.

April 1995. Hawkwind expand past their then trio state to include guitarist Jerry Richards and vocalist Ron Tree (both from the English free festival scene), afterward embarking on a 13-date North American tour.

June 20, 1995. The core contemporary Hawkwind trio—Dave Brock, Alan Davey and Richard Chadwick—team up with engineer Dave Charles (sampler, OCSI) to produce an album called *White Zone*, credited to band moniker Psychedelic Warriors. The record is instrumental electronic music, spanning Eno-esque ambient through loud techno but in total, sounding like the then-current definition of industrial music.

Summer 1995. Hawkwind work at Rockfield in Monmouth on tracks slated for their next album. Ron Tree is on board as a full band member, writing and singing; however guitarist Jerry Richards is essentially a guest, playing on three tracks.

July 27, 1995. Hawkwind record a BBC Radio 1 session, at Maida Vale.

October 1995. The band play 13 shows in the UK, followed by another seven dates in mainland Europe.

October 30, 1995. Emergency Broadcast System issues a 20th Hawkwind studio album, entitled *Alien 4*, which reaches No. 119 on the UK charts. *Alien 4* is officially credited to the four-piece Hawkwind configuration consisting of Dave Brock, Richard Chadwick, Alan Davey and Ron Tree, who figures prominently in the credits. "Death Trap" is a recording of a song originally found on *PXR5* while "Wastelands" is a new look at "Wastelands of Sleep" from *The Xenon Codex*.

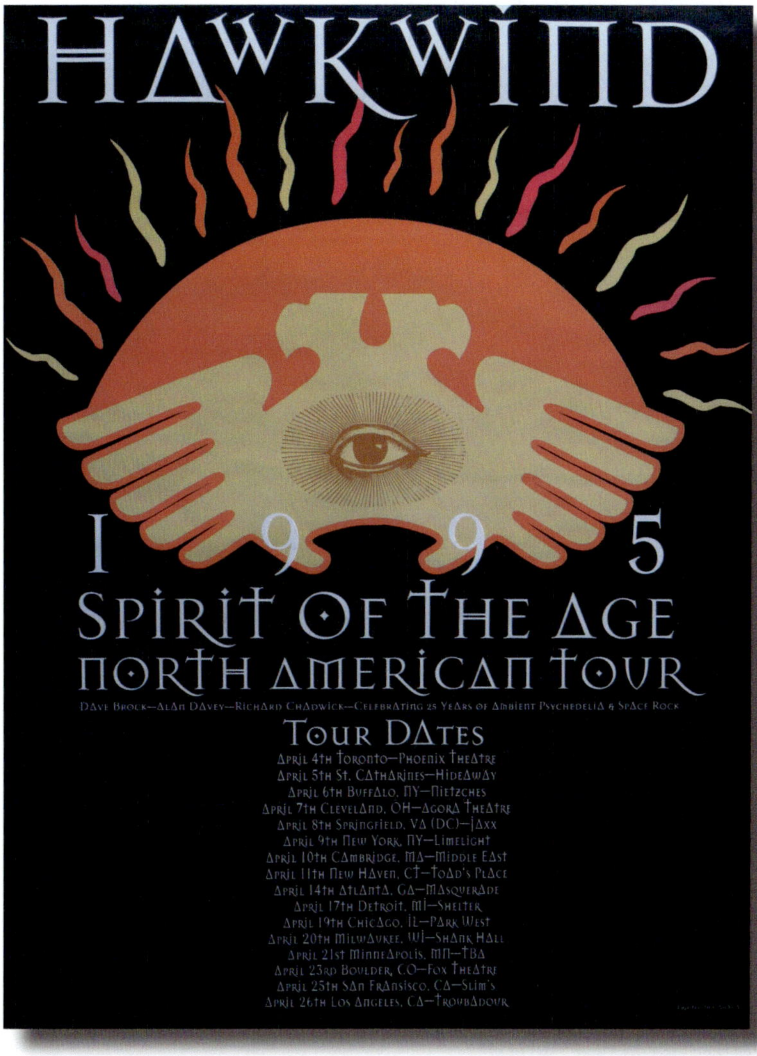

New Haven, Connecticut,
April 11, 1995.

UND
CO

ampeg

Strange Days Festival, Sherman, New York

August 31, 1997.

© Chris Green

Richard Chadwick
Strange Days Festival,
Sherman, New York
August 31, 1997.
© Chris Green

1998

August 1998. Castle Communications reissues *Live Chronicles* in a two-CD package with bonus tracks.

1999

January 5, 1999. Griffin in the US issues a part studio/part live Hawkwind album called *In Your Area*. On this release, the band's lineup was expanded with the addition of "Space Reggae Toaster" and community activist Captain Rizz. The first six of the record's 12 tracks come from a gig in Brussels, Belgium on November 20, 1997. The studio material was recorded at Earth Studios in 1998. With EBS shelved, Dave begins working with Rob Ayling's Voiceprint label, who puts the record out domestically in the UK in 2000.

July 1999. *The Xenon Codex* and *It Is the Business of the Future to Be Dangerous* both see digipak reissue through Essential.

August 1999. Representing what is probably the most official and corporate of Hawkwind compilations, EMI issues a three-CD box set called *Epocheclipse: 30 Year Anthology*. An abridged single CD version is also released, called *The Ultimate Best of*.

September 21, 1999. Thoughtful Aussie popsters The Church issue a covers album, which includes a rendition of "Silver Machine."

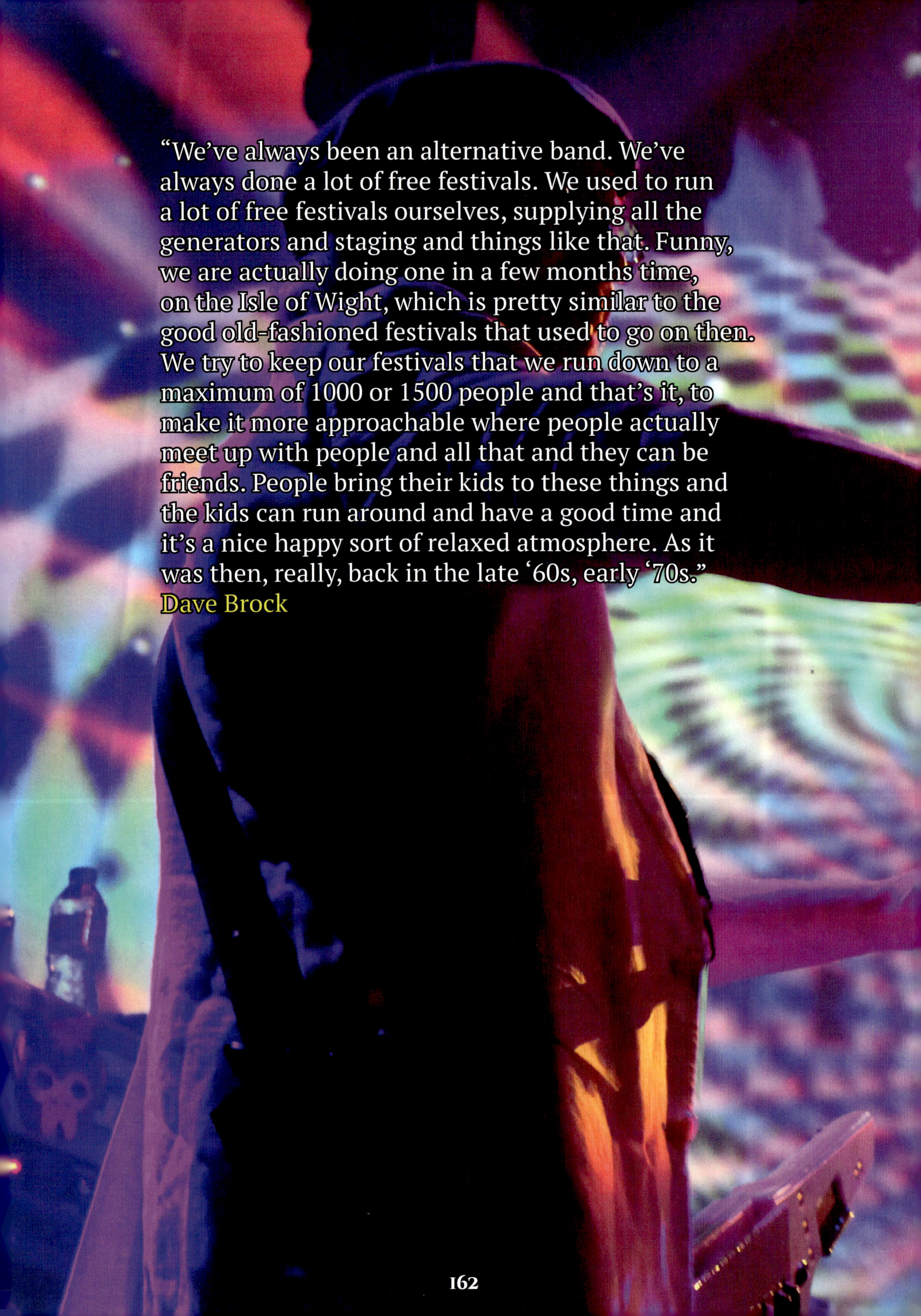

"We've always been an alternative band. We've always done a lot of free festivals. We used to run a lot of free festivals ourselves, supplying all the generators and staging and things like that. Funny, we are actually doing one in a few months time, on the Isle of Wight, which is pretty similar to the good old-fashioned festivals that used to go on then. We try to keep our festivals that we run down to a maximum of 1000 or 1500 people and that's it, to make it more approachable where people actually meet up with people and all that and they can be friends. People bring their kids to these things and the kids can run around and have a good time and it's a nice happy sort of relaxed atmosphere. As it was then, really, back in the late '60s, early '70s."
Dave Brock

THE 2000s

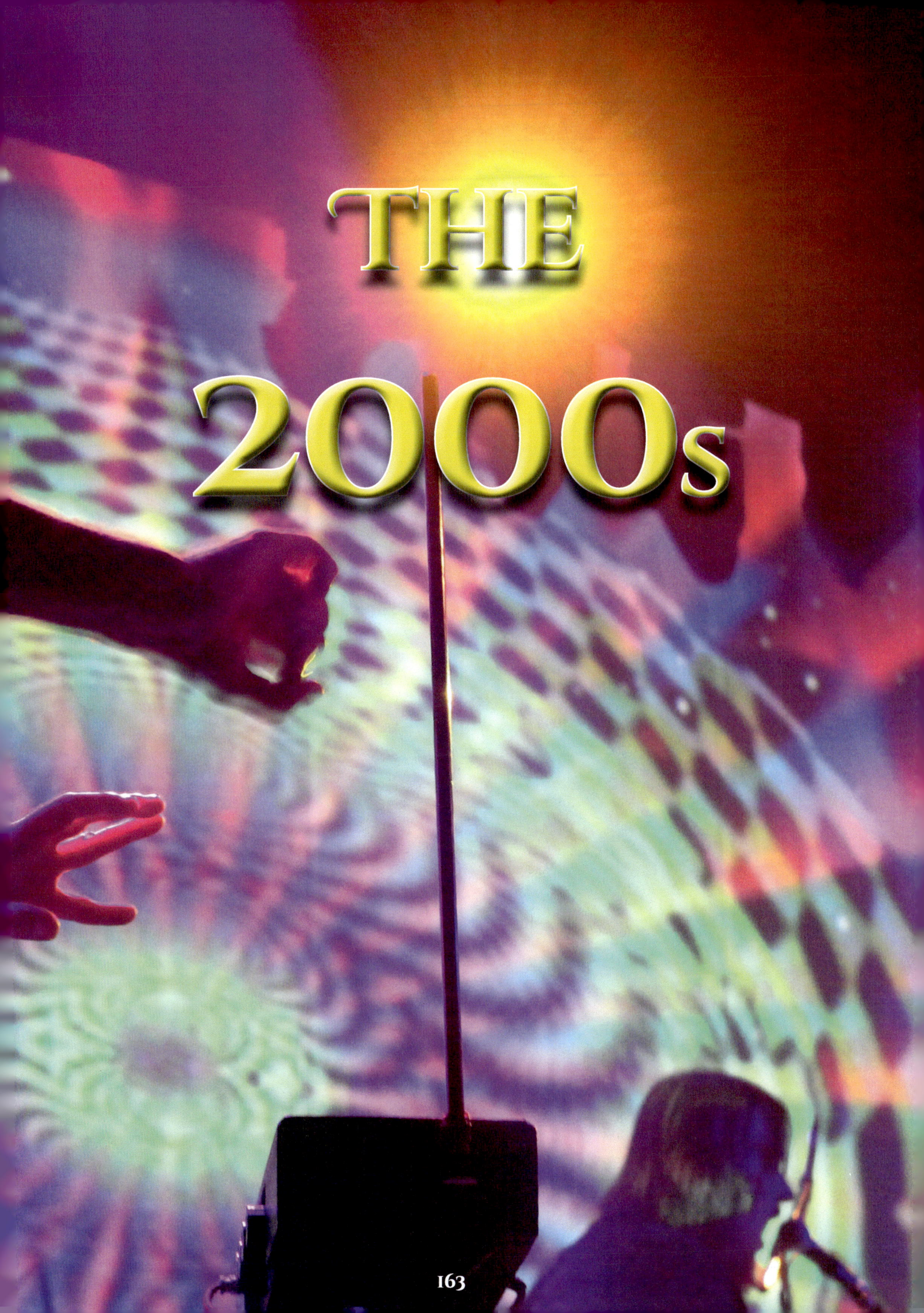

HAWKWIND
'TAKE ME TO YOUR LEADER'
Richard
www.hawkwind.com

Illogical as it may be, the 2000s for Hawkwind are going to pale in comparison vis-à-vis creativity and productivity compared to the 2010s, but such is life in the Brock multiverse. The decade kicks off with another casual and messy record that stirs up a fuss at categorization, namely *Spacebrock*, a Dave Brock solo album with a front cover that says big an' bold: Hawkwind and *Spacebrock*. Another tangle is *Take Me to Your Future*, leaving only *Take Me to Your Leader* in between to represent that band proper in terms of a bona fide studio album, loopy and Julian Cope-like as it is.

Maybe the theme of the new millennium is this then: reissuing. First there's *The Weird Tapes* and the Dave Brock solo stuff through Voiceprint, who are also good for a bunch of live albums plus the regular new Hawkwind items. But then there's the big Cherry Red deal, which kicks off at the end of the decade and continues into the next, with reverent look-ins at the original master tapes for sonic adjustments as well as rarities to include on expanded packages.

Another exciting marker on the dance card camp comes with the Hawkfest events that occur throughout the decade, endorsed and attended by the band and band members from over the years. These sorts of fan gatherings are community-building but there's also a strong collecting theme to the proceedings, codifying the substantial interest in Hawkwind as a collectible band, no surprise given the top-shelf graphics on the records (well, both top-shelf and bottom-cupboard with very little middle ground!) and the anarchic release history of the labyrinthine canon.

Other than that, Hawkwind tours as do Hawklords. There's also Hawkestra, and there are tribute concerts to both Robert Calvert and Barney Bubbles, both gone to soon. Also gone too soon is Jason Stuart who is in the band when he succumbs to a haemorrhage of the brain in September of 2008. Tim Blake, already part of the fold at that juncture, soldiers on as co-keyboardist with Dave and others (Dead Fred, Magnus Martin) over most of the ensuing years through to the present day. Through it all, Dave Brock, defying the advancing years and inspiring musicians half his age, continues to steward this band as it navigates a new millennium seeming built for his positive and life-affirming words of wisdom concerning how to make this planet a better place.

2000

2000. Black Widow Records out of Italy issues a Simon House album called *Spiral Galaxy Revisited.*

September 2000. Dave's archival cassette series, *The Weird Tapes* is issued on CD through Voiceprint, or rather seven of the original tapes are, with the eighth issued in March of 2006.

October 21, 2000. Voiceprint issues a 23rd Hawkwind album, entitled *Spacebrock*, which is essentially a Dave Brock solo trip. This coincides with the first Hawkestra event, a 30th anniversary concert, which takes place at the Brixton Academy with approximately 20 Hawkwind alumni participating in a show that goes three hours. Alan Davey is one party joining in, which paves the way for his return to the band.

December 29, 2000. Hawkwind play their annual Christmas show, at the Astoria in London. Brock, taking inspiration from the recent Hawkestra experience, involves a handful of ex-members in the proceedings.

2001

2001. Alan Davey rejoins Hawkwind, although also this year, his band Bedouin issue a studio album called *As Above So Below*. Also rejoining is Huw-Lloyd-Langton.

October 2001. Voiceprint issues a live album called *Yule Ritual*, which documents the annual Christmas gig of the previous year. Guesting on vocals are Michael Moorcock and Captain Rizz.

December 20, 2001. The Christmas show at the London Forum sees Tim Blake return, setting up his contribution to the band in 2002.

2002

May 2002. EMI keep their hand in the Hawkwind game, issuing a 14-track compilation in their *Masters of Rock* series.

July 19 – 21, 2002. Hawkwind (greatly expanded, with alumni) and various offshoot and related acts perform at the first Hawkfest, a three-day festival open exclusively to members of the fan club. The event takes place at Three Horseshoe Farms in Devon.

October 2002. Hawkwind are joined by fellow underground legend Arthur Brown, whose association with the band goes back to Calvert's *Captain Lockheed and the Starfighters*. Brown had guested at a festival in Canterbury the previous summer, and would remain until the following summer, bringing his own "Time & Confusion" and "Time Captives" to the set, along with his Captain Lockheed cameo "Song of the Gremlin." The December 4th Newcastle show is recorded and released on CD and DVD as *Out of the Shadows* in 2004. The December 13th London show is also recorded for the very limited edition *Spaced Out in London* CD, considered by most fans to be the better album.

December 10, 2002. Following a show in Nottingham, ill health forces Huw to leave the band, though he will make occasional guest appearances in future.

2003

2003. Alan Davey's Bedouin temporarily fold their tent.

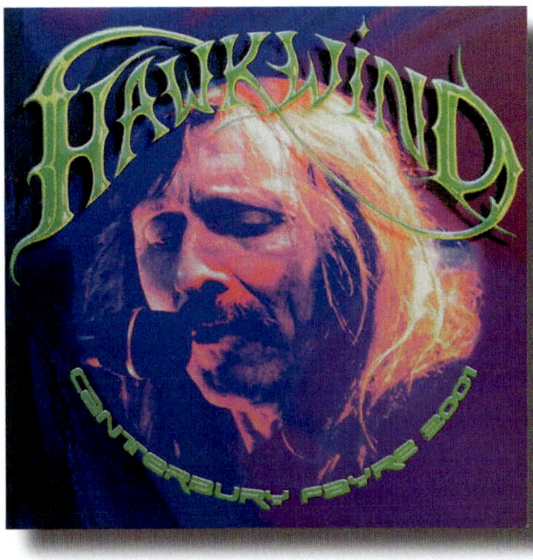

February 4, 2003. Voiceprint issues a live album called *Canterbury Fayre 2001*, which documents Hawkwind's show at the hippie fest, August 18, 2001.

July 2003. Voiceprint combine Dave's *Earthed to the Ground* and *Dave Brock and the Agents of Chaos* for a paired CD reissue package.

August 8 – 10, 2003. The second Hawkfest is held, in Garstang, Lancashire, England. Once again, an all-in-the-family version of Hawkwind play, but Arthur Brown does as well, headlining the Friday.

August 17, 2003. A four-piece Hawkwind, consisting of Brock, Chadick and Davey, along with Keith Barton, hop across the Channel for a gig at Amsterdam's Melkweg.

2004

May – July 2004. The year's round of UK touring is punctuated by shows in Greece, Sweden, Finland and Germany.

May 25, 2004. Monster Magnet issue their sixth album, *Monolithic Baby!*, which includes a cover of Robert Calvert solo track "The Right Stuff."

October 23, 2004. Keyboardist Jason Stuart performs his first gig with the band, at Cheltenham Town Hall.

2005

September 12, 2005. Hawkwind issue their first proper new studio album in five years, *Take Me to Your Leader*, on Voiceprint. The core band of Brock, Chadwick and Davey is augmented by guests including Jason Stuart, Lene Lovich, Arthur Brown, Simon House and TV presenter Matthew Wright on a version of "Spirit of the Age" which is also released as a single.

October 31, 2005. UK black metal act The Meads of Asphodel issue their fourth album, *Damascus Steel*. It includes a cover of Hawkwind's "Sword of the East." On and off, both Alan Davey and Huw Lloyd-Langton play with the band, Alan from 2002 to 2014, Huw from 2000 to 2007.

2006

September 24, 2006. Hawkwind issue, through Voiceprint, an odds 'n' sods audio/video album called *Take Me to Your Future*.

September 25, 2006. Alan Davey vehicle Bedouin issue *Extremely Live 2003*; this follows upon the indie released *Live and Beyond* from 2002 and *Live in Europe 1998*, from 1998, as well as a couple of live videos.

December 2006. Alan Davey leaves Hawkwind for a second time, reforming Gunslinger. He is replaced by long-time crew member Mr. Dibs.

2007

March 30, 2007. BBC 4's Original series airs an hour-long documentary called *Hawkwind: Do Not Panic*, running it again on August 10th. Brock pulls out of the project because of Turner's involvement.

June 15 – 17, 2007. A third Hawkfest is held, at Donington Park Farmhouse, Leicestershire, England. This represents Mr. Dibs' first gig as Hawkwind bassist.

October 8, 2007. Voiceprint reissues Robert Calvert's *Centigrade 232* book of poems and 1986 recitations thereof in a single package.

November 2007. Having worked with Hawkwind on and off over the years, synthesizer wizard Tim Blake begins a long and essentially continuous period of association with Hawkwind.

2008

January 2008. The band reverse their long-time ban on fans recording their live gigs, with stipulations.

May 26, 2008. Vision Music issues *Knights of Space*, documenting Hawkwind's annual Christmas gig in London, recorded at the Astoria on December 19th the previous year.

July 2008. Cherry Red acquire the rights to the entire Hawkwind catalogue from 1976 through to 1997, and create a new imprint called Atomhenge to re-constitute and reissue the material.

September 8, 2008. Current-era Hawkwind keyboardist Jason Stuart dies from a brain haemorrhage.

September 28, 2008. Nik Turner assembles a bunch of ex-Hawkwind members in Herne Bay for a concert in tribute to Robert Calvert, and a new version of Hawklords is born.

December 2008. Hawkwind mount a UK tour; new to the band is multi-instrumentalist Niall Hone, who mostly plays guitar on the campaign.

2009

March 2009. First off the mark as part of the vast Atomhenge reissue deal are the *Spirit of the Age* and *The Dream Goes On* anthologies, Robert Calvert's *Freq*, Hawklords' *25 Years On*, the *Live Chronicles* live album plus studio albums *Astounding Sounds, Amazing Music* and *Electric Teepee*.

June 29, 2009. Atomhenge reissues *The Chronicle of the Black Sword*, adding *The Earth Ritual Preview* EP from 1984. Also re-launched is 1996 live album *Love in Space*, Atomhenge adding to the package tracks from the *Love in Space* EP.

October 29, 2009. The loose consortium known as Hawklords reconvene for a concert in tribute to Barney Bubbles, at the 229 club in London.

© Oz Hardwick

"We called our new album *Blood of the Earth* because, well, the blood of the earth is the actual organic waste—the lava—that comes out of the earth. That's the blood. They always have this thing that oil is the blood of the earth, but it's not really. It's the lava. And it's always red, hence the title. And some of the tracks relate to it."

"Emphasized on this one, really, is the electronics. We use a lot of electronic oscillators and crossovers and things like that, which are quite unusual in a sense, for these high-frequency sounds that do make you go a bit wobbly (laughs), to get your senses going a bit strange. So it's a combination of that and, I suppose, good rhythms, solid rhythms pounding away. And there we are—that's pretty much what Hawkwind music is (laughs)."

"We've pretty much kept our style going all the way through, all these years. I mean, nowadays, we've been using obviously state-of-the-art gear. We used to use old EMS synthesizers, but obviously now you can get Apple computers where you can call up all the stuff on, really. So we moved on from using our old audio generators. Well, in fact we still do use them. I mean, I've got this big box of audio generators so even today I suppose we do use a combination of new Apple stuff—the modern technology—with the old stuff, really."

Dave Brock

THE 2010s TO 2023

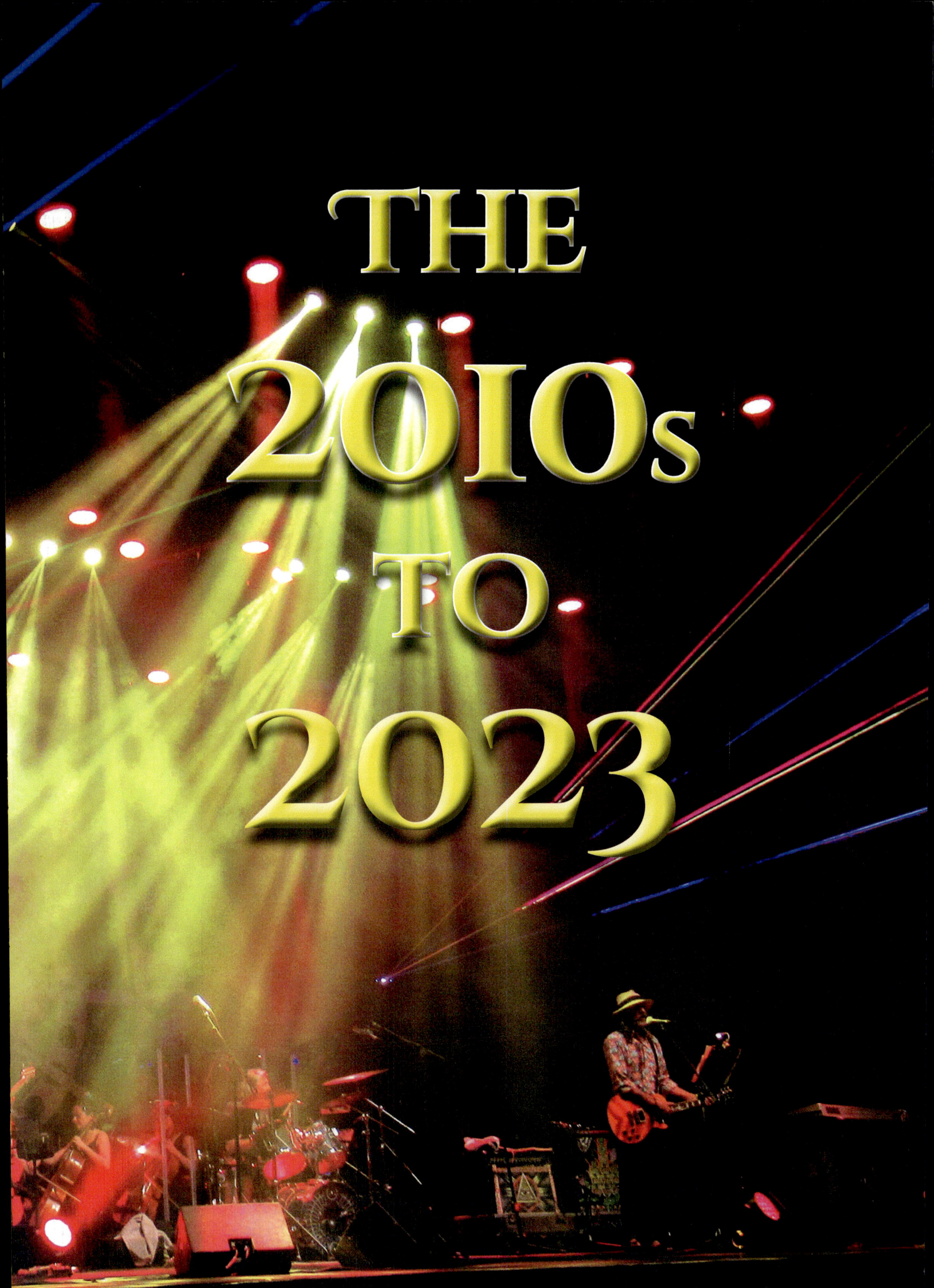

HAWKWIND

It's quite inspiring that Dave Brock spent most of the 2010s in his 70s producing efficient, well-appointed proper Hawkwind albums, overseeing classy reissues of the past catalogue and commandeering a band blessed with both maturity and stability. At his side as always is drummer Richard Chadwick, but the expanded cast also stays quite consistent, one or another of the duo's long-time collaborators hopping on and then off the spaceship, roles more pronounced one record, less pronounced another.

The decade kicks off in fine fashion with *Blood of the Earth*, complicated by the odd remake to be sure, but generally a bright, fresh and intellectually stimulating new Hawkwind record. Then, as if contemplating his impending mortality, Dave knuckles down, asking his band mates to pick up any slack necessary due to Brock's old age, to which they respond in spades. *Onward* (a double), *The Machine Stops* and *Into the Woods* (both concept albums), and *All Aboard the Skylark* (great album cover) deliver a wealth of new Hawkwind material to be studied and debated for decades to come, while *Stellar Variations*, *The Road to Utopia* and to some extent 2020's casual *Carnivorous* remind everyone of the previously ragged nature of the Hawkwind collective.

Part of that debate, invariably, will be the same one that applies to the likes of Deep Purple in later years, and closer to home, Motörhead until the end, and that is the idea of the band becoming too self-aware, too professional, too prolific, too plush, as if Hawkwind fans didn't complain about the opposite (if not continuously, continually) since the band's inception 54 years ago.

But strength to strength, Dave, now into his 80s, has delivered a new record called *The Future Never Waits*, and one can only marvel at the late-period rush of creativity we're getting from Hawkwind, which again, has been smartly commandeered by Brock involving alumni younger than him into the process. Indeed (and this is rare amongst band franchises), given the complexity and uniqueness of the sonic and lyrical world Hawkwind has constructed—and how through sheer multiplicity of dimension it seems bigger than any one member—it's not unreasonable to think the band can continue operating once Dave Brock experiences his own personal "10 Seconds of Forever." No one wishes that to be soon, but yes, I can't help but think Hawkwind can—and should—carry on doing what they're doing for thousands of years to come.

2010

2010. Hawklords conduct a short UK tour, following up with a more extensive campaign in 2011.

February 2010. *Alien 4*, from 1995, sees reissue as a two-CD package, through Atomhenge/Cherry Red.

March 2010. The BBC issues *At the BBC 1972*, which sees re-release on vinyl in 2020. This package included two mixes. The stereo mix was located at the prompting of Griffin boss Robert Godwin, who urged manager Doug Smith to listen to the various bootleg versions that had circulated for years. This mix was used, along with another key piece of Hawkwind history, two additional BBC tracks with Lemmy, who can be heard singing on a superlative live version of "Silver Machine."

March 15, 2010. *Lemmy*, directed and produced by Greg Oliver and Wes Orshoski, premieres at the South by Southwest film festival. Participating in the documentary are both Dave Brock and Nik Turner.

May 2010. *The Xenon Codex* sees reissue, through Atomhenge/Cherry Red.

June 21, 2010. Eastworld issues a 26th Hawkwind album called *Blood of the Earth*, which comes in regular and expanded two-CD editions, with the second CD consisting of live tracks and an interview.

2011

April 25, 2011. Atomhenge/Cherry Red reissues Dave Brock's *Earthed to the Ground* solo album, with five bonus tracks, following up the next month with a reissue of 1997 Hawkwind studio album *Distant Horizons*.

May 2011. Multi-instrumentalist Niall Hone, in the band since '08, grows into his role as the band's bassist, with Mr. Dibs also playing bass but increasingly serving as front man, given Brock's growing reluctance to take the spotlight.

October 11, 2011. William Shatner issues his fourth studio album, *Seeking Major Tom*, on Cleopatra. It includes a cover of "Sliver Machine."

Fall 2011. Hawklords play dates in mainland Europe.

December 2011 – May 2012. Hawklords work at various locales on tracks slated to appear on a reunion studio album.

2012

April 30, 2012. Eastworld issues Hawkwind's 27th studio album (depending on how one counts). *Onward* is a (short) double album, recorded at Earth Studios. Huw Lloyd-Langton guests on the track "The Hills Have Ears."

May 26, 2012. Original Hawkwind bassist John A. Harrison dies, two days before what would have been his 70th birthday. He had been diagnosed with Huntington's disease in 2005 and had been living in a long-term care home.

September 24, 2012. Hawklords issue a studio album called *We Are One*, which sounds like golden-era Hawkwind from the mid-'70s.

November 26, 2012. Hawkwind Light Orchestra—Dave Brock, Niall Hone and Richard Chadwick—issue *Stellar Variations*.

December 6, 2012. Huw Lloyd-Langton dies, age 61, at his home after a two-year battle with cancer.

2013

2013. Prog magazine bestow upon Dave a lifetime achievement award. It's a bitter pill, as Brock is in bad health due to stress throughout this period, cancelling North American tours as he battles Nik Turner in the courts over use of the Hawkwind name.

2013. Alan Davey forms The Psychedelic Warlords, initially to recreate the *Space Ritual* show in its entirety, with subsequent shows featuring the complete *Captain Lockheed and the Starfighters* and *Hall of the Mountain Grill* albums, before becoming a vehicle for Davey's compositions with an emphasis on the Hawkwind era. Three live albums are released following the band's dissolution in 2015.

2013. Hawkwind issues *Spacehawks*, an album comprised mostly of re-recordings and remixes. The band's re-recording of 1971's "Master of the Universe" constitutes Huw Lloyd-Langton's last recording session before his death.

October 25, 2013. Hawklords issue *Dream*, which again sounds like Hawkwind and Hawklords from the '70s, albeit a bit more progressive and produced than the album's predecessor, *We Are One*.

2014

February 14, 2014. The band execute a charity show for animal causes, at Shepherd's Bush Empire, at which they perform an almost complete re-telling of the original *Space Ritual* live set.

October 6, 2014. Hawklords issue *Censored*, which continues the band's tradition of delivering a facsimile of classic-era Hawkwind. Michael Moorcock contributes a poem called "Induction," rendered as a typical nightmarish spoken word performance over space noises.

2015

March 30, 2015. Gonzo Multimedia issues *Space Ritual Live 2014*, on both CD and DVD.

October 9, 2015. Hawklords issue *R:Evolution*.

December 28, 2015. Hoary heart of classic-era Hawkwind Lemmy Kilmister succumbs to cancer, just two days after his diagnosis.

© Oz Hardwick

Manchester
October 3, 2015.

© Oz Hardwick

Manchester

October 3, 2015.

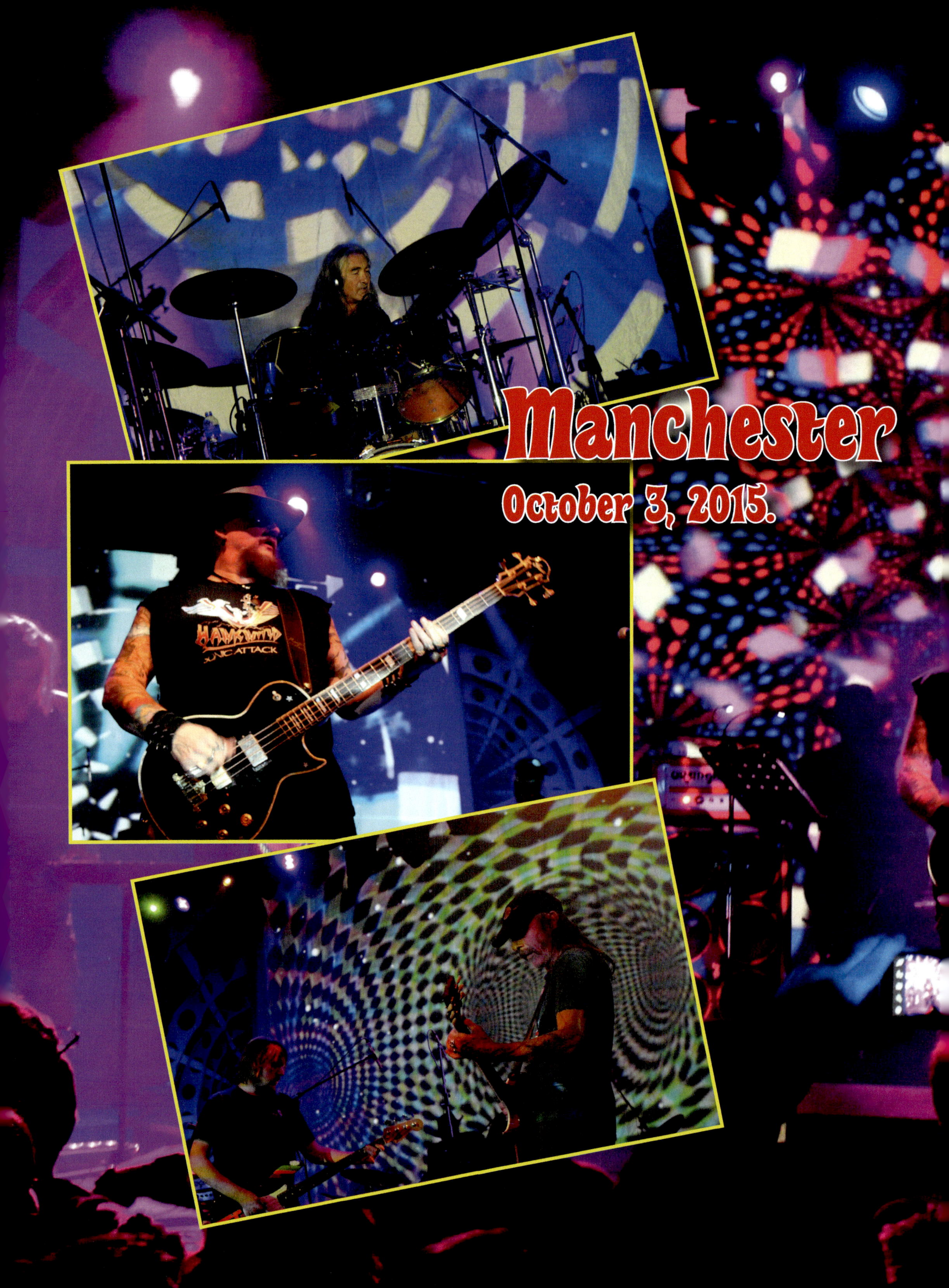

Manchester

October 3, 2015.

SONIC ATTACK

Manchester

October 3, 2015.

© Oz Hardwick

Manchester

October 3, 2015.

© Oz Hardwick

HAWKWIND
Roland

Manchester

October 3, 2015.

2016

February 26, 2016. Quebec progressive metal masters Voivod issue their *Post Society* EP, which features a cover of "Silver Machine."

April 15, 2016. Hawkwind issue a concept album called *The Machine Stops*, based on a short story by E.M. Forster from 1909. Haz Wheaton is the band's new bassist as Mr. Dibs concentrates on vocals. Synthesizer master Tim Blake is now gone from the band, intent on exploring further his Crystal Machine brand, with Niall Hone and Dead Fred picking up the slack. The album hit No. 29 on the UK charts, the band's highest placement since *Choose Your Masques* back in 1982.

October 7, 2016. Hawklords issue a fifth album (of the modern era), entitled *Fusion*.

2017

January 2017. Niall Hone leaves Hawkwind, soon to return.

May 5, 2017. Hawkwind issue what is considered their 30th album. *Into the Woods* is a concept record which, Dave states, continues the saga started on *The Machine Stops*. The album reaches No. 34 on the UK charts. The lineup of the band now consists of Dave Brock, Mr. Dibs, Magnus Martin, Haz Wheaton and Richard Chadwick. Gone since the last record are Niall Hone and Dead Fred.

May 26, 2017. Hawkwind play London's Roundhouse, home of "Silver Machine" and *Greasy Truckers Party*. The set, for which the band are joined on the encore by Motörhead's Phil Campbell, is released by Cherry Red later in the year as *At the Roundhouse*.

June 30, 2017. Dave Brock gets a sense of closure with a legal ruling over Nik Turner concerning ownership of the Hawkwind trademark.

Leeds
March 16, 2017.

BURMAN
BURMAN

Morecambe
March 30, 2018.

© Oz Hardwick

September 29, 2017. Nik Turner issues *Life in Space*, designed as a follow-up to 2015's *Space Fusion Odyssey*, both part of Turner's collaboration with Cleopatra Records.

October 6, 2017. Hawklords issue *Six*.

November 16, 2017. Michael "Dik Mik" Davis dies, with no cause of death reported.

2018

March 30 – April 1, 2018. Hawkeaster at Morecambe's Alhambra Theatre sees Hawkwind joined by friends and relations, including an ecstatically received set by Tim Blake and Friends (Blake, Brock, Davey and Steve Hillage) and rare performances of a number of Calvert's short plays.

May 2018. Hawkwind bassist Haz Wheaton leaves the band to join stoner rockers Electric Wizard; he is replaced by a returning Niall Hone, who now concentrates on electronic sound duties, as does Mr. Dibs.

August 28, 2018. Mr. Dibs leaves Hawkwind citing in an announcement "irreconcilable differences." He now moves on to Evil Blizzard, Strip Search Tramp and solo projects.

September 14, 2018. Hawkwind issue *Road to Utopia*, a record of reworked classics with arrangements by Mike Batt. Featured are radically different and substantially lush interpretations of the songs, augmented by strings, brass section and much vigorous acoustic guitar strumming. Eric Clapton, long-time friend of Dave Brock, guests on "The Watcher."

October 26, 2018. Hawklords issue *Brave New World*.

November 4 – 5, 2018. The UK tour, with Mike Batt conducting the orchestra and guest vocals by Arthur Brown, culminates in two sold-out shows at London's famous Palladium. Dave Brock recalls having busked the queues outside in the '60s.

Hawkwind

Morecambe

March 30, 2018.

© Oz Hardwick

Laney
Laney

November 4, 2018.

© Oz Hardwick

© Oz Hardwick

© Oz Hardwick

KORG

© Oz Hardwick

2019

March 8, 2019. Purple Pyramid, a sub-imprint of Cleopatra, issues a Nik Turner album called *The Final Frontier*, which represents Turner's continued collaboration with the UK Subs' Nicky Garratt.

March 29, 2019. Alan Davey's Bedouin issue *Time Is Made of Gold*, on Purple Pyramid. Davey plays all the guitar, bass and keyboards plus programs the drums; on vocals is Michelle Jimenez-Alder.

July 2019. Stacia makes a surprise appearance on stage with Nik Turner at Kozfest.

October 18, 2019. The prolific Hawklords issue *Heaven's Gate*, their eighth album in eight years. The last three had been designed as a trilogy on the subjects of war, peace and love.

October 25, 2019. Cherry Red issues a 32nd Hawkwind studio album, entitled *All Aboard the Skylark*, which reaches No. 34 on the UK charts. Some versions of the album include a second disc titled *Acoustic Daze*, which is comprised of the original basic tracks used to sculpt *Road to Utopia* plus live recordings. *Acoustic Daze* is also issued as a stand-alone vinyl LP. The official band at this juncture consists of Dave Brock, Magnus Martin, Niall Hone and Richard Chadwick.

November 14, 2019. The band perform four songs for Marc Riley's BBC Radio 6 Music show.

November 25, 2019. Eric Clapton joins Hawkwind onstage for nearly an hour at the band's show in Guildford. The gig is part of a 15-date tour of the UK promoting the new album, culminating in a show at the Royal Albert Hall.

York

November 11, 2019.

© Oz Hardwick

© Oz Hardwick

HAWKWIND 50
BLACK SWORD
HAWKWIND 50
HAWKWIND
© Oz Hardwick

© Oz Hardwick

2022

May 30, 2022. Nik Turner & The Trance Dimensionals (essentially a Steve Hillman vehicle) issue an album through Italy's Black Widow Records called *Synchronicity*.

September 9 – 11, 2022. It's another Hawkfest! This one takes place at Morecambe, Lancashire.

October 7, 2022. Hawkwind issue a double live album called *We Are Looking In on You*.

November 10, 2022. Dave Brock nemesis Nicholas Robert "Nik" Turner dies at the age of 82.

2023

April 28, 2023. For the author's 60th birthday, Hawkwind deliver 'round about their 35th album, entitled *The Future Never Waits*. The band creating these new sound collages consists of Magnus Martin, Thighpaulsandra, Doug MacKinnon, Richard Chadwick and, as always, Dave Brock. As for the future, wait and find out.

© Oz Hardwick

Special Thanks

I'd like to thank Jerry, Gary and Andy back at the Wymer compound for coaxing this book out of deep space and into the light.

But it's really Hawkwind angel Oz Hardwick that has made these pages sing. His myriad visual contributions as well as his impressive second-pass peer review scholarship on all things Brock an' Hawk were crucial to this project's success.

Finally, I'd like to thank Griffin Music boss and world-renowned Hawkwind expert Robert Godwin for his primary peer review of my text. His conscientious work on this manuscript has made sure that it is a fitting tribute to all that Dave Brock has accomplished in keeping Hawkwind firing on all cylinders through a quantity and quality of adversity that would have killed a lesser man.

The Publisher would like to thank Chris Green, Oz Hardwick and Steve LIvesley for their contributions.

About the Author

At approximately 7900 (with over 7000 appearing in his books), Martin has unofficially written more record reviews than anybody in the history of music writing across all genres. Additionally, Martin has penned approximately 115 books on hard rock, heavy metal, classic rock and record collecting. He was Editor-In-Chief of the now retired Brave Words & Bloody Knuckles, Canada's foremost metal publication for 14 years, and has also contributed to Revolver, Guitar World, Goldmine, Record Collector, bravewords.com, lollipop.com and hardradio.com, with many record label band bios and liner notes to his credit as well. Additionally, Martin has been a regular contractor to Banger Films, having worked for two years as researcher on the award-winning documentary *Rush: Beyond the Lighted Stage*, on the writing and research team for the 11-episode Metal Evolution and on the ten-episode Rock Icons, both for VH1 Classic. Additionally, Martin is the writer of the original metal genre chart used in *Metal: A Headbanger's Journey* and throughout the Metal Evolution episodes. Martin currently resides in Toronto and can be reached through martinp@ inforamp.net or www.martinpopoff.com.

Martin Popoff – A Complete Bibliography

2023: Nazareth: A Visual Biography, Dominance and Submission: The Blue Öyster Cult Canon, Wild Mood Swings: Disintegrating The Cure Album by Album, AC/DC at 50

2022: Pink Floyd and The Dark Side of the Moon: 50 Years, Killing the Dragon: Dio in the '90s and 2000s, Feed My Frankenstein: Alice Cooper, the Solo Years, Easy Action: The Original Alice Cooper Band, Lively Arts: The Damned Deconstructed, Yes: A Visual Biography II: 1982 – 2022, Bowie @ 75, Dream Evil: Dio in the '80s, Judas Priest: A Visual Biography, UFO: A Visual Biography

2021:Hawkwind: A Visual Biography, Loud 'n' Proud: Fifty Years of Nazareth, Yes: A Visual Biography, Uriah Heep: A Visual Biography, Driven: Rush in the '90s and "In the End," Flaming Telepaths: Imaginos Expanded and Specified, Rebel Rouser: A Sweet User Manual

2020: The Fortune: On the Rocks with Angel, Van Halen: A Visual Biography, Limelight: Rush in the '80s, Thin Lizzy: A Visual Biography, Empire of the Clouds: Iron Maiden in the 2000s, Blue Öyster Cult: A Visual Biography, Anthem: Rush in the '70s, Denim and Leather: Saxon's First Ten Years, Black Funeral: Into the Coven with Mercyful Fate

2019: Satisfaction: 10 Albums That Changed My Life, Holy Smoke: Iron Maiden in the '90s, Sensitive to Light: The Rainbow Story, Where Eagles Dare: Iron Maiden in the '80s, Aces High: The Top 250 Heavy Metal Songs of the '80s, Judas Priest: Turbo 'til Now, Born Again! Black Sabbath in the Eighties and Nineties

2018: Riff Raff: The Top 250 Heavy Metal Songs of the '70s, Lettin' Go: UFO in the '80s and '90s, Queen: Album by Album, Unchained: A Van Halen User Manual, Iron Maiden: Album by Album, Sabotage! Black Sabbath in the Seventies, Welcome to My Nightmare: 50 Years of Alice Cooper, Judas Priest: Decade of Domination, Popoff Archive – 6: American Power Metal, Popoff Archive – 5: European Power Metal, The Clash: All the Albums, All the Songs

2017: Led Zeppelin: All the Albums, All the Songs, AC/DC: Album by Album, Lights Out: Surviving the '70s with UFO, Tornado of Souls: Thrash's Titanic Clash, Caught in a Mosh: The Golden Era of Thrash, Rush: Album by Album, Beer Drinkers and Hell Raisers: The Rise of Motörhead, Metal Collector: Gathered Tales from Headbangers, Hit the Lights: The Birth of Thrash, Popoff Archive – 4: Classic Rock, Popoff Archive – 3: Hair Metal

2016: Popoff Archive – 2: Progressive Rock, Popoff Archive – 1: Doom Metal, Rock the Nation: Montrose, Gamma and Ronnie Redefined, Punk Tees: The Punk Revolution in 125 T-Shirts, Metal Heart: Aiming High with Accept, Ramones at 40, Time and a Word: The Yes Story

2015: Kickstart My Heart: A Mötley Crüe Day-by-Day, This Means War: The Sunset Years of the NWOBHM, Wheels of Steel: The Explosive Early Years of the NWOBHM, Swords and Tequila: Riot's Classic First Decade, Who Invented Heavy Metal?, Sail Away: Whitesnake's Fantastic Voyage

2014: Live Magnetic Air: The Unlikely Saga of the Superlative Max Webster, Steal Away the Night: An Ozzy Osbourne Day-by-Day, The Big Book of Hair Metal, Sweating Bullets: The Deth and Rebirth of Megadeth, Smokin' Valves: A Headbanger's Guide to 900 NWOBHM Records

2013: The Art of Metal (co-edit with Malcolm Dome), 2 Minutes to Midnight: An Iron Maiden Day-by-Day, Metallica: The Complete Illustrated History, Rush: The Illustrated History, Ye Olde Metal: 1979, Scorpions: Top of the Bill - updated and reissued as Wind of Change: The Scorpions Story in 2016

2012: Epic Ted Nugent, Fade To Black: Hard Rock Cover Art of the Vinyl Age, It's Getting Dangerous: Thin Lizzy 81-12, We Will Be Strong: Thin Lizzy 76-81, Fighting My Way Back: Thin Lizzy 69-76, The Deep Purple Royal Family: Chain of Events '80 – '11, The Deep Purple Royal Family: Chain of Events Through '79 - reissued as The Deep Purple Family Year by Year books

2011: Black Sabbath FAQ, The Collector's Guide to Heavy Metal: Volume 4: The '00s (co-authored with David Perri)

2010: Goldmine Standard Catalog of American Records 1948 – 1991, 7th Edition

2009: Goldmine Record Album Price Guide, 6th Edition, Goldmine 45 RPM Price Guide, 7th Edition, A Castle Full of Rascals: Deep Purple '83 – '09, Worlds Away: Voivod and the Art of Michel Langevin, Ye Olde Metal: 1978

2008: Gettin' Tighter: Deep Purple '68 – '76, All Access: The Art of the Backstage Pass, Ye Olde Metal: 1977, Ye Olde Metal: 1976

2007: Judas Priest: Heavy Metal Painkillers, Ye Olde Metal: 1973 to 1975, The Collector's Guide to Heavy Metal: Volume 3: The Nineties, Ye Olde Metal: 1968 to 1972

2006: Run for Cover: The Art of Derek Riggs, Black Sabbath: Doom Let Loose, Dio: Light Beyond the Black

2005: The Collector's Guide to Heavy Metal: Volume 2: The Eighties, Rainbow: English Castle Magic, UFO: Shoot Out the Lights, The New Wave of British Heavy Metal Singles

2004: Blue Öyster Cult: Secrets Revealed! – update and reissue 2009); updated and reissued as Agents of Fortune: The Blue Öyster Cult Story 2016, Contents Under Pressure: 30 Years of Rush at Home & Away, The Top 500 Heavy Metal Albums of All Time

2003: The Collector's Guide to Heavy Metal: Volume 1: The Seventies, The Top 500 Heavy Metal Songs of All Time

2001: Southern Rock Review

2000: Heavy Metal: 20th Century Rock and Roll, The Goldmine Price Guide to Heavy Metal Records

1997: The Collector's Guide to Heavy Metal

1993: Riff Kills Man! 25 Years of Recorded Hard Rock & Heavy Metal

See martinpopoff.com for complete details and ordering information.

© Oz Hardwick

釈迦三尊像

Triade de Śākyamuni

1

釈迦如来像

Bouddha Śākyamuni

文殊菩薩像

Bodhisattva Mañjuśrī

3

普賢菩薩像

Bodhisattva Samantabhadra

動植綵絵

Le Royaume coloré des êtres vivants

1

芍薬群蝶図

Pivoines et papillons

11

梅花小禽図

Prunier en fleur et petits oiseaux

III

雪中鴛鴦図

Canards mandarins dans la neige

IV

秋塘群雀図

Millet d'automne et moineaux

V

向日葵雄鶏図

Tournesols et coq

VI

紫陽花双鶏図

Hortensias, coq et poule

VII

大鶏雌雄図

Coq et poule

VIII

梅花皓月図

Fleurs de prunier et lune

IX

老松孔雀図

Vieux Pin et paon

X

芙蓉双鶏図

Hibiscus, coq et poule

XI

老松白鶏図

Vieux Pin, coq et poule blancs

XII

老松鸚鵡図

Vieux Pin et cacatoès

XIII

芦鵞図

Oie et roseaux

XIV

南天雄鶏図

Nandina et coq

XV

梅花群鶴図

Prunier en fleur et grues

XVI

棕櫚雄鶏図

Palmiers de Chine et coqs

XVII

蓮池遊魚図

Étang aux lotus et poissons

XVIII

桃花小禽図

Fleurs de pêcher et petits oiseaux

XIX

雪中錦鶏図

Faisans dorés dans la neige

XX

群鶏図

Coqs

XXI

薔薇小禽図

Roses et petit oiseau

XXII

牡丹小禽図

Pivoines et petits oiseaux

XXIII

Étang aux insectes

池辺群虫図

XXIV

貝甲図

Coquillages

XXV

Vieux Pin et phénix blanc

老松白鳳図

XXVI

芦雁図

Oie sauvage et roseaux

XXVII

諸魚図

Poissons

XXVIII

Poissons 群魚図

XXIX

Chrysanthèmes et ruisseau

菊花流水図

XXX

紅葉小禽図

Érable et petits oiseaux

JAKUCHŪ 1716–1800

若冲－〈動植綵絵〉を中心に

Le Royaume coloré des êtres vivants

Sous la direction de Manuela Moscatiello et Aya Ōta

Petit Palais
Paris Musées

Japonismes 2018

En cette année 2018, qui marque le cent soixantième anniversaire des relations diplomatiques entre la France et le Japon, le Petit Palais lève le voile sur l'un des secrets les mieux gardés de l'archipel nippon, dans le cadre d'une exposition d'envergure consacrée au peintre Itō Jakuchū.

Figure singulière de la période d'Edo (1603-1867), artiste indépendant en quête de réalisme pictural, Jakuchū demeure unique en son genre. Originaire de Kyōto, il a passé sa vie à étudier la nature, voyant sans doute en elle une source inépuisable d'inspiration.

Observateur et prolifique, il est l'auteur d'un œuvre reconnu, dont une partie a intégré les collections impériales. Au Japon, les expositions qui lui sont consacrées ne manquent jamais d'attirer les foules, au point que l'on y parle d'un «phénomène Jakuchū».

Celle qui s'ouvre à Paris aujourd'hui offre au public l'occasion unique de prendre part au phénomène. Présentant pour la première fois en Europe les trente rouleaux de peinture polychrome sur soie connus sous le nom de *Royaume coloré des êtres vivants*, emblématiques de l'œuvre de Jakuchū, elle s'annonce comme un événement.

Cet ensemble monumental, qui a nécessité près d'une décennie de travail et dont la fragilité limite l'exposition à un mois, est présenté avec la triade bouddhique provenant du temple Shōkoku-ji de Kyōto.

L'exposition, et l'ouvrage qui l'accompagne, ont pu voir le jour grâce à un prêt exceptionnel de l'Agence de la Maison impériale du Japon, que je remercie de sa confiance. Il s'agit là d'un cadeau magnifique à l'attention des Parisiens.

Anne Hidalgo
Maire de Paris

C'est un immense honneur que de voir s'ouvrir cette exposition consacrée à Itō Jakuchū, organisée par la Fondation du Japon, Nikkei Inc., l'Agence de la Maison impériale, avec le concours de Paris Musées et du Petit Palais.

Cette exposition constitue l'un des événements phares organisés dans le cadre de «Japonismes 2018», une série de manifestations culturelles de grande ampleur décidée d'un commun accord par les plus hautes autorités de nos deux pays en cette année 2018 qui marque le 160e anniversaire des relations d'amitié entre la France et le Japon.

Itō Jakuchū, peintre né à Kyōto au XVIIIe siècle, est un artiste qui, ces dernières années, jouit d'une étonnante popularité au Japon. L'exposition organisée à Tōkyō en 2016 – l'année du tricentenaire de sa naissance – a battu tous les records d'affluence avec 450 000 visiteurs durant un mois. L'exposition de Paris constitue la première occasion de présenter en Europe les peintures les plus représentatives du génie de l'artiste et qui ont retenu l'attention du public et des spécialistes : l'ensemble composé de la *Triade de Śākyamuni* et des rouleaux du *Royaume coloré des êtres vivants*.

Le *Royaume coloré des êtres vivants* – le plus grand chef-d'œuvre de Jakuchū – au cœur de cette exposition, désigne une série de trente rouleaux relevant du genre des peintures de fleurs et d'oiseaux. Fleurs, arbres, oiseaux, insectes et poissons : devant cette œuvre où la richesse de toutes les formes du vivant est représentée avec fraîcheur et élégance, « hommes et femmes » quel que soit leur âge comme le veut l'expression classique japonaise – en bref, tout un chacun – ne peut s'empêcher d'être captivé et attiré par la surface des soies peintes. Que ce soit la richesse des couleurs de chaque motif, la minutie infinie des descriptions picturales ou encore les techniques d'expression propres à la peinture japonaise : à mesure que l'on regarde son œuvre, tout concourt à nous faire découvrir le charme de Jakuchū.

À l'origine, le *Royaume coloré des êtres vivants* a été peint comme un ornement censé magnifier la *Triade de Śākyamuni*, placée au centre de l'ensemble. L'œuvre représente une foule d'êtres vivants réunis pour écouter l'enseignement du Bouddha. Cet ensemble offert par Jakuchū lui-même au grand monastère zen du Shōkoku-ji à Kyōto a été préservé avec le plus grand soin. Donné à la Maison impériale en 1889, il est aujourd'hui conservé au musée des collections impériales, Sannomaru Shōzōkan, à Tōkyō placé sous l'égide de l'Agence de la Maison impériale. Dans cette exposition, la série des rouleaux est présentée avec la *Triade de Śākyamuni* qui, aujourd'hui encore, fait partie des collections du Shōkoku-ji.

Notre vœu le plus cher est que, grâce à cette exposition, le Japon et la France et, au-delà, les visiteurs venus de chaque pays, à travers le regard qu'ils porteront sur les peintures de Jakuchū, puissent enrichir de leur dialogue commun et élargir encore les horizons d'une inspiration, vers une création nouvelle liée à un avenir pacifique. Nous aimerions ici remercier Anne Hidalgo, maire de Paris, Delphine Lévy, directrice générale de Paris Musées, et Christophe Leribault, directeur du Petit Palais, dont le concours précieux a permis de mener à bien cette exposition, ainsi que toutes les personnes qui ont participé à sa réalisation.

Fondation du Japon, Nikkei Inc., Agence de la Maison impériale

Faire découvrir un immense artiste resté inconnu en France jusqu'à présent est un privilège unique. C'est donc une fierté pour le Petit Palais de pouvoir présenter, pour la première fois en Europe, l'art d'un des plus grands maîtres de la peinture japonaise du XVIIIe siècle.

Longtemps oublié en raison de la brièveté de sa carrière et de la rareté de ses œuvres, Jakuchū bénéficie d'un engouement extraordinaire depuis quelques années au Japon. C'est la méticuleuse restauration et la présentation de son chef-d'œuvre, le cycle du *Royaume coloré des êtres vivants*, longtemps préservé dans le secret des collections impériales, qui a révélé l'artiste au public. Il revient aux éminents spécialistes qui ont rédigé les articles du catalogue de mieux expliquer la spécificité de l'art de Jakuchū, dans son temps et dans le contexte religieux qui imprègne ses créations.

Grâce à la générosité de l'Agence de la Maison impériale qui a accordé ce prêt en tout point exceptionnel des trente rouleaux du *Royaume coloré des êtres vivants*, et celle du prêtre du temple Shōkoku-ji pour la *Triade de Śākyamuni* restée conservée à Kyōto, l'ensemble est ainsi recréé dans son intégralité pour le public parisien et international. Ce miracle n'aurait pu avoir lieu sans le soutien de la Fondation du Japon, de son président, M. Hiroyasu Ando, et celui de Nikkei Inc. et de son président, M. Naotoshi Okada, auxquels vont également nos remerciements les plus chaleureux. Ceux-ci s'adressent aussi au ministère des Affaires étrangères du Japon, à son ambassadeur à Paris, son Excellence M. Masato Kitera, à la Maison du Japon, son président, M. Tsutomu Sugiura, et à tous les relais enthousiastes qui ont permis la réalisation complexe de cette exposition dont le commissariat est assumé par Mme Aya Ōta, conservatrice en chef du musée des collections impériales Sannomaru Shōzōkan à Tōkyō et Mme Manuela Moscatiello, responsable des collections japonaises du musée Cernuschi, à Paris.

Fleuron des manifestations de la saison « Japonismes 2018 », cette exposition vient saluer la passion française pour la culture japonaise, aussi vivante de nos jours qu'au moment de sa redécouverte, à partir de 1868. Gageons que le raffinement et l'inventivité de l'art de Jakuchū sauront toucher le cœur des visiteurs du Petit Palais, et que ces derniers seront reconnaissants envers l'Agence de la Maison impériale d'avoir su choisir pour écrin parisien un musée qui abrite en son centre un jardin suspendu et des bassins d'eau claire où viennent parfois s'ébrouer des canards sauvages.

Christophe Leribault
Directeur du Petit Palais

Ouvrage sous la direction de Manuela Moscatiello et Aya Ōta.

Contributeurs

Tadashi Kobayashi
Directeur du musée d'art Okada

Manuela Moscatiello
Responsable des collections japonaises au musée Cernuschi,
musée des arts d'Asie de la Ville de Paris

Aya Ōta
Conservatrice en chef du musée des collections impériales,
Sannomaru Shōzōkan

Jean-Noël Robert
Professeur au Collège de France, membre de l'Académie
des Inscriptions et Belles-Lettres

Nobuo Tsuji
Professeur émérite de l'université de Tōkyō

Traductions par François Lachaud des textes en japonais de Aya Ōta,
Tadashi Kobayashi et Nobuo Tsuji

Chronologie et bibliographie par Élodie Pascal

Sommaire

Un porte-drapeau du japonisme en 2018, Itō Jakuchū

La politique de fermeture du pays adoptée par les shoguns Tokugawa (*sakoku*), après plus de 200 années d'existence, s'acheva sous la pression des navires de guerre américains en 1854. À la suite de cet événement, les productions culturelles japonaises qui, jusqu'alors étaient restées méconnues des pays étrangers, se mirent à inonder l'Europe, comme si une digue avait été rompue, et leurs charmes, inconnus et étranges, suscitèrent un immense intérêt au sein du Vieux Continent. Ce fut le monde des arts français qui se montra le plus immédiatement réceptif à ceux-ci ; ainsi, entre les années 1860 et les années 1900, apparurent des phénomènes de mode tels que les japonaiseries ou le japonisme. Les œuvres de Kitagawa Utamaro (1753-1806), Katsushika Hokusai (1760-1849), Utagawa Hiroshige (1797-1858) ou encore Ogata Kōrin (1658-1716) furent présentées au public avec un cortège d'éloges et furent la source de diverses inspirations nouvelles qui infléchirent les principes régissant leur création, chez les peintres tels Monet, Degas, Van Gogh, Gauguin ou Cézanne – la liste est loin d'être exhaustive.

Cependant, le nom d'Itō Jakuchū ne figure pas parmi les artistes japonais mentionnés ci-dessus. L'on ne saurait s'en étonner. À l'époque où le japonisme prospère, le *Royaume coloré des êtres vivants* (*Dōshoku sai-e*), l'une des œuvres majeures de Jakuchū, était conservée à la cour impériale et n'était que fort rarement montrée au public. Le nom de l'artiste était tombé dans l'oubli, même chez les Japonais. Or, voici qu'à l'orée du XXIe siècle, celui-ci fait soudain l'objet de toutes les attentions chez les amateurs d'art au Japon et suscite une vague d'enthousiasme fort étonnante ; vague dont la retombée s'étend au-delà des mers. En 2012, lorsque la National Gallery of Art de Washington présente les trente rouleaux composant le *Royaume coloré des êtres vivants*, l'événement attire plus de 300 000 visiteurs en quatre semaines correspondant à la courte durée de l'exposition. Celle-ci devait d'ailleurs battre les records d'entrée du musée le jour de son ouverture. «C'est l'une des plus belles expositions qu'il m'a été donné de voir.» Ces éloges dithyrambiques sous la plume du critique d'art du *New York Times*, Holland Cotter, eurent une grande influence sur le succès rencontré.

L'année de naissance d'Itō Jakuchū (1716-1800) coïncide avec celle de la mort d'Ogata Kōrin (1658-1716). Tous les deux sont les descendants de marchands de Kyōto. Cependant, lorsque Jakuchū vient au monde, l'élite marchande à laquelle appartient la famille de Kōrin est en plein déclin, tandis que les marchands issus des couches plus humbles – comme la famille de Jakuchū – voient leur richesse matérielle s'accroître. D'ailleurs, ce n'est qu'après la ruine qui frappe l'activité familiale que Kōrin a montré toute l'étendue de son génie artistique et que ce qui n'était pour lui qu'une passion (*shumi*) devint un moyen de subsistance. À l'inverse, même si, à la mort de son père, Jakuchū reprend l'activité familiale à l'âge de vingt-trois ans, c'est aussi pour se consacrer à la peinture – son seul centre d'intérêt. L'on ne sait pas très précisément auprès de qui Jakuchū a commencé à apprendre la peinture. Pour l'essentiel, il semblerait que ce soit en autodidacte.

La peinture d'Asie orientale, qui a ses origines en Chine, se répartit en trois thèmes principaux : le paysage (*sansui*) ; les personnages (*jinbutsu*) – portraits et anecdotes représentant des figures célèbres de la Chine ancienne – et les fleurs et oiseaux (c. *huaniao hua* ; j. *kachōga*). Parmi ces genres, c'est le troisième vers lequel Jakuchū se tourne. Il copie des peintures de fleurs et d'oiseaux des dynasties Yuan (1279-1368) et Ming (1368-1644) conservées dans les monastères bouddhiques de Kyōto. Nagasaki constitue alors le seul port où les navires commerciaux chinois sont autorisés à entrer au Japon; c'est à bord de ceux-ci qu'arrivent Shen Nanpin (Shin Nanpin, vers 1682 - après 1760) et Song Ziyan (Sō Shiseki, 1715-1786), deux peintres du Continent qui vont enseigner l'art pictural aux Japonais durant leur séjour dans la ville ; leur nouvelle manière de traiter la peinture de fleurs et d'oiseaux fut également transmise à Kyōto et connut une grande popularité ; Jakuchū s'est voué à l'étude de celle-ci avec un zèle à nul autre pareil.

Lorsqu'il prit ses distances avec l'activité familiale, Jakuchū était déjà une figure célèbre parmi les habitants de la capitale en tant que peintre de fleurs et d'oiseaux. Son œuvre la plus représentative, le *Royaume coloré des êtres vivants*, consiste en une série appartenant à ce genre pictural ; lorsqu'il eut terminé le vingt-quatrième rouleau sur les trente finalement réalisés, il ajouta à l'ensemble la *Triade de Śākyamuni* (*Shaka sanzon*) – et en fit don au grand monastère zen du Shōkoku-ji. Il faut sans doute chercher les raisons de ce choix dans la mort prématurée de son plus jeune frère. Jakuchū avait alors cinquante ans en 1765. Dans la lettre qui accompagne sa donation, il déclare à propos des motifs qui lui ont inspiré celle-ci : « Mon acte n'est aucunement motivé par un quelconque souci de renommée mondaine ; je souhaite que ces peintures soient longtemps transmises comme autant d'instruments et de décors cultuels servant lors des cérémonies religieuses. » La rétribution que le monastère accorda à Jakuchū en remerciement de ce don précieux, considéré par les autorités monastiques telle une contribution spontanée d'un marchand de la ville, fut une simple boîte de gâteaux... Conformément aux volontés de Jakuchū, les peintures furent présentées chaque année au sixième mois lors des cérémonies de confession collectives (*senpō kō*) selon le dispositif suivant : la triade de Śākyamuni au centre, flanquée de chaque côté de quinze peintures du *Royaume coloré des êtres vivants*.

L'exposition présentée à Paris reste fidèle à la disposition choisie par le monastère.

Cet acte pieux entièrement désintéressé de Jakuchū, ainsi que la splendeur de l'œuvre devinrent, de manière assez surprenante, très populaires chez les habitants de Kyōto. Dans les cercles de peintres (*gadan*), Jakuchū ne fit que gagner en notoriété, ne le cédant qu'à Maruyama Ōkyo (1733-1795). Durant les quatre décennies suivantes, il continua de peindre et de dessiner.

Lorsque le grand incendie qui frappa Kyōto en 1788, réduisit en cendres la maison et l'atelier de Jakuchū, alors âgé de 70 ans, l'artiste fut confronté à une réalité nouvelle : devoir peindre pour gagner sa vie. Il lui arriva souvent d'échanger un lavis à l'encre noire contre un boisseau de riz (environ 18 litres).

La vie de Jakuchū, ce bouddhiste fervent, abonde en épisodes dignes d'être développés : le fait qu'il refusa de se marier et qu'il resta célibataire sa vie durant ; son naturel agréable qui le portait à aimer tous les êtres vivants ; sa profonde amitié pour le moine zen Daiten (1719-1801) du Shōkoku-ji. Nous passerons ici sur ces aspects de sa personnalité pour évoquer le caractère contemporain du *Royaume coloré des êtres vivants*. Ainsi que nous l'avons mentionné plus haut, son style de peintures de fleurs et d'oiseaux se fonde sur son étude de ce genre pictural chez les peintres chinois. Cependant, si l'on fait exception des œuvres célèbres des dynasties Yuan et Ming conservées dans les grands monastères de Kyōto, Jakuchū n'a pu copier et observer que les œuvres destinées à la vente composées par des peintres professionnels contemporains de la dynastie Qing (1644-1912). On s'accorde à penser que ces peintures reposent sur la technique « d'après nature » (c. *xiesheng* ; j. *shasei*) exposée dans les propos sur la peinture (c. *hualun* ; j. *garon*) de la dynastie Song (960-1279) ; cette pratique consiste à se placer face à un être vivant, à l'observer minutieusement, puis à reproduire ses formes et son mode de vie. Jakuchū aurait acquis ces connaissances très tôt, grâce à son ami Daiten. Et en effet, les rouleaux du *Royaume coloré des êtres vivants* témoignent de ce procédé.

Mais l'art de Jakuchū ne saurait être circonscrit à l'intérieur du vocabulaire traditionnel des arts picturaux en Chine ou au Japon, qu'il s'agisse de peinture de fleurs et d'oiseaux, d'après nature, ou encore de l'école de Shen Nanpin (Nanpin-ha). En définitive, cet art n'est autre que le produit d'un regard et d'une conscience (ou d'une inconscience) qui n'appartiennent qu'à lui. S'il fallait lui appliquer un seul qualificatif, celui qui conviendrait le mieux serait celui d'«excentrique». Mais ce dernier terme ne dit pas tout. Les adjectifs «naïf», «primitif», «surréaliste» – en somme, tout le vocabulaire de la peinture du XXe siècle s'avère étonnamment adapté à son œuvre.

Le regard des Japonais, qui a fini par s'accoutumer à l'art moderne du siècle précédent, a découvert *a posteriori*, de la manière la plus fortuite, des formes d'expressions picturales qui correspondent à ce dernier, dans la peinture nipponne du XVIIIe siècle.

Cette exposition du *Royaume coloré des êtres vivants* à Paris constitue la première présentation de l'œuvre en Europe. Quels échos va-t-elle susciter ? Et si elle devenait l'occasion d'un deuxième Japonisme ? Sans doute est-ce un vain espoir que de nourrir pareille attente...

Nobuo Tsuji

III

III

IV

VI

V

La peinture japonaise au XVIIIe siècle

Itō Jakuchū a exercé son art de peintre au milieu de l'époque d'Edo (1603-1867), dans la seconde partie du XVIIIe siècle – à Kyōto.

Le gouvernement des shoguns Tokugawa (le *bakufu*), à la tête du pays, se situait à Edo (l'actuelle Tōkyō) durant cette période féodale qui a pris ce nom. C'est depuis cette ville qu'il exerçait son autorité sur plus de deux cent soixante gouverneurs féodaux (*daimyō*). Le pouvoir politique véritable était entre les mains de la classe sociale des «guerriers» (*bushi*), en dessous desquels se situaient les paysans, les artisans et les marchands (en d'autres termes : ceux qui fabriquaient les objets et ceux qui en assuraient la distribution) ; ainsi la société d'Edo reposait-elle sur un système hiérarchique au sein duquel une séparation entre les «quatre occupations» (classes sociales) – guerriers, paysans, artisans et marchands (*shinōkōshō*) – était maintenue avec fermeté.

Sur le principe, le système dépendait d'un empereur (*tennō*), vivant à Kyōto – alors capitale du pays connue sous le nom de Heian-kyō – qui confiait l'administration de la politique du pays au shogun ; *de facto* l'empereur et sa cour, même s'ils en tiraient quelque gloire, n'avaient aucun pouvoir politique ; ce n'est qu'à l'extrême fin de l'époque d'Edo (Bakumatsu) qu'il lui revint, quand s'écroula l'autorité des shoguns.

Les guerriers placés sous l'autorité du shogun et des gouverneurs féodaux avaient, en tant que classe dominante, une position vis-à-vis de la culture, fondée sur le respect des enseignements du confucianisme, lesquels peuvent se résumer par l'expression tirée des *Entretiens de Confucius* (c. Lunyu ; j. Rongo): «transmettre sans inventer» (c'est-à-dire recevoir et transmettre la parole des anciens sans y ajouter de création ou d'invention nouvelles); autrement dit, le maintien d'une attitude «conservatrice» s'appuyant sur les classiques chinois et japonais. Dans le monde des arts – et plus particulièrement celui de la peinture –, ils faisaient appel aux peintres officiels (*goyō eshi*) de l'école Kanō, dont le lignage remontait à l'époque précédente et dont le style pictural reposait sur l'application des canons de la peinture chinoise, mais également sur le respect stylistique de la peinture traditionnelle japonaise (Yamato-e), élaboré depuis l'époque de Heian (794-1185).

À l'opposé des guerriers, en quête de raffinement et d'élégance (*miyabi*), les classes populaires, au fur et à mesure du temps, virent leur pouvoir économique s'élever et développèrent une culture originale, pleine de créativité, en réaction à celle des guerriers. Cette culture se distinguait par son caractère populaire, et ses principaux acteurs réactifs aux diverses modes, toujours avides de nouveautés ; c'était tout particulièrement le cas dans les grands centres urbains et prospères de la capitale et des provinces – Edo, Kyōto, Ōsaka, Nagoya. Ces villes virent, sous des formes les plus diverses, l'éclosion de la liberté d'expression et des idées des «citadins» (*chōnin*)[1]. En cette époque partagée entre deux cultures – celle «raffinée» (*ga*) de la classe dominante des guerriers et celle, «vulgaire» (*zoku*), issue des couches populaires –, Jakuchū ouvrit de nouveaux horizons à l'art pictural. Par son appartenance au milieu des citadins de Kyōto, il devint l'une des personnalités représentatives de la culture et des arts de cette catégorie sociale.

1 - Ce terme désigne les commerçants mais aussi, dans une moindre mesure, les artisans (NDT).

2 - Hideyoshi, qui exerça la tutelle de son successeur, eut le titre honorifique de Taikō, à l'origine de l'anglais *tycoon*.

3 - Akira Hayami, *Rekishi jinkōgaku de mita Nihon* [Histoire démographique d'un village japonais], Tōkyō, Bungeishunjū, 2001.

De nouvelles opportunités pour les artistes amateurs

Avant que Tokugawa Ieyasu (1542-1616) n'instaure le gouvernement des shogun à Edo (fig. 1), la période de conflits entre les seigneurs de la guerre (les guerriers les plus puissants) pour exercer leur domination sur le pays avait duré presque un siècle. L'ensemble du pays connut une succession de guerres motivées par des velléités d'extension territoriale ; les paysans furent eux aussi entraînés dans ces conflits ; champs et rizières furent dévastés. Toyotomi Hideyoshi (1537-1598), qui avait unifié le pays avant Ieyasu, fit mesurer les zones cultivables de tout le Japon et détermina pour chacune d'entre elles leur niveau moyen de production de riz. En calculant la quantité de riz obtenue, dont le volume avait été fixé par le «Cadastre de Hideyoshi[2]», on estime que la population du pays devait se situer aux alentours de 12 millions d'habitants. Toutefois, au milieu de l'époque d'Edo – plus précisément lors de l'ère Kyōhō (1716-1736) – avec la fin de la période des guerres civiles et l'augmentation de la production dans les zones rurales, la population se serait accrue à un rythme très rapide, soit d'environ deux fois et demie pour atteindre 30 millions d'habitants[3].

À cette époque, les ressources du pays se développèrent de façon telle que les bienfaits, seulement possibles en période de paix et de stabilité, en furent ressentis non seulement par les guerriers mais aussi par le peuple. C'est ainsi que la population alphabétisée augmenta et que la culture du livre et de l'écrit devint florissante, donnant ainsi naissance à une classe d'intellectuels – le mot devant être pris au sens large – et à des amateurs d'art.

Alors qu'aux époques précédentes, le métier de peintre était réservé à des familles bien identifiées, de génération en génération, ou à des artistes issus d'écoles réputées, le nombre d'amateurs qui se vouaient à la peinture et aux arts appliqués (*kōgei*) connurent alors un accroissement considérable. Ce fut un moment propice à l'éclosion de disciplines très diverses, et beaucoup d'artistes non-professionnels émergèrent dans plusieurs disciplines. L'année de naissance de Jakuchū coïncide précisément avec la première année de l'ère Kyōhō (1716) ; en ce sens, il fut véritablement l'enfant de son temps, de cette génération qui avait su profiter des opportunités offertes à ceux qui n'étaient pas des artistes professionnels au départ.

Positivisme et peinture d'après nature

Tokugawa Yoshimune (1684-1751), huitième shogun de la dynastie, fut l'homme qui contribua à ouvrir la voie de cette époque nouvelle par ses positions politiques originales. Il parvint au rang de shogun en 1716 – année de naissance de Jakuchū – et mit en application des réformes dont on se contentera ici de mentionner celles qui entretiennent un rapport direct avec la culture et les beaux-arts.

Les données démographiques concernant l'ensemble de la population japonaise, auxquelles nous avons déjà fait référence, étaient le résultat d'un recensement conduit en 1721 sur ordre de Yoshimune, avec la collaboration de nombreux gouverneurs féodaux. Par la suite, des recensements

1

2

Fig. 1 Attribué à Kanō Tan'yū (1602-1674), *Portrait de Tokugawa Ieyasu, connu sous le nom de Tōshōgū* [le sanctuaire qui lui est dédié], 17 septembre 1645, 201 x 70 cm, rouleau vertical, encre et couleurs sur papier. Tōkyō, Fondation-Mémorial de la famille Tokugawa.

Fig. 2 Tani Bunchō (1763-1840), Copie de *Fleurs et oiseaux* de Willem van Royen, fin XVIIIe siècle, 231,9 x 96,5 cm, rouleau vertical, couleurs sur papier. Musée municipal de Kōbe.

de l'ensemble de la population japonaise furent dirigés par les autorités shogunales à intervalles réguliers – tous les six ans, jusqu'en 1846 – alors que ce régime approchait de son terme. De même, la faune et la flore de l'ensemble des régions furent inventoriées dans toutes les provinces du pays, en collaboration avec de nombreux savants et érudits parmi lesquels le naturaliste Noro Genjō (1694-1761) et le spécialiste d'« études néerlandaises » (*Rangaku*)[4] Aoki Konyō (1698-1769) ; ces inventaires firent progresser significativement l'histoire naturelle. Cette démarche visait à acquérir une connaissance des phénomènes du monde réel et encourageait à suivre les préceptes du positivisme ; il faudrait ajouter à celui-ci une incitation à étudier les sciences occidentales, à l'exclusion de la religion et l'établissement des bases des études néerlandaises. C'est ainsi que Yoshimune transforma le climat intellectuel de son époque.

Dans le domaine des arts, Yoshimune demanda que le négociant en chef (en néerlandais *opperhoofd*), envoyé dans l'île artificielle de Dejima à Nagasaki fît venir des peintures occidentales authentiques ; il fit également en sorte que le peintre chinois Shen Nanpin (vers 1682 - après 1760) vienne au Japon. Il en résulta, d'une part, la présentation au public au monastère du Gohyaku rakan-ji de peintures de fleurs et d'oiseaux (datées de 1725), réalisées par le peintre de cour néerlandais Willem van Royen (1654-1728), fournissant au shogun l'occasion d'observer directement les techniques de composition des huiles occidentales (fig. 2). D'autre part, Shen Nanpin vint à Nagasaki, accompagné d'un de ses disciples au douzième mois de l'année 1731. Durant son séjour, qui allait durer pratiquement deux ans – il retourna sur le continent au neuvième mois de l'année 1733 –, il enseigna les techniques de la représentation d'après nature à plusieurs peintres japonais parmi lesquels Kumashiro Yūhi (1712-1773). Ces nouvelles techniques, inspirées du style de Shen Nanpin, suscitèrent un vif enthousiasme dans tout le Japon et se développèrent dans chaque province, exerçant ainsi une influence très importante sur les peintres japonais, à commencer par Jakuchū.

Grâce à l'esprit positiviste de l'époque et à l'étude – directe et indirecte – de la peinture européenne et chinoise, il fut possible de se détacher de la tradition conservatrice japonaise – qui consistait à étudier en copiant des peintures de maîtres anciens – par la prise de conscience de l'importance de l'exécution de la peinture d'après nature. L'apparition de peintres à l'occidentale (fig. 3) installés à Edo, tels Shiba Kōkan (1747-1818), et d'artistes travaillant d'après nature à Kyōto, à l'instar de Maruyama Ōkyo (1733-1795) et d'Itō Jakuchū, résulta d'un éveil à une peinture dont la plus haute ambition consistait en la représentation objective du réel.

Subjectivité et peinture de lettrés, l'école excentrique

D'un autre côté, le climat de liberté intellectuelle que l'on commençait à voir éclore au sein du peuple – tout particulièrement parmi les populations citadines – devait jouer également en faveur d'une valorisation de l'individualité de l'artiste, à travers la transmission des impressions propres à chacun. Grâce aux théories portant aux nues la subjectivité

4 - Ce terme désigne les diverses formes livresques de la connaissance des sciences occidentales (NDT).

de la peinture de lettrés chinoise, ainsi qu'aux illustrations des albums xylographiés (c. *huapu ; j. gafu*) servant de modèle aux artistes japonais, autant qu'aux œuvres importées du Continent, une nouvelle démarche artistique vit le jour. Celle-ci – qui consistait à accorder plus de valeur à la mise à nu de l'intériorité de l'artiste, plutôt qu'aux techniques de peinture proprement dites –, fut reçue avec beaucoup d'enthousiasme par le plus grand nombre ; l'intérêt porté à la peinture de lettrés (*bunjinga*) s'étendit à un public de plus en plus large. Ike no Taiga (1723-1776) – issu de la classe marchande de Kyōto (fig. 4) – ou encore Yosa Buson (1716-1784) – né dans une famille de paysans des environs d'Ōsaka – qui ont transmis le plus fidèlement possible les impressions suscitées par la nature japonaise au fil des quatre saisons comme les émotions ressenties à son contact, furent des représentants très actifs de cette peinture. Taiga excellait également dans le domaine de la calligraphie, tandis que Buson était aussi connu comme poète de haiku.

Soga Shōhaku (1730-1781) et Nagasawa Rosetsu (1754-1799), grâce à leur inspiration singulière, hors de portée du commun des mortels, et à l'excentricité de leur art (techniques de peinture sortant de l'ordinaire) causèrent l'étonnement du public et furent regardés comme des peintres «hérétiques», allant le plus loin possible dans l'expression de leur subjectivité. Sans doute n'est-il pas exagéré de dire que ces artistes jugés comme appartenant à l'école des excentriques (kisōha) furent les précurseurs de cet esprit de liberté, allègre et énergique, du monde des peintres considérés comme amateurs dans le Japon au XVIIIe siècle.

Le temps du grand public

À Edo, à partir de la seconde moitié du XVIIIe siècle, l'ukiyo-e, mouvement artistique rencontrant un vif succès auprès des populations urbaines, connaît un âge d'or. En 1765, Suzuki Harunobu (1725 ?-1770) concevait la technique xylographique permettant l'impression d'estampes polychromes connues sous le nom d'«images de brocart» (*nishiki-e*). Cette innovation technique fut accueillie très favorablement et l'on vit apparaître une succession d'artistes populaires tels que Torii Kiyonaga (1752-1815), Kitagawa Utamaro (1753 ?-1806) (fig. 5), Katsukawa Shunshō (1726-1792), Tōshūsai Sharaku (actif en 1794 et 1795), Utagawa Toyoharu (1735-1814), Katsushika Hokusai (1760-1849). Il était désormais possible d'acheter, pour un prix modique, des estampes aux belles couleurs. Ce qui provoqua un fort engouement chez les habitants d'Edo.

Tous les styles de l'estampe japonaise dans lesquels sont traités les thèmes les plus divers, se développèrent en tant que «médias» artistiques et acquirent une grande renommée au sein des classes populaires de la population. Pour ce faire, les artistes se fondaient sur l'étude des techniques de la perspective à l'occidentale : des «images de belles dames» (*bijinga*) de Kiyonaga ou d'Utamaro (qui montrent sous des abords attrayants les femmes des quartiers des plaisirs (*iromachi*) – courtisanes (*yūjo*) et geishas – ainsi que les mœurs des lieux), aux «images d'acteurs» (*yakusha-e*) de Shunshō comme de Sharaku, qui décrivent avec

4

3

Fig. 3 Shiba Kōkan (1747-1818), *Vue de la plage de Shichiri dans la province de Sagami*, 1796, 95,7 x 178,4 cm, paravent à deux panneaux, huile sur papier. Musée municipal de Kōbe (ancienne collection Ikenaga Takeshi).

Fig. 4 Ike no Taiga (1723–1776), *Enfants sous les saules*, XVIIIe siècle, 129,8 x 343,4 cm, paravent à huit panneaux, encre et couleurs légères sur papier. Préfecture de Kyōto, collection du musée Ike Taiga.

5

6

Fig. 5 Kitagawa Utamaro (1753 ?-1806), *Dix types dans l'étude de la physionomie des femmes : l'adultère*, XVIIIe siècle, 37,8 x 24, 3 cm, xylographie polychrome. Musée national de Tōkyō.

Fig. 6 Itō Jakuchū, *Chiot et balai*, seconde moitié du XVIIIe siècle, 99,5 x 27,8 cm, rouleau vertical, encre sur papier. Poème d'éloge composé par le moine Musen Jōzen (1693-1764), de son nom d'artiste Tangai. Kyōto, musée Hosomi.

un grand réalisme le jeu des vedettes les plus populaires, actives sur la scène du kabuki, en passant par les représentations de paysages (*fūkeiga*) saisis avec une précision infinie.

Dans les grandes villes de la région du Kansai, telles Kyōto ou Ōsaka, le développement de l'estampe fut plus tardif, mais il semble que les peintures proprement dites circulaient sur le marché à des prix modérés. Jakuchū utilisait comme l'un de ses noms de pinceau (*gō*) Tobei'an (Boisseau de riz), indiquant ainsi qu'il acceptait une mesure de riz (environ 18 litres) quand on lui passait commande d'une peinture. En réalité, ce «tarif» ne s'appliquait que pour des lavis à l'encre de Chine très simplifiés (fig. 6).

Le XVIIIe siècle marque donc l'avènement de la popularisation des arts, grâce à laquelle on ne percevait plus de si grande distinction entre les amateurs d'estampes conçues par les meilleurs maîtres et les amateurs de peinture et des beaux-arts (au sens noble du mot). Chacun pouvait avoir accès aux œuvres d'art pour un prix assez modique.

Quand Jakuchū s'adonnait à la peinture

Sans aborder la question du sens à donner à l'œuvre pictural de Jakuchū, nous nous contenterons de mettre en ordre les étapes de sa carrière de peintre. Fils aîné d'un grossiste en légumes (*aomono tonya*), Jakuchū, conformément au calendrier traditionnel, dut succéder à son père après la mort de ce dernier, en 1738, à la tête de la maison Masuya, située dans la rue étroite où se trouve Nishiki (*Nishiki kōji*), un marché spécialisé principalement dans les produits alimentaires et qui existe toujours. Les grossistes en légumes – en «choses vertes» (*aomono*) si l'on traduit littéralement l'expression japonaise – étaient de grandes maisons de commerce qui achetaient leurs denrées chez les producteurs agricoles et, en tant que grossistes, les vendaient par lots séparés aux marchands ambulants (*gyōshō*). Or, il semble que chez celui pour qui l'étude de l'art pictural avait constitué sa passion (*shumi*) depuis qu'il avait quinze ans, la perspective de manier le pinceau l'ait emporté car en 1755, à l'âge de quarante ans, il prit son indépendance.

En 1766, à cinquante ans, Jakuchū, après avoir fait don l'année précédente du *Royaume coloré des êtres vivants* et de la *Triade de Śākyamuni* au monastère zen du Shōkoku-ji, fit graver sur sa future stèle funéraire un texte contenant une biographie traitant de la première moitié de son existence, ainsi que des anecdotes sur son caractère et ses goûts excentriques. L'auteur de ce texte était un moine du Shōkoku-ji, Daiten Kenjō (1719-1801) avec lequel il partageait une profonde amitié. La partie concernant les étapes de sa formation de peintre consignée par Daiten, en se fondant directement sur le récit de Jakuchū, s'avère des plus intéressantes.

Comme une majorité de ceux qui étudiaient alors la peinture, Jakuchū affirme avoir appris les techniques de l'école Kanō, représentante de l'académisme. L'enseignement de cette école reposait sur la copie d'œuvres de maîtres anciens reproduites dans des manuels de peinture ; l'on comprend aisément qu'il n'était pas évident de faire preuve d'originalité dans le cadre imposé par cette école. Jakuchū aurait copié environ mille modèles de peintures chinoises (notamment les peintures des dynasties Song et Yuan, mais également les peintures de la dynastie suivante – celle des Ming), qu'il convenait alors d'étudier. Du point de vue de l'artiste, rien ne valait la peinture d'après nature, puisque l'on copiait des manuels de peinture chinoise conçus ainsi. Et Jakuchū de déclarer : «Les choses ! Les choses !». Cela explique que, durant plusieurs années, il se soit consacré entièrement à la reproduction des attitudes et de la morphologie des poules et des coqs qu'il élevait dans son jardin.

On comprend ainsi que les peintures de Jakuchū – à commencer par celles du *Royaume coloré des êtres vivants* – ne se limitent pas à de simples reproductions d'après nature mais qu'en réalité elles ont ouvert une voie originale à l'art pictural dans lequel sa personnalité se manifeste dans tout son éclat.

Somme toute, Itō Jakuchū fut un peintre amateur, sans appartenance à un mouvement académique. Il parvint à naviguer entre l'objectivité (le positivisme) et la subjectivité, ces deux pôles que seul le XVIIIe siècle japonais pouvait produire.

Tadashi Kobayashi

VI

VII

IX

IX

XI

XIV

La vie d'Itō Jakuchū

Itō Jakuchū (1716-1800) (fig. 1) portait le nom (*mei*) de Jokin et avait pour surnom (*ji*) Keiwa. Jakuchū est l'un de ses noms de pinceaux (*gō*) et on l'appelle également Tobei'an (Boisseau de riz) ou Beitō (Le Vieil Homme au boisseau de riz), ses autres noms de pinceau.

Fils aîné d'un grossiste en légumes dont la maison était appelée Masuya et située dans le quartier de Nishiki-Takakura à Kyōto, Jachukū est né dans cette ville le huitième jour du deuxième mois de l'an 1716 (Shōtoku, 6) et a grandi dans un environnement privilégié. D'après les sources écrites qui nous sont parvenues, il se serait familiarisé avec l'art pictural dès l'âge de deux ans et en aurait appris les techniques fondamentales auprès d'Ōoka Shunboku (1680-1783) – un peintre formé au sein de l'école Kanō, actif entre Ōsaka et Kyōto. Des recherches récentes mentionnent la possibilité d'un apprentissage chez Aoki Saemon Genmei qui, très tôt, se démarqua par son habileté dans la représentation naturaliste du réel (*shajitsusei*)[1].

À la suite de la mort de son père, Itō Genzaemon (Munekiyo) III, en 1738 (Genbun, 3) Jakuchū, alors âgé de vingt-trois ans, reprit les affaires familiales sous le nom d'Itō Genzaemon IV. Mais, après plus de quinze ans à la tête de cette grande enseigne dont il assurait la gestion au quotidien, il céda, à quarante ans, la direction de l'entreprise à son frère cadet et, désormais retiré des affaires, se consacra à la peinture. Si cette année-là marque ses véritables débuts dans le métier de peintre, force est de reconnaître que sa sensibilité de créateur se manifesta dès sa prime jeunesse. L'œuvre la plus ancienne de Jakuchū est *Coqs parmi les pins* (*Shōju bankei zu*). Elle fut composée lorsque l'artiste de trente-sept ans, gérait encore la maison Masuya; elle est reproduite dans le numéro 129, daté de 1900, de la revue *Kokka*[2]. On ignore où cette œuvre est conservée aujourd'hui. Elle est signée «Jakuchū koji» (Jakuchū, pieux laïc) et comporte deux sceaux, l'un avec l'inscription «Tō Jokin» et l'autre, de forme carrée et aux caractères vermillon, avec «Jakuchū». La présence de cette signature et de ces sceaux permet d'établir que le peintre se faisait appeler de ses noms de pinceau «Jakuchū» ou «Jakuchū koji» avant cette date. «Jakuchū» a pour origine une phrase du *Laozi* : «La plus grande plénitude est comme vide ; alors elle est intarissable.» Ce texte est très populaire dans les écoles zen et apprécié des moines ; le choix de ce nom est vraisemblablement dû à Daiten, moine du grand monastère zen du Shōkoku-ji. Celui-ci connaissant fort bien Jakuchū, savait qu'il ne se satisfaisait de rien en ce bas monde et cherchait à adhérer à de plus hautes valeurs, tout en se consacrant à la peinture. Daiten – Baisō Kenjō (1719-1801) de son nom de moine – qui exerça une influence très grande sur Jakuchū, outre ses recherches sur le Zen, a laissé des travaux remarquables sur les lettres et le confucianisme ainsi que de nombreuses œuvres de belle facture en prose et en vers. En son temps, l'on disait de lui qu'il était le moine-poète (*shisō*) le plus accompli dans les monastères des Cinq Montagnes ; ecclésiastique éminent, il devint le cent quatorzième supérieur du Shōkoku-ji. À son contact, Jakuchū se cultiva énormément et devint un bouddhiste pieux et dévot. On pense que Jakuchū rencontra Daiten vers l'âge de trente ans. Tout en se détachant du tumulte de l'existence quotidienne, Jakuchū se familiarisait auprès de Daiten

1 – Mariko Yamaguchi, «Itō Jakuchū no shoki kaika kōsatsu» (Une étude des premières peintures d'Itō Jakuchū) dans *Hōjō no Nihon bijustsu – Kobayashi Tadashi sensei koki kinen ronbunshū* (Abondance des arts du Japon : volume présenté en hommage au professeur Kobayashi Tadashi à l'occasion de ses soixante-dix ans), Tōkyō, Geika shoin, 2012.

2 – La plus ancienne revue japonaise consacrée aux arts de l'Asie et du Japon (NDT).

1

Fig. 1 Kubota Beisen (1852-1906), *Portrait d'Itō Jakuchū*, 1885, encre et couleurs sur soie, 55 x 35 cm. Kyōto, Shōkoku-ji.

2

Fig. 2 Itō Jakuchū, *Couple de phénix et soleil levant*, 1755. Tōkyō, musée des collections impériales, Sannomaru Shōzōkan.

avec le bouddhisme qui devint son soutien spirituel et, en même temps, il noua de nouvelles relations avec les lettrés et les artistes de l'ancienne capitale qui faisaient partie des connaissances de Daiten.

Une autre personnalité intervenue dans la carrière de Jakuchū est Baisaō (1675-1763) «Le Vieil Homme qui vendait du thé» – également connu sous le nom lettré de Kō Yūgai et sous son nom de moine Gekkai Genshō – qui, après avoir abandonné la carrière ecclésiastique, menait une existence hors normes, détaché des plaisirs terrestres. Il jouissait des faveurs des personnalités du monde de la culture et des arts et vécut, un temps, dans l'un des temples secondaires (*tatchū*) du Shōkoku-ji[3].

Les heures délicieuses passées dans ce nouvel univers auquel l'entraînaient l'érudition comme l'esprit de Daiten et de Baisaō contribuèrent à enrichir la sensibilité de Jakuchū. Quand il décida de travailler à plein temps à la peinture et déploya des trésors d'ingéniosité dans son expression plastique, l'artiste eut l'occasion de voir diverses peintures japonaises et chinoises dans les monastères et s'essaya ensuite à la copie des œuvres qui l'avaient marqué. Par ailleurs, il reproduisait sans cesse d'après nature les coqs qui vivaient en liberté dans son jardin et tous les êtres vivants qu'il avait l'occasion d'observer. C'est en portant à un raffinement extrême son expression artistique et son art de la composition, qu'il parvint à exceller dans sa technique.

Il s'agissait d'une quête inlassable de formes d'expression picturale qui progressait avec chaque nouvelle peinture. Quand Jakuchū embrassa le métier de peintre, son choix correspondait à un ardent désir de s'immerger avec bonheur dans la recherche de nouvelles formes d'art. Son approche différait de celle des peintres professionnels ; elle lui permit de concevoir des œuvres pleines de charme, attestant sa singulière créativité, mais aussi d'asseoir sa réputation.

En 1755 (Hōreki, 5), lorsque Jakuchū céda les affaires familiales à son frère le deuxième mois (*kisaragi*) de la même année, il peignit *Pruniers sous la lune* (*Getsubai zu*)[4] ; au quatrième mois, période appelée «début d'été» (*shuka*) dans l'ancien calendrier luni-solaire japonais, *Couple de phénix et soleil levant (Kyokujitsu hōhōzu)* (fig. 2) et *Tigre*[5]. Ces œuvres sont constituées de couleurs sur soie de grand format ; on peut s'étonner que l'artiste soit parvenu à les exécuter en l'espace de quelques mois. On y voit assurément l'expression d'un désir débordant et encore inassouvi de peindre, alors qu'il vient de se décharger des responsabilités incombant à la direction d'une grande enseigne. La minutie donnée au moindre détail et au choix des couleurs, la présence de motifs recouvrant l'ensemble de l'œuvre dans *Pruniers sous la lune* ou *Couple de phénix et soleil levant* laissent deviner la plénitude spirituelle extraordinaire de Jakuchū. L'acte de peindre et sa possible expression reposent sur une grande maîtrise des procédés picturaux qui sera mise à profit dans le *Royaume coloré des êtres vivants*.

Jakuchū allait commencer à travailler à son grand œuvre environ deux ans plus tard, en 1757 (Hōreki, 7). En 1759 (Hōreki, 9), il peignit cinq rouleaux du *Royaume coloré des êtres vivants* et cinquante peintures sur cloisons coulissantes (*fusuma*) pour la grande salle d'étude

3 - Sur ce personnage, voir François Lachaud, *Le Vieil Homme qui vendait du thé*, Paris, Cerf, coll. «Conférences de l'École pratique des hautes études», 2010 (NDT).

4 - Ancienne collection Mary Griggs Burke, aujourd'hui au Metropolitan Museum of Art.

5 - États-Unis, collection Etsuko et Joe Price.

3

4

Fig. 3 Itō Jakuchū, *Grappes de raisins*, 1759, quatre panneaux sur *fusuma* (cloisons coulissantes), encre sur papier, 168,5 x 93 cm (chacun). Kyōto, Rokuon-ji.

Fig. 4 Statues des *Cinq cents arhats*. Kyōto, temple Sekihō-ji.

6 - Littéralement «Salle d'audience retirée» (NDT).
7 - Actuel département de Kagawa, sur l'île de Shikoku (NDT).

(*daishoin*) du monastère du Rokuon-ji – plus connu sous son nom de «Pavillon d'or» (Kinkaku-ji). Aux vifs coloris employés pour le *Royaume coloré des êtres vivants* s'opposent les peintures du Rokuon-ji (fig. 3), réalisées uniquement à l'encre de Chine. Ainsi, durant la même période, Jakuchū se consacrait avec enthousiasme aussi bien à la recherche d'expressions picturales pour des œuvres richement colorées qu'à des peintures à l'encre de Chine. De surcroît, en 1764 (Meiwa, 1) il composa des peintures sur cloisons coulissantes pour l'Okushoin[6] du grand sanctuaire shintō de Kotohiragū[7]. L'année suivante, il fit don des vingt-quatre premiers rouleaux du *Royaume coloré des êtres vivants* et des trois rouleaux de la *Triade de Śākyamuni (Shaka sanzon)* – tous de format vertical – au monastère du Shōkoku-ji. L'énergie créatrice de Jakuchū, au cours des dix premières années qui suivent son retrait des affaires familiales, laissent penser que, tout en ayant confié celles-ci à son frère, il ne souffrait guère de problèmes financiers et qu'il vivait dans un environnement suffisamment privilégié pour pouvoir acheter couleurs de haute qualité et soies onéreuses. Les œuvres de cette période sont souvent des peintures sur soie de grand format aux coloris très riches.

Entre l'âge de quarante et cinquante ans, Jakuchū a peint de nombreuses œuvres dont la richesse des coloris et les motifs sont très caractéristiques. On compte parmi les premières datées, exécutées après ses trente-cinq ans, diverses peintures monochromes à l'encre, fortement influencées par l'ingéniosité de ce genre en vogue dans la peinture chinoise de l'époque. Jakuchū maîtrisa très tôt les contrastes de densité (*nōtan*) de l'encre et leur utilisation, engendrant un nombre infini de tons et créant une grande variété d'expressions picturales. La sensibilité exceptionnelle de Jakuchū devant ces variations lui permit de concevoir des œuvres originales et élégantes, grâce à l'emploi de la technique du *sujimegaki* qui exploite la capacité de l'encre à imprégner le papier ; il parvint également à exprimer l'intérêt de compositions reposant sur un simple contraste entre noir et blanc comme l'album d'images en négatif (*takuhanga*) connu sous le nom de *Fleurs précieuses du jardin mystérieux* (*Genpo yōka*, **voir p. 140-142**) qui fait appel à la technique de l'estampage venue de Chine. Il se lança aussi le défi technique de créer des œuvres au rendu expressif singulier par l'emploi de pointillés reposant sur des jeux de densité de l'encre.

Les œuvres pour lesquelles la technique appelée «peinture en mosaïque » (*masumegaki*) est utilisée, sont autant d'exemples par lesquels Jakuchū démontre son génie débordant pour la composition, le caractère décoratif et l'innovation. C'est au cours de cette période que l'artiste atteignit l'apogée de son art : il poursuivit sa quête de couleurs toujours plus éclatantes et joua des contrastes produits par l'opposition entre le noir et le blanc. Sa création, hautement originale, se fonde sur la combinaison de plusieurs des procédés techniques ingénieux qu'il a développés.

L'un des tournants majeurs de la vie de Jakuchū a été le grand incendie de l'ère Tenmei (*Tenmei no taika*) qui se produisit le dernier jour du premier mois de l'an 1788 (Tenmei, 8). À la suite de cette catastrophe qui réduisit en cendres la ville de Kyōto, il perdit sa demeure et son atelier. Privé de son lieu de vie et de travail, l'artiste, qui avait alors soixante-dix ans passés, séjourna chez des amis et des connaissances ou dans des monastères et parvint à continuer à composer des œuvres. Deux ans après ce sombre événement, sans doute à cause de la fatigue endurée par la poursuite de son œuvre de peintre, malgré le traumatisme psychologique subi et les déménagements à répétition auxquels il lui avait fallu se résoudre, il tomba gravement malade. Désormais confronté à des difficultés matérielles pour assurer son existence quotidienne, Jakuchū se retira au monastère du Sekihō-ji, dans la ville de Fushimi au sud de Kyōto. On rapporte qu'il y vécut en compagnie de sa sœur cadette, devenue veuve, et de son enfant. C'est alors qu'il se mit à vivre en échangeant une peinture contre un boisseau de riz et à composer des œuvres à l'encre de Chine, répondant aux demandes de ses clients. Avec l'argent ainsi obtenu, il demanda à un tailleur de pierres de fabriquer une série de statues des *Cinq cents arhats* (*Gohyaku rakan*) qu'il avait conçue pour créer un monde bouddhique en miniature sur la colline située derrière le monastère (fig. 4).

Jakuchū est mort le dixième jour du neuvième mois de l'an 1800 (d'autres sources mentionnent la date du huitième jour du neuvième mois). Sur le lieu de la cérémonie de crémation, au Sekihō-ji – désormais entouré des *Cinq cents arhats* –, se trouve sa tombe. Le vingt-septième jour du dixième mois – c'est-à-dire le quarante-neuvième jour suivant le décès selon l'usage bouddhique[8] –, une cérémonie eut lieu au Shōkoku-ji, à l'occasion de laquelle furent accrochés la *Triade de Śākyamuni* et le *Royaume coloré des êtres vivants*. Jusqu'à la fin de sa vie, Jakuchū eut le loisir d'exprimer sa vision en faisant preuve d'une intense créativité.

Aya Ōta

8 – Cette durée (sept semaines) est celle de l'existence intermédiaire (s. *antarābhava* / j. *chūin*) entre la vie du défunt et son incarnation dans une nouvelle existence. Des cérémonies sont célébrées tous les sept jours et s'achèvent le quarante-neuvième jour – la septième semaine (NDT).

XV

XVII

XIX

XIX

XX

XX

XXI

Le Royaume coloré des êtres vivants

Déjà connu, Jakuchū commença son travail sur le *Royaume coloré des êtres vivants* autour de 1757 (Hōreki, 7). À quarante-deux ans – âge auquel énergie créative et vitalité atteignent leur sommet – l'artiste mena à bien une œuvre d'une ampleur considérable en trente rouleaux verticaux.

Le premier jour du neuvième mois de l'an 1765 (Meiwa, 2), avant que l'ensemble des trente peintures soit achevé, l'artiste fit une donation de vingt-quatre rouleaux du *Royaume coloré des êtres vivants* au monastère du Shōkoku-ji, ainsi que d'une *Triade de Śākyamuni* que, vraisemblablement, Jakuchū avait réalisée lorsqu'il débuta son chef-d'œuvre. Une lettre de donation (*kishinjō*) était jointe aux peintures de cet ensemble. Dans les premières lignes de celle-ci, Jakuchū écrit qu'au terme de longs efforts, aussi bien spirituels que techniques, la pratique régulière de la peinture d'après nature et de la copie [d'œuvres célèbres] lui ont permis d'acquérir une maîtrise technique par laquelle il put exprimer la beauté du monde végétal, représenter celle des oiseaux, des insectes, des reptiles et des poissons. Il poursuit en mentionnant que, transporté par l'habileté extraordinaire des peintures des trois Vénérés généralement attribuées à Zhang Sigong montrant le bouddha Śākyamuni (*Shaka*) et les bodhisattvas Mañjuśrī (*Monju*) et Samantabhadra (*Fugen bosatsu*), il les avait copiées. Celles-ci étaient anciennement dans les collections du monastère du Tōfuku-ji, mais aujourd'hui la peinture de Śākyamuni est au Cleveland Museum of Art et celles de Mañjuśrī et de Samantabhadra sont dans les collections du Seikadō Bunko à Tōkyō. Par ce don, il souhaitait que ces œuvres contribuent à orner l'intérieur (*shōgon / sōgon*) du monastère pour toujours. On dit que cette donation fut motivée par la mort de son plus jeune frère, une dizaine de jours auparavant. Bouddhiste convaincu et fortement influencé par Daiten, Jakuchū entretenait un commerce amical avec de nombreux moines et éprouvait un sentiment de dévotion profonde à l'égard du Bouddha. Sans doute est-ce la raison pour laquelle il imagina un projet pictural dans lequel serait représentée une foule d'êtres vivants rassemblés pour recevoir les enseignements de Śākyamuni, formant ainsi la vision d'un monde organisé autour du Bouddha. Ce type de décor existait dans les monastères zen depuis le Moyen Âge. On disposait au centre le bouddha Śākyamuni ou l'un de ses Grands Disciples (c. *luohan* ; j. *rakan*) et, à droite et à gauche, on les flanquait d'une série de peintures de paysages, de fleurs et d'oiseaux, généralement sans aucun rapport avec les images des Vénérés. Ces formes de décor de l'intérieur des pavillons des monastères durent exercer une influence sur Jakuchū. Pareille conception est propre aux représentations du monde développées dans le Zen : les paysages reproduits constituent un éloge et une représentation de l'enseignement des vertus du Bouddha tandis que celles de fleurs et oiseaux ont pour signification la vision d'un cosmos en miniature ; en voyant les motifs de ces peintures, le spectateur pouvait observer ainsi le monde fourmillant qui se trouvait à l'arrière-plan. Jakuchū aurait-il entendu Daiten parler des enseignements ayant trait à ce type d'ornementation ? Toujours est-il qu'il se sentait en profonde harmonie avec les enseignements du Bouddha, affirmant que tous les êtres vivants et toutes les formes d'existence étaient dignes de vénération. Cette notion au cœur de la composition du *Royaume coloré des êtres vivants*, permit à Jakuchū de proposer une décoration intérieure correspondant à l'image d'un monde inspiré par le bouddhisme.

La maîtrise technique de Jakuchū

Le *Royaume coloré des êtres vivants* avait pour ambition d'exprimer toute la pureté, la beauté et la force vitale des végétaux, des oiseaux, des insectes, des reptiles et autres poissons qui peuplent le monde naturel. Les idées de Jakuchū, dont témoigne son emploi méticuleux et admirable du pinceau, trouvèrent leur écho dans la magnificence de cet ensemble. Quelles furent les innovations techniques qui permirent à l'artiste de représenter les divers motifs très colorés, irradiant l'ensemble des surfaces peintes ? J'aimerais en présenter ici l'ingéniosité[1].

La principale caractéristique du *Royaume coloré des êtres vivants* tient en la maîtrise complète d'effets remarquables rendus possibles par la peinture sur soie. Pour peindre (*eginu*) sur soie, on utilise un tissage uni (*hiraori*) – une armure où le fil de trame croise en alternance le fil de chaîne –, avec des espaces ménagés dans la trame. Lorsqu'on applique des couleurs au revers de cette soie ayant pour particularité une transparence similaire à celle de la gaze, les coloris qui apparaissent sur l'avers à travers l'étoffe semblent adoucis. Cette technique de coloration et la façon très subtile de poser des couleurs obtenues par l'usage conjoint de la coloration du revers et de l'avers du support de soie, donne un effet d'épaisseur des surfaces peintes. Cette technique était connue sous le nom de « coloration du revers » (*urazaishiki*). Elle avait été pratiquée au Japon à l'époque Heian (794-1185), autour du IXe siècle, principalement pour les peintures à sujets bouddhiques. Il s'agit d'une technique traditionnelle de représentation tout à fait remarquable qui s'est perpétuée. Si l'on connaît un nombre d'œuvres – principalement des peintures bouddhiques – de belle facture pour lesquelles elle a été employée jusque vers le XIVe siècle, on ignorait qu'elle fût encore utilisée dans la peinture de l'époque d'Edo, après la seconde moitié du XVIIe siècle. Ce fait est à mettre en rapport avec la production et la diffusion du papier à partir du XIVe siècle au Japon, qui débouchèrent sur une augmentation massive des peintures sur papier qui l'emportèrent sur tous les autres supports. Cette tendance eut pour effet que l'on cessa de s'interroger sur le mode de transmission de la coloration du revers propre à la peinture sur soie, ainsi que sur la catégorie des peintres employant celle-ci et leur méthode ; remarquons également l'absence d'études consacrées aux techniques picturales dans la peinture de l'époque d'Edo. Les travaux de restauration du *Royaume coloré des êtres vivants*, qui commencèrent en 1999 et durèrent six ans, ont confirmé que Jakuchū a utilisé la coloration du revers et fait prendre conscience de la transmission ininterrompue de techniques propres à la peinture traditionnelle au cours des siècles. Ce constat a également permis de comprendre comment on a pu imaginer de nouvelles formes d'expressions, au fil des époques, apportant un élan créatif novateur.

1 - Lors du démontage et de la restauration du *Royaume coloré des êtres vivants*, entre 1999 et 2004, une étude systématique des techniques picturales ainsi que des couleurs a été menée. Les résultats de ce travail ont été publiés dans les ouvrages suivants auxquels plusieurs études ont été adjointes. *Kachō : mederu kokoro, irodoru gi (Fleurs et oiseaux) : Dōshoku sai-e wo chūshin to shite* [Passions du cœur et technique de la couleur : autour du *Royaume coloré des êtres vivants*, Tōkyō, catalogue d'exposition du musée des collections impériales / Sannomaru shōzōkan], nº 40, 2006. Dōshoku sai-e : *Jakuchū byōsha no myōgi* [*Le Royaume coloré des êtres vivants* : virtuosité des descriptions picturales de Jakuchū], Tōkyō, Agence de la Maison impériale, 2006. *Itō Jakuchū Dōshoku sai-e shūri jigyō hōkokusho* (Rapport sur les travaux de restauration du *Royaume coloré des êtres vivants* d'Itō Jakuchū), Agence de la Maison impériale, 2009. Agence de la Maison impériale / Institut du patrimoine de Tōkyō éd., *Itō Jakuchū Dōshoku sai-e zen sanjuppuku* [*Le Royaume coloré des êtres vivants* d'Itō Jakuchū : l'ensemble des trente rouleaux verticaux], Tōkyō, Shōgakukan, 2010.

La richesse des matériaux de la palette de couleurs de Jakuchū et l'habileté remarquable dont il fait preuve en la maniant est très caractéristique de son œuvre. Les matières colorantes que Jakuchū utilise, en dehors de celles issues de pigments broyés (*ganryō*) – notamment des pigments minéraux (*iwaenogu*) –, sont obtenues à partir de teintures naturelles (*senryō*). L'usage conjoint qu'il fait des deux, avec sa connaissance très précise de leur nature, constitue une autre singularité de son travail. Les pigments résultant de la pulvérisation de minéraux ou de coquilles ont pour propriété de ne pas être solubles dans l'eau et sont appliqués à la surface de la soie en utilisant de la colle animale (*nikawa*) produite à partir de la peau, des os, des tendons ou encore des viscères. À l'inverse, les teintures naturelles, qui proviennent de végétaux, de mollusques ou d'insectes et sont solubles dans l'eau, imprègnent les fils de soie. Ces types de couleurs aboutissent à des différences de rendu : ainsi une légère superposition de couches de pigments à la surface de la soie va donner un aspect de granulation irrégulière ; au contraire, on observera une surface plane et dépourvue d'aspérités quand les teintures naturelles ont imprégné les fils de cette même soie. Par exemple, dans les parties colorées avec des pigments, les minuscules pointillés que l'on aperçoit sur les pistils et les étamines résultent de la superposition d'une couche de blanc de perle (*gofun*)[2], qui renforce encore l'impression de relief des couleurs. Pour les feuilles des végétaux, Jakuchū emploie presque toujours des pigments naturels, mais il peint avec du vert malachite (*rokushō*) les nervures des feuilles, ce qui accentue l'expression de leur volume. Cette subtilité extrême des couleurs et son effet jouent sur la beauté des contrastes expressifs (*nōtan*) en fonction des tonalités et de la granulation ; en même temps, il utilise avec maîtrise les teintures naturelles.

Une autre spécificité de l'art de Jakuchū vient de son ingéniosité à combiner les couleurs afin d'obtenir une expression particulière – par exemple, en mélangeant celles-ci ou par la surimpression de plusieurs couches – fondée sur sa connaissance précise de la nature des différentes couleurs employées. Ainsi, dans l'expression des blancs, les pétales des pivoines de Chine (fig. 1) (*shakuyaku*) et pivoines arbustives (*botan*) ; des fleurs de pruniers (fig. 2), des chrysanthèmes ou des roses sont représentés avec une sensibilité exquise, jouant sur une gradation d'intensité entre la lumière quasi transparente du centre de la fleur jusque vers son rebord extérieur, là où la teinte se fait plus dense. De même, le rendu du pourtour des yeux de l'oie dans *Oie et roseaux* (*Roga zu*, fig. 3, voir cat. XIII), épaissi par l'application de trois couches successives de blanc de perle, fait ressortir avec force les yeux du volatile et est caractéristique du peintre. Dans *Nandina et Coq* (*Nanten yūkei zu*, cat. XIV), des changements subtils dans la pose des couleurs – ainsi les innombrables baies des nandines domestiques (j. *nanten* ; l. *nandina domestica*) – se distinguent des autres grâce à la technique de la coloration du revers. De même, les rouges sur l'avers du support de soie sont différents selon que l'artiste a employé un simple pigment rouge ou bien a empâté celui-ci de teintures naturelles de la même couleur. Il crée une

2 – Le terme désigne un pigment blanc composé de poudre de carbonate de calcium produite en chauffant et en pulvérisant les coquilles d'huîtres et d'autres coquillages.

1

2

3

Fig. 1 *Pivoines et papillons (Shakuyaku gunchō zu)*, détail (voir cat.1)

Fig. 2 *Prunier en fleur et petits oiseaux (Baika shōkin zu)*, détail (voir cat.II)

Fig. 3 *Oie et roseaux (Roga zu)*, détail (voir cat.XIII)

 interaction entre le premier et le second plan, rendant ainsi l'impression de volume des grappes de baies. En outre, les pétales des fleurs pour lesquelles Jakuchū employait avec prédilection un rose transparent d'une grande élégance sont recouverts d'une mince couche de blanc elle-même légèrement empâtée de blanc et de rouge et, par endroits, couverts encore de teintures naturelles rouges. La représentation des feuilles se fonde, pour la plus grande partie, sur des teintures naturelles de couleur verte qui, par endroits, gagnent en expressivité par la superposition de couleurs plus denses obtenues à partir de pigments verts et rouges. Afin de faire ressortir l'expression propre à chacun des objets représentés, Jakuchū a recours à nombre de moyens techniques ingénieux pour la pose des couleurs.

La peinture de l'artiste se caractérise également par l'absence de délinéation des motifs. Cette technique consiste à ne pas utiliser de lignes de contours préliminaires, mais est basée sur des gradations d'intensité de l'encre et sur la pose des couleurs. Cela correspond assez bien à la technique picturale traditionnelle appelée « sans os » (c. *mogu* ; j. *mokkotsu*). Cette dernière apparaît dans la Chine de l'époque des Tang (618-907), entre le VIIIe et le IXe siècle et, à partir du siècle suivant, elle est largement employée dans la peinture de fleurs et d'oiseaux. Jakuchū a sans doute étudié cette façon de disposer des couleurs ; malgré une concentration d'aussi nombreux motifs, il ne les cerne pas et rend les formes de chaque motif par l'application de couleurs sur le support de soie. Cette approche laisse supposer l'existence de dessins préparatoires (*shitazu*) dessinés avec le plus grand soin par l'artiste.

De fait, les surfaces peintes de cette manière par Jakuchū, avec leurs teintes éclatantes, ont en réalité pour fondement des techniques traditionnelles, qu'il mélange par son sens exceptionnel de la couleur, auxquelles il ajoute des procédés originaux qui lui sont propres, sans être particulièrement complexes. En dehors de la coloration du revers, il fait appel à des techniques transmises au sein des écoles de peinture traditionnelles – principalement l'école Kanō –employées par de nombreux peintres : gradation d'encre (*bokashi*), estompage pour créer une forme (*katabokashi*), dégradé inversé (*teriguma*), application uniforme de la couleur (*hiranuri*) ; effacement des contours (*tsuketate*) ou encore application d'une couche de couleur sur une autre encore humide (*tarashikomi*). Jakuchū fusionne ces techniques et parvient au type d'expression picturale qu'il recherche. Dans le *Royaume coloré des êtres vivants*, Jakuchū démontre sa maîtrise des matériaux et des techniques apprises jusqu'alors ; l'ensemble constitue son plus grand chef-d'œuvre dans lequel il réussit à allier virtuosité technique et réflexion spirituelle.

Pour exprimer la fraîcheur et la vitalité des êtres vivants, l'artiste a conçu un ensemble de procédés subtils qu'aucun autre artiste ne saurait imiter. Il est fort vraisemblable que, pour Jakuchū qui avait employé autant d'expressions picturales aux charmes puissants, la *Triade de Śākyamuni* et *Le Royaume coloré des êtres vivants* présenté autour d'elle atteignaient au sublime. Sur la soie de chacun des rouleaux est appliqué un fond conçu à partir d'une couche fine d'encre de Chine et de teintures naturelles à dominante sombre pour donner du relief aux couleurs. De surcroît, pour le « papier de revers » (*hadauragami*) tendu au dos de chacun des supports en soie, Jakuchū employait un papier obtenu à partir de fibres de bambou (*chikushi*) d'un gris profond – couleur encre de Chine. Celui-ci accentue encore le relief des couleurs. Tels sont les divers exemples de ressources ingénieuses dont joue le peintre pour accroître l'effet produit par les représentations du *Royaume coloré des êtres vivants*. En effet, prenant un papier de revers couleur d'encre grise, il colore le revers, utilise de la soie et des couleurs posées à la surface se répartissant en pigments et en teintures naturelles. Le *Royaume coloré des êtres vivants* atteste la connaissance approfondie de Jakuchū de la peinture sur soie et sa capacité à exploiter au mieux matériaux et techniques. Il sait donner à l'ensemble une puissance expressive tout à fait exceptionnelle : il ne fait aucun doute que cette série est l'un des chefs-d'œuvre les plus remarquables de l'art japonais.

La représentation du réel au cœur de l'œuvre

La représentation des formes au moyen du blanc qui apparaît dans le *Royaume coloré des êtres vivants*, semble avoir fait l'objet d'une attention toute particulière chez Jakuchū, aussi bien en termes de technique qu'en termes d'expression artistique. À commencer par son phénix blanc – *Vieux Pin et phénix blanc* (fig. 4) – qui fait l'admiration des critiques pour sa beauté semblable à celle d'une dentelle. Son paon blanc, dans Vieux *Pin et paon* (*Rōshō kujaku zu*, cat. IX), montre la couleur blanche que l'on retrouve pour les coqs et les poules, les grues ou encore les perroquets ; Jakuchū représente le corps de l'oiseau couvert de plumes blanches au moyen de lignes fines et délicates puis pose les couleurs selon la technique de la coloration du revers, avec des ocres tirant vers le jaune et, sur l'avers, avec l'application minutieuse de blanc de perle pour chaque plume. L'ocre de la coloration du revers, grâce aux reflets des aspérités de la trame de l'étoffe et les particules lumineuses de blanc de perle brillent d'un éclat d'or à nos yeux. Nulle part ailleurs dans l'histoire de la peinture on ne trouve ce véritable tour de magie qui consiste à créer une impression visuelle de la couleur dorée (*konjiki*), sans faire appel à celle-ci. En utilisant conjointement des lignes fines tracées délicatement pour restituer les plumes et une ingénieuse coloration du revers par l'application d'ocre, Jakuchū parvient à donner un aspect brillant aux plumes blanches qui recouvrent le corps de l'oiseau, donnant du volume au plumage et une impression de plasticité.

L'expression picturale de la neige que l'on observe dans *Canards mandarins dans la neige* (*Setchū en'ō zu*, fig. 5) ou dans *Faisans dorés dans la neige* (*Setchū kinkei zu*, cat. XIX) est, elle aussi, tout à fait remarquable : l'usage de la coloration du revers est la preuve d'une grande maîtrise technique. En appliquant du blanc de perle sur les deux côtés de la soie dont le fond est gris (*usuzumi*), Jakuchū, invente une manière adéquate de restituer une impression de profondeur et de volume à la neige elle-même. Le blanc qui résulte de la coloration du revers à travers la soie semble avoir une légère couleur thé ; l'application successive de

4

5

6

Fig. 4 *Vieux Pin et phénix blanc (Rōshō hakuō zu), détail* (voir cat.XXV) vue du revers.

Fig. 5 *Canards mandarins dans la neige (Setchū en' ō zu)*, détails : avers (à droite) et revers (à gauche), (voir cat. III)

Fig. 6 *Fleurs de pêcher et petits oiseaux (Tōka shōkin zu)*, détail en cours de restauration (voir cat. XVIII)

couches de blanc de perle sur l'avers font ressortir encore plus vivement la couleur blanche. Jakuchū ne s'en tient pas au seul rendu de la neige accumulée après une chute ; les flocons poudreux qui tourbillonnent sont restitués grâce à la technique dite de pulvérisation des couleurs (*fukitsuke*) des deux côtés de la soie peinte : la différence d'aspect entre les flocons poudreux dont le blanc apparaît très nettement et ceux qui ont une couleur un peu plus sombre contribue efficacement à retranscrire l'espace.

De même, chacun des pétales – pivoines de Chine, pivoines arbustives, roses ou fleurs de pêcher – procure une impression de douceur et d'élasticité obtenues grâce à des gradations dans l'usage du blanc de perle. Appliqué depuis le bord extérieur du pétale jusque vers l'intérieur, il présente un volume arrondi pour l'ensemble des fleurs. L'artiste utilise scrupuleusement son pinceau. Il applique du blanc de perle extrêmement clair au centre, puis il superpose des couches plus légères de ce pigment, se rapproche du bord du pétale et, enfin, ajoute une autre couche de blanc de perle foncé sur le bord extérieur.

Les motifs du *Royaume coloré des êtres vivants* – à commencer par les fleurs et oiseaux – ont pour autre singularité la répétition du même être vivant, ou de formes identiques. Pétales, fleurs, feuilles, plumes, écailles de poissons, moineaux : en réalité, la répétition du dessin est omniprésente. Mais Jakuchū, en représentant chaque motif avec soin et méticulosité et en déployant des trésors d'ingéniosité dans les variations qu'il introduit dans la pose des couleurs, ne tombe jamais dans le piège de l'uniformité. Sans doute faut-il y voir, jusque dans les moindres détails de l'œuvre, l'expression d'une idée selon laquelle il n'est pas deux êtres semblables parmi les êtres vivants et que chacun possède une apparence qui lui est propre et lui donne sa beauté. Les fleurs de pêcher que l'on retrouve sur toute la surface peinte de *Fleurs de pêcher et petits oiseaux* (fig. 6) se répartissent en quatre couleurs différentes : blanc, rose, rose pâle, rose foncé. Pistils et étamines des deux premiers types de couleur sont colorés en jaune et, ceux des deux autres, avec un jaune plus intense opérant ainsi une nette distinction dans la manière de rendre ces fleurs sur la surface peinte. Dans *Érable et petits oiseaux* (fig. 7 et cat. XXX), l'on ne compte pas moins de 570 feuilles d'érable arborant les couleurs rouges de l'automne. La coloration du revers est utilisée pour la quasi-totalité des feuilles et les couleurs employées pour celle-ci vont du rouge, au rouge avec des nuances de jaune, au rouge-rosé, et à l'orange (*daidai iro*) avec divers tons de jaune, offrant ainsi une grande hétérogénéité d'aspects des feuilles représentées. Ces procédés pour distinguer des objets identiques atteignent leur sommet avec les lignes des nervures des feuilles de palmier dans *Palmiers de Chine et coqs* (*Shuro yūkei zu* cat. XVI). Certaines sont étirées en ligne droite, d'autres sont tracées avec de fines dentelures, d'autres encore, également dentelées, sont légèrement plus longues : Jakuchū parvient ici à peindre des nervures de feuilles très composites. C'est grâce à la répétition de ces infimes variations qu'il obtient un mode de représentation dans lequel des formes qui pourraient apparaître semblables s'avèrent, en réalité, fort différentes. L'obsession de

7

Fig. 7 *Érable et petits oiseaux (Kōyō shōkin zu)*, détail, vue de l'avers (en haut) et du revers (en bas), (voir cat. XXX)

Jakuchū pour ce genre de descriptions éclaire d'autant mieux la nature unique des idées ayant présidé à la conception du *Royaume coloré des êtres vivants*.

Son obsession pour la couleur se trouve encore renforcée si l'on prend en compte l'emploi d'un produit importé qui était très rare à l'époque. En effet, durant la dernière phase de la composition du *Royaume coloré des êtres vivants*, la peinture *Poissons* (*Gungyo zu*, cat. XXVIII), conçue vers 1766 (Meiwa, III), un poisson appelé dans la langue courante « savon à bande jaune » (l. *Aulacocephalus temmincki*) est coloré avec du bleu de Prusse. Cette couleur, dont la présence a été formellement identifiée lors des contrôles scientifiques des travaux de restauration, a été introduite au Japon par des navires néerlandais au milieu du XVIIIe siècle. Jusque-là, on savait cette couleur fréquemment utilisée dans l'École de peinture néerlandaise d'Akita (Akita ranga) – dont la courte période d'activité s'étend de la fin 1772 à 1780 ; les artistes de cette école employaient des techniques occidentales pour rendre des motifs de composition japonais – dans la peinture à l'occidentale de l'époque d'Edo et dans les ukiyo-e[3]. Cependant, personne n'avait imaginé que Jakuchū ait pu utiliser cette couleur à une époque bien antérieure pour peindre sur soie. Ce fut l'une des grandes découvertes de ces travaux de restauration. Cette couleur a des grains très fins et le bleu foncé et profond qui la caractérise est très différent de celui employé jusqu'alors : il en est ainsi de l'azurite (*gunjō*), d'une vive intensité ou de l'indigo (*ai*) aux tonalités sobres et maîtrisées. À travers l'usage de cette couleur par le peintre, on perçoit son obsession et l'intensité de son désir de relever le défi que pose l'utilisation de ce nouveau pigment dans sa palette.

L'observateur du *Royaume coloré des êtres vivants* est saisi par l'impression que, dans chacun des rouleaux qui composent l'ensemble, Jakuchū a représenté les formes du vivant – animaux ou plantes – avec une grande tendresse. L'extrême subtilité de ses capacités d'expression lui permet de représenter les détails les plus difficiles à saisir visuellement. Dans *Millet d'automne et moineaux* (*Shūtō gunjaku zu*, cat. IV), des touches oranges parsèment ainsi la partie allant de la gorge à la poitrine des moineaux qui s'amusent dans le millet dont les tiges ploient sous les graines, comme on le remarque également dans *Étang au lotus et poissons* (*Renchi yūgyo zu*, cat. XVII) ; on retrouve ces touches sur la bouche des *ayu* et les nageoires des chevesnes ornithorynques (*oikawa*). Ce sont en fait les grains d'un pigment appelé « minium » (*entan*). Jakuchū utilise une méthode de fixation qui ne consiste pas à faire adhérer le pigment après en avoir recouvert la surface à peindre, mais à en enduire la pointe du pinceau et à utiliser celui-ci comme une brosse pour le disperser. En somme, cette technique s'apparente à celle que l'on applique dans la dernière étape du maquillage d'un visage en ajoutant du fard à joues qui donne du contraste. On notera encore dans *Étang aux insectes* (*Chihen gunchū zu*, cat. XXIII) la présence de petits points noirs sur les vrilles rameuses sous une toile d'araignée. Ces points si minuscules qu'on ne leur prête pas attention au premier abord représentent de toute évidence des pattes d'insectes. Si ceux-ci faisaient partie de la représentation d'insectes en

3 - Le bleu de Prusse (a. *Preußigblau*) – connu également sous le nom de « bleu de Berlin » (a. *Berliner Blau*), désigne un pigment artificiel découvert vraisemblablement en 1706 par le marchand de couleurs et de peinture berlinois Johann Jakob von Diesbach. Son développement eut lieu plus de vingt ans après sa découverte, lorsque les secrets de sa composition furent dévoilés ; il fut, fréquemment utilisé dans le domaine de la céramique et occasionna ce que l'on a pu appeler la « révolution du bleu ». Il arriva au Japon dans les cargaisons d'un navire néerlandais en 1752 (Hōreki, 2) et fit l'objet d'une présentation détaillée par le pharmacologue, satiriste, dramaturge et... meurtrier Hiraga Gennai (1728-1779) dans son ouvrage *Variété de produits avec leurs spécificités (Butsurui hinshitsu)*. L'on savait qu'à partir de la fin du XVIIIe siècle il fut utilisé comme couleur par les peintres de l'École d'Akita, par les peintres à l'occidentale tels Shiba Kōkan (1747-1818) et par les créateurs d'estampe – ainsi Katsushika Hokusai (1760-1849) – mais nombre de détails quant aux circonstances de son utilisation avant cette date restent inconnus. La découverte de sa présence dans le *Royaume coloré des êtres vivants* est, à ce jour, l'exemple le plus ancien attesté de son utilisation au Japon.

mouvement – ainsi des fourmis – l'œil s'y arrêterait mais Jakuchū met ici l'accent sur une forme d'insectes noirs qui, tout en étant statiques, n'en sont pas moins des êtres vivants. Ce regard plein de compassion et de tendresse du peintre à l'égard du vivant s'étend à ces créatures considérées habituellement comme indignes de recevoir une quelconque attention.

Au premier coup d'œil, le *Royaume coloré des êtres vivants*, œuvre d'une grande beauté, procure un plaisir intense au spectateur par la richesse de ses coloris et son cortège d'êtres vivants – végétaux et animaux. Mais, le charme étrange qui attire spectatrices et spectateurs – tous âges confondus – vers ces peintures s'explique sans doute par cette expression de la beauté et de l'exubérance des formes du vivant qui avaient frappé Jakuchū et touche la sensibilité de ceux qui regardent son travail.

Pour Jakuchū, il n'était sans doute d'éloge plus grand du *Royaume coloré des êtres vivants* que celui de Baisaō – le Vieil homme qui vendait du thé – résumé en une ligne de calligraphie (*ichigyōsho*) : « La suprême habileté de la main qui compose ces peintures communique avec le divin » (*tansei no kasshu no myō kami ni tsūzu*). La fierté que l'artiste éprouva lorsqu'il lut ces mots fut telle qu'il les grava sur un sceau qu'il allait apposer désormais sur ses œuvres. À l'harmonie entre Baisaō, admirateur inconditionnel du *Royaume coloré des êtres vivants* et de Jakuchū, son auteur, fait écho la fascination de celles et ceux qui regardent ce chef-d'œuvre plus de deux cents ans après sa création.

Aya Ōta

XXIII

XXIV

XXVI

XXVI

XXV

Jakuchū et le bouddhisme ou l’Éveil du radis

 En tant que peintre et bouddhiste, Itō Jakuchū partage avec les artistes et poètes japonais de son temps une conception de l'art qui, sans être explicitement formulée, influe pourtant en profondeur sur le sens que l'on peut trouver dans leurs œuvres. La grande originalité de ses représentations repose sur des principes qu'il convient de mettre en lumière si l'on veut mieux en comprendre la portée.

L'esprit comme peintre

Si l'idée de Dieu comme architecte de l'univers se trouve déjà chez des auteurs classiques comme Cicéron avant d'être reprise dans le christianisme, où l'on trouve encore le Créateur appelé «semeur» ou «planteur» du monde (*sator* en latin), la métaphore du peintre semble inconnue dans les Écritures sacrées de l'Europe ancienne. Ce n'est pas le cas dans le bouddhisme d'Extrême-Orient. L'un des textes canoniques les plus fondamentaux pour la pensée de l'Asie orientale, le *Sūtra de l'Ornement de splendeur*, dont le titre se prononce *Kegon-kyō* en japonais, transmis en plusieurs versions chinoises à partir d'un original indien en grande partie disparu, comporte un célèbre quatrain, légèrement différent selon les versions, mais que l'on peut traduire ainsi : «L'esprit est comme un peintre / capable de représenter les différents mondes / les cinq agrégats en sont tous issus / aucune entité qu'il ne crée.» Une version ajoute : «De même que l'esprit, ainsi est le Bouddha, de même que le Bouddha, ainsi sont les êtres vivants. Esprit, Bouddha, êtres, les trois sont indistincts les uns des autres.»

Dans le bouddhisme, ce n'est pas Dieu qui est architecte, mais l'esprit qui est peintre. La différence est essentielle. L'esprit de qui, demandera-t-on ? La réponse est dans la dernière phrase : esprit, bouddha, êtres ne sont pas séparables les uns des autres. Ce n'est pas l'esprit de tel ou tel individu, ce l'est aussi cependant, car tout être n'est individualisé que dans la mesure où l'ignorance fondamentale (*mumyō*) qui l'enveloppe l'empêche d'aller au bout de son identité avec l'esprit de Bouddha (*busshin*), lequel gîte au plus profond de son être. Nous serions tentés de croire que cette pensée qui peint l'univers, cette pensée cosmogonique, dans cette grandiose conception noétique, est le summum de l'être. Elle l'est d'une certaine façon, si on la considère à partir de la dimension, ou du plan d'existence suprême qu'est le Plan de Loi (*hokkai*), bien qu'une telle perception nous soit bien sûr impossible. En fait, pour nous aussi, les êtres vivants, l'esprit est peintre, mais à notre dimension. La stance le dit expressément d'ailleurs en parlant des cinq agrégats (*go.un*). Il faut rappeler que pour le bouddhisme, toutes les entités du monde phénoménal, les «choses» donc, qui nous entourent et dont nous faisons partie, sont composées de cinq agrégats. Ces cinq éléments peuvent se regrouper en deux : l'élément «physique» ou «visible» (*shiki*), et l'élément «psychique» (*shin*), ce dernier terme étant celui que nous traduisons aussi par «esprit». Tout existant a donc deux dimensions qui sont partie intégrante de son être au monde, mais où situer la dimension psychique ? Si l'on nous dit qu'une chaise a une dimension physique, nous pouvons le comprendre, mais comment concevoir que la même chaise ait une dimension psychique ? Une chaise pense-t-elle, sent-elle ? On pensera avec quelque raison qu'il n'en est rien, et il est bien évident que cette dimension psychique n'est pas dans la chaise, mais du côté de celui qui la perçoit : une chaise n'est pas chaise objectivement, c'est l'esprit qui la structure comme chaise à partir de sa dimension physique, qui n'est qu'un amas de bois et de métal. De même que l'amour, ou la beauté, dont le dicton anglais dit qu'ils sont dans l'œil de l'admirateur, la chaise est dans la faculté visuelle de celui qui la voit. On comprend alors que le *Sūtra de l'Ornement de splendeur*, après avoir comparé l'esprit à un peintre, mentionne à ce sujet les cinq agrégats : même dans le plus simple acte de perception de notre monde phénoménal, c'est l'esprit, quel que soit son niveau, qui peint la réalité qu'il croit apercevoir. Elle n'est pas hors de lui, et il peint lui-même le décor de son monde.

Il est dommage qu'il n'y ait pas de terme adéquat pour rendre en français toute la richesse sémantique du caractère chinois que nous traduisons par «esprit», lu *shin* ou *kokoro* en japonais. Il signifie tout à la fois la pensée, l'esprit, la conscience, le cœur, et il est un trait d'union, se trouvant à la fois individualisé en chaque être mais aussi, au tréfonds de son être, en communion avec l'esprit de Bouddha. Chaque être est en effet pourvu de la nature de Bouddha qui ne demande qu'à se déployer.

L'idéalisme bouddhique : le monde comme représentation

La métaphore de l'esprit-peintre est l'illustration d'une idée essentielle qui imprègne tout spécialement le bouddhisme japonais et que l'on pourrait appeler l'idéalisme, ou la noétique, bouddhique : le «rien-que-pensée» (*yuishin*), qui établit une ontologie générale de l'univers, dont le fondement est la Pensée, indistincte du Bouddha originel, le grand Bouddha universel qu'est Mahāvairocana (Dainichi-nyorai en japonais). Cette idée n'est pas propre à l'école de l'*Ornement de splendeur*, mais est reprise dans les traditions ésotériques, l'école Shingon et l'école Tendai entre autres. Le Zen japonais n'est pas resté en dehors de ce courant général, lui dont l'une des maximes principales était de «viser directement l'esprit de l'homme» (*jikishi ninshin*), ou de «transmettre d'esprit à esprit» (que l'on peut traduire aussi «de cœur à cœur», *ishin denshin*).

L'expression la plus originale du Zen japonais se trouve certainement dans l'œuvre de Dōgen (1200-1253), en particulier dans son chef-d'œuvre religieux et littéraire, le *Réceptacle de l'œil de la Loi correcte* (*Shōbōgenzō*). On y trouve un chapitre intitulé «Une galette en peinture» (*Gabyō*) dont la lecture est édifiante dans la perspective idéaliste que nous venons d'esquisser. Ce sermon de Dōgen part d'une citation d'un moine chinois du IXe siècle : «Ce n'est pas l'image d'une galette qui va vous rassasier». Ce genre de propos est typique du Chan (Zen) chinois, tout en s'inscrivant dans une longue série d'anecdotes sur la puissance de représentation du peintre (tel cet artiste qui peint un dragon si réel qu'il finit par prendre son essor vers le ciel…). On ne peut rien comprendre à ce sermon, déjà fort peu compréhensible, si l'on ne saisit d'emblée la clef que nous en donne Dōgen dès les premiers mots : «C'est parce que les bouddhas réalisent l'Éveil que les choses phénoménales [y compris les êtres] réalisent l'Éveil.» Dōgen déploie ensuite toutes les possibilités combinatoires, et il fait bien sûr appel à la notion des cinq agrégats et de la double dimension physique-psychique, pour nous amener à concevoir, en un tourbillon démonstratif qui donne le vertige comme à l'accoutumée, que la galette et sa représentation peinte peuvent être comprises comme un bouddha et l'image d'un bouddha. Une fois admis qu'ils sont projetés – peints – par l'esprit, comment peut-on distinguer le réel et le représenté, œuvres l'un et l'autre du même peintre ?

Itō Jakuchū et le Zen

Itō Jakuchū vit et peint dans le Japon du XVIIIe siècle, à l'époque où la pensée et l'œuvre de Dōgen connaissent un renouveau d'intérêt considérable dans l'école qu'il a fondée, l'école Sōtō. Il est peu probable que Jakuchū ait lu Dōgen, lui qui, une fois qu'il eut décidé de renoncer aux affaires mondaines pour se consacrer à son art, à quarante ans passés (après 1755), entretint des contacts très étroits avant tout avec le monastère Shōkoku-ji de Kyōto. C'était en effet l'un des hauts lieux de l'école Rinzai, principale rivale du Sōtō, et antérieure à celle-ci, tout en ayant également des relations avec le courant le plus récent du Zen, arrivé de Chine à l'époque d'Edo, après la chute des Ming et la prise de pouvoir des Manchous qui fondent la dynastie Qing. Ce courant, appelé Ōbaku, et dont le centre était le Manpuku-ji, temple proche de Kyōto, se situe lui aussi pleinement dans la lignée Rinzai, et le portrait que Jakuchū fait du moine Hoan Jōei, son contemporain, nous montre sa proximité avec ce milieu. Il ne faut cependant pas se représenter la rivalité entre le Rinzai et le Sōtō comme une fracture irréductible entre deux visions du bouddhisme. Certes, les temps modernes nous ont habitués à placer le Sōtō sous le signe du *zazen* ou «méditation assise», avec l'exclusive de la pratique annoncée par Dōgen lui-même : *shikan taza* «Il n'y a qu'à s'asseoir», et le Rinzai sous celui des *kōan* ou «énigmes à méditer». Il suffit de parcourir le *Shōbōgenzō* pour constater que chez Dōgen, les *kōan* sont partout, et que le récit même de son accès au *satori*, à la compréhension suprême, est fondée sur un *kōan*.

De plus, le sermon de la galette en peinture ne peut se comprendre qu'à la lumière de cette doctrine idéaliste du «rien-que-pensée», qui est bien antérieure aux deux courants du Zen. En tant que peintre profondément imprégné par le bouddhisme, Jakuchū ne pouvait qu'être sensible à cette conception de l'esprit comme peintre : qu'en est-il alors de l'esprit d'un peintre ? L'artiste conscient de son art, dans cet univers mental du bouddhisme japonais, ne peut que se concevoir lui-même comme esprit peignant le phénoménal, dans les deux sens : il le peint et il le crée (c'est le sens du quatrième vers du *Sūtra de l'Ornement de splendeur*).

1

Fig. 1 Itō Jakuchū, *Śākyamuni sortant de la montagne*, rouleau vertical, encre et couleurs sur soie, XVIIIe siècle, 154,2 × 54,9 cm. Collection particulière.

2

Fig. 2 Itō Jakuchū, *Nirvāna des légumes*, XVIIIe siècle, rouleau vertical, encre sur papier, 181,7 x 96,1 cm.
Musée national de Kyōto.

Les Fleurs précieuses du -din mystérieux. Itō Jakuchū, troduction et légendes Manuela Moscatiello, Arles, ilippe Picquier, 2015, p. 23.

Que Jakuchū ne se soit senti contraint par les dogmes d'aucune école, c'est l'évidence même. Sa splendide *Triade de Śākyamuni (Shakasanzon)* (cat. 1-3) conservée au Shōkoku-ji, monastère zen, reproduit celle du Tōdai-ji, où le Bouddha est flanqué des deux grands bodhisattvas Samantabhadra (Fugen) et Mañjuśrî (Monju), alors que très souvent, dans les représentations zen du Bouddha historique, privilégié dans cette tradition, il se trouve accompagné de *rakan* ou arhat en sanscrit, les «Méritants» qui ont un statut en quelque sorte plus humain que ces bodhisattvas déjà au-delà de notre dimension. Cela n'empêche pas Jakuchū d'avoir fait aussi des *rakan* l'un de ses thèmes bouddhiques favoris, parfois sous la forme des seize arhats, d'autres fois en de grandioses représentations des cinq cents arhats. On peut d'ailleurs penser qu'il influença également des peintres postérieurs : ne retrouve-t-on pas dans les processions de moines d'un peintre zen comme Nantenbō (1839-1925) des échos des défilés de *rakan* ou des figurines de Fushimi *(Fushiminingyō)* de Jakuchū ? Le *Śākyamuni sortant de la montagne* de Gōchō (1749-1835), avec son halo caractéristique, pourrait aussi bien s'inscrire dans la lignée de celui de Jakuchū (fig. 1). Toutes ces images reflètent des thèmes classiques de l'iconographie bouddhique et ne sont pas révélatrices d'une attitude religieuse particulière de ce peintre.

Le *Nirvāna des légumes*

Il n'en est pas de même de l'une de ses peintures les plus fameuses, et peut-être la moins bien comprise, des Occidentaux comme des Japonais, son *Nirvāna des légumes (Yasai nehan zu,* fig. 2). On serait tenté d'y voir encore une image satirique comme il s'en trouve beaucoup dans la tradition illustrée japonaise, ainsi le célèbre rouleau médiéval des *Caricatures des animaux humanisés (Chōjū-jinbutsu giga)*, mais, comme le souligne Manuela Moscatiello, il n'y a ici rien d'ironique ni de blasphématoire[1]. Il s'agit même de la mise en image d'une très ancienne doctrine bouddhique, déjà reprise par Dōgen. Cette doctrine, élaborée essentiellement dans l'école Tiantai chinoise puis développée dans sa version japonaise, le Tendai, est celle de la présence de la nature de Bouddha non seulement chez les êtres vivants, ceux qui renaissent dans les six voies, mais également dans l'inanimé, c'est-à-dire le végétal et le minéral. Résumée le plus souvent en une formule qui ne concerne que le végétal : *sōmoku jōbutsu*, «les plantes deviennent bouddha», sentence qui ne peut se penser que si l'on admet, encore une fois, que le monde qui nous entoure, celui du minéral et du végétal, est le produit de notre esprit : avec l'esprit qui accède à l'Éveil, c'est le monde phénoménal tout entier, dont il n'est que la projection, qui arrive à la délivrance. Qui dit Éveil et délivrance, dit forcément entrée dans l'Extinction suprême, dans le *nirvāna*. Si l'on parle le plus souvent de l'Éveil des plantes, Jakuchū ne fait que mener l'idée à son terme en représentant ce qui doit forcément suivre leur Éveil, leur entrée dans l'Extinction. À travers ce *Nirvāna des légumes*, Jakuchū nous rappelle encore ce qu'est le *nirvāna* dans le bouddhisme du Grand Véhicule : non pas la fin ultime, mais une manière de prêcher la Loi aux êtres : le Bouddha est en réalité depuis toujours en *nirvāna*, et la scène, dépeinte ici de façon aussi décalée, est bien cette prédication au sein du phénoménal prise à la lettre. Chacun peut reconnaître l'idée qu'elle exprime : celle de la prédication de la Loi bouddhique par l'inanimé *(mujō-seppō)*. Vieille idée de l'école Tendai, reprise, comme toujours de façon éclatante et déroutante par Dōgen dans l'un des sermons les plus importants de son *Shōbōgenzō*. Cela peut nous amener à nous demander si Jakuchū n'a pas eu, d'une façon ou d'une autre, la possibilité de prendre connaissance des sermons du grand moine médiéval.

Éveil et calembour

Mais, se demandera-t-on, pourquoi le rôle principal dans cette image, celui du Bouddha en nirvāna, est-il accordé à un vulgaire radis ? D'autant plus que ce mot peut avoir, en japonais comme en français, des connotations fort terre à terre. Il faut bien sûr se rapporter à la langue japonaise pour comprendre cette image surprenante, car dans la culture japonaise prémoderne, pourrait-on dire, tout passe par l'auto-exégèse que le langage effectue sur lui-même grâce à la constante interaction entre ses deux dimensions langagières, la japonaise et la chinoise. «Radis» se dit en japonais *daikon*, terme sino-japonais qui signifie littéralement la «grosse racine». Cela, en japonais de tous les jours. Mais dans le vocabulaire bouddhique, le même terme, prononcé et écrit exactement de la même façon, désigne les «grandes facultés», les facultés supérieures d'intelligence qui permettent aux êtres qui en sont pourvus de comprendre les doctrines plus subtiles du bouddhisme, c'est-à-dire celles du Grand Véhicule. Et c'est naturellement à la lumière de ces doctrines que l'Éveil et le *nirvāna* de l'inanimé sont concevables et représentables. Le radis qui gît au centre de l'image est la représentation de l'intellect de celui qui a saisi l'enseignement qu'elle illustre. Extraordinaire effet de va et vient entre l'image et le spectateur, l'esprit qui regarde et l'esprit qui crée, la pensée qui se pense elle-même par l'intermédiaire du monde phénoménal[2].

On voit ainsi que le rapport qu'a Jakuchū avec le bouddhisme est bien loin d'être superficiel. Si le religieux ne représente pas, en terme de quantité, la plus grande part de son œuvre, on ne peut qu'être frappé par la variété des thèmes bouddhiques qu'il a illustrés, non pas dépendants d'une seule école ou tradition, mais tels qu'ils sont vécus et compris par un artiste qui a pleinement compris la métaphore fondamentale de l'esprit comme peintre.

Jean-Noël Robert

2 - On trouvera une interprétation voisine de la nôtre, avec de notables différences, dans l'essai de Yoshiaki Shimizu, « Multiple Commemorations: The Vegetable Nehan of Ito Jakuchu » dans *Flowing Traces: Buddhism in the Literary and Visual Arts of Japan*, James H. Sandford (dir.), Princeton University Press, 1992, p. 201-233.

XXVII

XXVII

XXVIII

XXIX

XXX

Explorer sans cesse...

Le renouvellement des techniques chez un peintre d'exception

Contrairement à d'autres artistes contemporains comme Yosa Buson (1716-1784) ou Ike no Taiga (1723-1776), Jakuchū ne fut pas un grand voyageur, malgré son ouverture d'esprit et son sens de l'indépendance, et passa l'essentiel de sa vie entre Kyōto et ses alentours. Son voyage ne fut pas à travers le monde, mais consista en un parcours intérieur, une immersion totale dans sa plus grande passion : la peinture.

Tout au long de ce que l'on pourrait définir comme un périple spirituel, loin des bruits de la vie mondaine, la culture chinoise classique fut son point de repère, un phare qui lui ouvrit de nouvelles perspectives en stimulant sans cesse son talent surprenant. Cependant, cette source d'inspiration inépuisable n'empêcha jamais les idiosyncrasies de l'artiste de marquer ses œuvres d'une touche distinctive, en particulier d'adapter les emprunts de genres ou de techniques à son langage stylistique personnel, leur donnant un caractère unique.

Son amitié profonde avec Baisō Kenjō (1719-1801), moine lettré (*bungakusō*) du Shōkoku-ji mieux connu sous le nom de Daiten, philosophe sinisant et auteur de recueils poétiques et de prose, a joué un rôle crucial dans ses choix artistiques[1]. De même, sa rencontre avec la culture Ōbaku, et en particulier avec le poète calligraphe et amateur de thé infusé (*sencha*) Baisaō (litt. «Le vieil homme qui vend du thé», 1675-1763), qui avait abandonné la vie monastique pour vivre en ermite, exerça une influence certaine sur son évolution personnelle et stylistique[2].

En général, Jakuchū quittait l'ancienne capitale lorsque son désir de se retirer du monde devenait trop fort ou quand il devait répondre à des commandes d'œuvres. Ce fut le cas lors de son séjour dans l'île de Shikoku, où il réalisa la décoration des cloisons coulissantes (*fusuma*) et des parois des salles de l'un des deux édifices principaux (Okushoin) du sanctuaire shintō de Kotohiragū, aussi appelé Konpira-san[3].

Pour ses créations à sujet floral (*hanamaruzu*, fig. 1), l'artiste s'inspira d'un type de composition chinoise dit à «branches coupées» (c. *zhezhi hua* ; j. *ori-eda*)[4]. Appartenant au genre pictural académique des «Fleurs et oiseaux» (c. *huaniao hua* ; j. *kachōga*), le *zhezhi* est une sorte d'évocation idéalisée de la plante qui consiste à l'isoler de son contexte naturel en représentant une ou quelques branches fleuries se détachant sur un fond neutre.

Jakuchū a mis en valeur l'aspect décoratif de ces peintures aux couleurs brillantes en appliquant des particules de feuille d'or (*kinpaku*) sur le papier, sans négliger pour autant le rendu naturaliste, obtenu par une profusion de détails pour les fleurs et les feuilles, comme en témoigne l'utilisation d'un vert tendre pour l'envers des feuilles et d'une tonalité plus foncée pour l'endroit.

En observateur attentif de la nature, y compris des moindres aspects botaniques, il est allé jusqu'à représenter les trous laissés par les insectes et le changement de pigmentation que présentent la plupart des feuilles avec des taches marron clair, parfois circulaires et souvent concentrées sur les bords, annonçant la fin du cycle végétatif. Ces détails fidèles à la réalité, évoquant le caractère transitoire et éphémère de la vie des plantes, ont probablement trouvé leur inspiration dans les créations des

1 - Sur le lien entre Jakuchū et Daiten voir : [Arima Raitei, dir.], *Daiten zenji to Jakuchū*, Kyōto, Shōkokuji Jōtenkaku Bijutsukan, 2001.

2 - La figure fascinante de Baisaō mérite un approfondissement, voir François Lachaud, *Le Vieil homme qui vendait du thé. Excentricité et retrait du monde dans le Japon du XVIIIe siècle*, Paris, Éditions du Cerf, 2010.

3 - Kōno Motoaki, « Les peintures modernes de Konpira-san et leur contexte historique », *Konpira-san, Sanctuaire de la mer. Trésors de la peinture japonaise*, Paris, Musée national des arts asiatiques Guimet, Kagawa-ken, Kotohira-gū, 2008, p. 19.

4 - Ce type de composition fit son apparition vers la fin des Tang (618-907) et prospéra à l'époque des Cinq Dynasties (907-960) et sous la dynastie des Song (960-1279).

peintres de la dynastie des Song du Sud (1127-1279), comme le montre une feuille célèbre de Lin Chun[5] (fig. 2).

Il faut toutefois préciser que dans l'œuvre de Jakuchū, les feuilles rongées, trouées et tachées deviennent un motif récurrent et obsessionnel, et dans certains cas, le germe de la maladie envahit d'autres éléments végétaux (**cat. XXIII**), en insufflant une atmosphère inquiétante à la composition. Néanmoins, d'un point de vue purement formel, ces aspects perdent leur apparence maladive, se transformant en modules décoratifs d'une incroyable puissance évocatrice.

Au printemps 1767 (Meiwa, 4), le peintre âgé de cinquante-deux ans entreprit, en compagnie de Daiten, un voyage de plaisance en barque depuis la ville portuaire de Fushimi, au sud de Kyōto, jusqu'à Ōsaka, au pont Tenmabashi, où ils débarquèrent en pleine nuit. La beauté du paysage des deux rives de la Yodogawa l'enchanta au point qu'il y consacra un rouleau horizontal (*emakimono*), un long support capable de rendre à la fois le rythme narratif d'une croisière fluviale et la dimension spirituelle, presque onirique, du voyage[6].

Les Plaisirs de voyager en barque (*Jōkyōshū*, fig. 3)[7] est le fruit d'une collaboration spontanée avec Daiten, laissant une large place aux émotions ressenties sur le moment par les deux amis[8]. Dans un esprit conforme à l'idéal chinois d'une vie dédiée à l'érudition, Daiten composa de brèves inscriptions en style classique chinois (*kanbun*) destinées à accompagner les esquisses à l'encre qui avaient permis à Jakuchū de saisir rapidement le paysage défilant sous ses yeux. Cette œuvre exceptionnelle a été exécutée selon un procédé particulier de gravure inspiré de la technique de l'estampage, pratiquée en Chine (*taben*) pour copier sur le papier les inscriptions gravées sur les stèles. Connu au Japon sous le néologisme de *takuhanga*, ce procédé fut choisi par l'artiste pour reproduire ses dessins en négatif, c'est-à-dire en blanc sur un fond noir profond, leur conférant ainsi une allure archaïque. Ce résultat est obtenu à l'aide de planches de bois (*hangi*) sur lesquelles on applique le papier où l'on passe un linge humide afin de le faire adhérer parfaitement à la surface, avant d'étaler l'encre à l'aide d'un pinceau. À la différence de la méthode xylographique traditionnelle japonaise, c'est le recto et non le verso de la feuille qui est posé sur la planche, de manière à réaliser une impression de face.

De surcroît, le recours à deux autres procédés sophistiqués, le *ukontaku* (ou *ukintaku*) et le *senyokutaku*, fait de cette œuvre un exemple magistral des possibilités expressives du *takuhanga*. Grâce à la première technique, sans doute suggérée par Jakuchū, l'imprimeur obtint un noir sans nuances, si compact qu'il évoque le plumage du corbeau, tandis qu'avec la seconde, il parvint à créer deux tons différents de gris, dont la délicatesse est comparable à la transparence des ailes de la cigale[9].

Probablement stimulé par la réussite admirable du *Jōkyōshū* et encouragé par Daiten, avec lequel il partageait non seulement le détachement spirituel, mais aussi une vision artistique nourrie par la tradition chinoise, Jakuchū se consacra à une étude plus approfondie du *takuhanga*. Au cours des années suivantes, il en expérimenta le potentiel fabuleux sur des formats différents tel que le rouleau vertical (*kakejiku*)[10].

Né à Qiantang (Hangzhou), Chun fut peintre à la cour empereur Xiaozong durant Chunxi (1174-1190). Il reçut tre honorifique de *daizhao* récompense prestigieuse de einture d'or.
La Yodogawa a fait l'objet euvres antérieures à celle akuchū, l'exemple le plus narquable en est le rouleau Maruyama Ōkyo (1733-1795), ourd'hui au musée Hara Arc Gunma.
Le commentaire de cette œuvre le celles réalisées selon un même océdé (cf. *infra*) reprend les herches entreprises pour rédaction de l'ouvrage : *Les Fleurs écieuses du jardin mystérieux. Jakuchū*, Introduction et gendes de Manuela Moscatiello, les, Picquier, 2015. Voir aussi mikichirō Tokuriki, Fumio aekawa, Chōzō Yamanouchi, *kuchū no takuhanga*, Tōkyō, uri Shōbo, 1981.
– Ōnishi Hiroshi, *On a Riverboat urney. A handscroll by Ito Jakuchu ith poems by Daiten*, New York, eorge Braziller, 1989, p. 27.
– Kobayashi Tadashi, Ōta Aya lir.), *Seitan sanbyakunen kinen kuchū ten, The 300th Anniversary f his birth: Jakuchū*, Tōkyō, ōkyōto bijutsukan, 2016, p. 285.
0 – Il s'agit du rouleau conservé u temple Hōzōji de Kyōto où sont eprésentés deux crânes blancs ur un fond noir au-dessous d'une nscription de Baisaō. L'illustration st reproduite dans *Les Fleurs précieuses du jardin mystérieux*, *op. cit.*, p. 31.

C'est dans cette même technique qu'il réalisa en 1768 (Meiwa, 5) deux albums en accordéon (*hōjō*), que l'on pourrait classer dans le genre pictural des fleurs, plantes et légumes (*kakisosai*), mais qui puisent également dans l'iconographie chinoise, en particulier dans la peinture de «plantes et insectes» (c. *caochong hua*), avec la présence de petits animaux invertébrés.

Ces deux œuvres, *Les Fleurs précieuses du jardin mystérieux* (*Genpo yōka*, **ill. p. 140-142**) et l'*Album de dessins élégants sur un fond simple* (*Sokenjō*)[11], s'inspirent des traités traditionnels de botanique chinoise très répandus dans le Japon de l'époque d'Edo (1603-1867), où ils contribuèrent largement au développement des études en pharmacognosie (*honzōgaku*) et à l'intérêt pour l'histoire naturelle.

Marqué par une intense tension dramatique due notamment à l'abandon de la polychromie et aux cadrages très audacieux, le *Genpo yōka* constitue l'exemple le plus réussi parmi les créations *takuhanga* du peintre. Son titre, probablement suggéré par Daiten, fait référence dans sa première partie au Xuanpu, lieu légendaire de la cordillère du Kunlun où sont censés habiter les immortels, tandis que «*yōka*» évoque des fleurs belles comme le jade.

Vingt-neuf pages sur quarante-huit sont accompagnées de brèves annotations poétiques (*tanji*) de Daiten. Animées d'une grande spiritualité, elles témoignent de l'échange esthétique entre les textes et les compositions de l'artiste. Les sujets représentés, fleurs, plantes, fruits et légumes ainsi qu'insectes et animaux de petite taille, sont placés au tout premier plan, vus de très près et caractérisés par une mise en page et des solutions formelles originales qui font de cet album un chef-d'œuvre d'art graphique. Par ailleurs, quelques motifs sont à mettre en relation avec les rouleaux du *Royaume coloré des êtres vivants*, comme dans l'*Étang aux insectes* (**cat. XXIII**), d'où a été tirée la grenouille flottant sur l'eau de la page consacrée au nénuphar nain (*Nymphaea tetragona Georgi*; *hitsujigusa*)[12].

Poursuivant ses recherches dans le domaine de la gravure, Jakuchū se lança en 1771 (Meiwa, 8) dans la réalisation d'autres dessins destinés à cette technique. Bien que ses liens avec le *takuhanga* ne soient pas certains dans ce cas-là, ce procédé a sans doute joué un rôle important dans les images polychromes de fleurs et oiseaux (*kachōzu*), dont on ne connaît que six exemplaires, où les silhouettes d'oiseaux exotiques se détachent sur un fond noir[13]. La technique xylographique, utilisée notamment pour le fond noir de jais, est ici combinée au *kappazuri*, une méthode qui permet d'appliquer la couleur sur le papier à l'aide de pochoirs servant d'habitude pour la teinture de textiles Yūzen[14].

Dans cinq de ces œuvres, le dessin, qui se développe en diagonale à partir d'un angle créant une sorte de ligne idéale marquée par la présence d'éléments végétaux, n'est pas sans rappeler les compositions si chères aux peintres de la dynastie des Song du Sud. La sixième œuvre se distingue des autres par son format circulaire (fig. 5). Elle représente sur un perchoir délicieusement coloré un cacatoès blanc, dont la ligne souple du corps, dessiné de manière simplifiée, fait écho au contour de la sphère noire.

11 - D'après la postface de l'exemplaire appartenant à la maison d'édition Seishōdō shoten, le Sokenjō fut publié au début de l'été 1768 alors que le colophon indique la fin de l'hiver 1767. L'exemplaire de la New York Public Library est daté lui aussi de l'été 1768, voir Nobuo Tsuji (dir.), *Jakuchū wandārando, Jakuchū wonderland*, Shiga, Miho Museum, 2009, p. 282, n° 8.

12 - Cette même page inspira Sakai Hōitsu (1761-1828), qui en fit une réélaboration personnelle pour son *Album de modèles* (*Tekagamijō*). Dans cette œuvre figurent onze compositions empruntées au *Genpo yōka*.

13 - Kobayashi Tadashi, Ōta Aya (dir.), *Seitan sanbyakunen kinen : Jakuchū ten, op. cit.*, p. 286-287.

14 - L'utilisation du kappazuri dans la gravure fut expérimentée en 1767 par Kitao Sekkōsai (actif 1745-1780) dans sa *Sélection de dessins colorés (Saishiki gasen)*.

1

2

Fig. 1 Itō Jakuchū, *Fleurs*, 1764, couleurs sur papier avec feuille d'or éparpillée, ensemble de quatre panneaux sur *fusuma* (cloisons coulissantes), 177,5 cm x 91 cm (chaque panneau), Okushoin (salle d'étude intérieure), Jyōdan no ma (chambre supérieure), Kotohiragū, préfecture de Kagawa, Shikoku.

Fig. 2 Lin Chun (actif dans la seconde moitié du XIIe siècle), *Raisins et insectes*, 1174-1190, feuille d'album, encre et couleurs sur soie, 26,2 cm x 27 cm. Pékin, musée du Palais.

3

4

Fig. 3 Itō Jakuchū, *Les Plaisirs de voyager en barque*, 1767, détail, rouleau horizontal, xylographie de type *takuhanga*, 28, 7 cm x 1151,8 cm, Musée national de Kyōto.

Fig. 4 Itō Jakuchū, *Lanternes en pierre*, XVIIIe siècle, paire de paravents à six volets, encre et laver d'or sur papier, 159 x 363 cm, Musée national de Kyōto.

山長

5

6

7

Le rapprochement de celle-ci avec une peinture, aujourd'hui montée en rouleau horizontal, de l'empereur Xuanzong (1398-1435)[15], d'une souris qui mange des myriques (*Myrica rubra* ; *yangmei*), est très évocateur (fig. 6). Les deux œuvres ne partagent pas seulement le format arrondi et le fond noir, mais également une conception de l'image marquée par la présence au centre d'un animal blanc ainsi que la gamme chromatique[16].

Quant à l'invention de la technique connue sous le nom de «peinture en mosaïque» (*masumegaki*)[17], la critique est unanime pour en accorder la paternité à Jakuchū, bien que l'on ne compte qu'une seule œuvre attribuée avec certitude à l'artiste parmi celles réalisées à l'aide de petits carreaux semblables aux tessères d'une mosaïque[18]. Il s'agit de l'*Éléphant blanc et autres animaux* (*Byakuzō gunjūzu*)[19] caractérisé par une gamme chromatique restreinte et sombre. La palette de tons se fait plus étendue et brillante dans la paire de paravents de la collection Price (fig. 7), où plusieurs espèces d'oiseaux et d'animaux peuplent un paysage imaginaire encadré par une frise, elle aussi peinte selon le même procédé. Une grille obtenue par le tracé à l'encre des lignes verticales et horizontales sur toute la surface du papier y a produit des petits carrés d'environ neuf millimètres de côté. À l'intérieur de chaque carré, deux autres ont été peints avec une grande précision, utilisant tantôt deux nuances de la même couleur, tantôt deux couleurs différentes. C'est la totalité de ces petits carrés qui permet de reconstituer l'image.

Diverses théories ont été formulées sur l'origine de cette technique. La plus répandue souligne l'intérêt de Jakuchū pour les dessins préparatoires employés pour les décors des tissus[20]. Cette hypothèse repose sur les rapports de l'artiste avec Kaneda Chūbei, un marchand de Nishijin, le quartier de Kyōto réputé pour la fabrication de textiles en soie[21].

Principalement apprécié pour sa sensibilité à la couleur, Jakuchū est également l'auteur d'œuvres monochromes, en premier lieu de l'ensemble du Rokuon-ji (fig. 3, p. 82), où le dialogue entre le souffle créateur du peintre et sa dextérité atteint un sommet artistique rare. Pour ce qui est du lavis, il expérimenta une variété extraordinaire de procédés qu'il perfectionna de manière novatrice en apportant toujours sa touche personnelle. C'est le cas de la méthode dite *sujimegaki*. Celle-ci met à profit la grande capacité d'absorption du papier chinois de type *xuan* (*gasenshi*), qui évite la dispersion de l'encre lorsque l'on trace, par exemple, des traits successifs pour évoquer les pétales des fleurs[22].

Parmi les innovations techniques de l'artiste, on compte aussi le pointillisme (*tenbyō*), consistant à créer une image avec de petites touches d'encre ou de couleur juxtaposées. La paire de paravents représentant des cloisons et des lanternes en pierre (*ishidōrō*), dans laquelle l'arrière-plan est marqué par le profil délicat de montagnes (fig. 4), en constitue un exemple remarquable[23]. La texture du granite est ici suggérée par une myriade de points disposés de manière homogène, créant un effet de tridimensionnalité à travers le jeu du clair-obscur.

Il convient de préciser que les peintres chinois se sont souvent servis de petits points (c.*dian*), en particulier pour restituer le feuillage. Dans le deuxième livre des *Enseignements de la Peinture du Jardin grand*

15 - Cinquième empereur de la dynastie des Ming (1368-1644), Xuanzong régna de 1426 à 1435 sous le nom d'ère de Xuande. Il fut un poète et un peintre talentueux.
16 - Il n'est pas sans intérêt de signaler une autre gravure représentant un cacatoès blanc sur un fond noir dessiné, vers 1931-1941, par Ohara Koson (1877-1945).
17 - Le terme a été forgé par Kobayashi Tadashi, voir son article : « Itō Jakuchū dokusō no ikkaku hyōhō ni tsuite», *Museum*, n° 359, février 1981, p. 31-40.
18 - Selon Satō Yasuhiro, deux de ces œuvres, les paires de paravents de la collection Price et du musée préfectoral de Shizuoka, ne seraient pas à attribuer à Jakuchū.
19 - L'illustration est reproduite dans *Les Fleurs précieuses du jardin mystérieux, op. cit.*, p. 18.
20 - Hypothèse d'abord soutenue par Kanō Hiroyuki et partagée ensuite par Izumi Miho dans « Itō Jakuchū no masume-gaki sakuin o saikō suru – Nishijin-ori shō-e to no kankei kara – », *Geijutsugaku gakuhō* 6, [1999], où les croquis originaux pour les textiles sont mis en relation avec ces peintures.
21 - Une autre théorie associe le *masumegaki* aux images folkloriques coréennes : Yukio Lippit (dir.), *Colorful Realm. Japanese Bird-and-Flower Paintings by Itō Jakuchū*, Washington, National Gallery of Art, Chicago et Londres, University of Chicago Press, 2012, p. 183.
22 - Kobayashi Tadashi, « Itō Jakuchū: A Man Rejoicing in Painting », *Orientations*, vol. 43, n. 3, avril 2012, p. 39.

Fig. 5 Itō Jakuchū, *Cacatoès*, 1771, xylographie polychrome, diam. 26,5 cm, Tōkyō, Fondation Hiraki Ukiyo-e.

Fig. 6 Xuanzong (1398-1435), *Souris qui mange des myriques*, vers 1427-1431, encre et couleurs sur papier, Pékin, musée du Palais.

Fig. 7 Itō Jakuchū, *Oiseaux, animaux, fleurs et arbres dans un paysage imaginaire*, paire de paravents à six volets, XVIIIe siècle, couleurs sur papier, 168,7 x 374,4 cm (chaque paravent). États-Unis, collection Etsuko et Joe Price.

comme un Grain de Moutarde (*Jieziyuan huazhuan*, 1679) – que Jakuchū connaissait certainement –, il est question de la méthode pour évoquer les feuilles avec des points comparés à la trace des pieds du rat (c. *shuzu*). L'emploi des points sert également à dessiner des arbres situés au loin ou des petites pierres sur les rochers et les montagnes[24]. Loin de recréer l'impression éthérée, impalpable, des paysages chinois animés par un souffle universel et caractérisés par une perspective aérienne, qui ont tant inspiré le pinceau de Taiga, Jakuchū adopta cette méthode pour rendre la solidité des lanternes dans leur matérialité et leurs formes géométriques, dont la variété retient l'attention.

À bien l'observer, cette œuvre fascine à plusieurs égards. Sa perception de la réalité comme suspendue dans le temps et enveloppée par le silence, où il est difficile de déterminer l'heure et la saison, pourrait presque faire penser à l'atmosphère magique de la peinture métaphysique italienne du début du XXᵉ siècle.

Il serait difficile de terminer cet inventaire rapide des principales innovations techniques de Jakuchū sans soulever quelques questions. On peut notamment se demander si cette quête inlassable, cette expérimentation constante, qui caractérise l'œuvre du maître dès ses débuts, ne cache pas des attentes plus ambitieuses, allant au-delà des aspirations d'un artiste talentueux. Ne pourrait-il avoir fait de la peinture la voie privilégiée pour parvenir à la connaissance de soi et à l'épanouissement personnel ? En liant de manière si étroite son chemin artistique à son parcours spirituel, Jakuchū semble dévoiler une exigence profonde, un désir puissant de déambuler dans les méandres de son intériorité.

Manuela Moscatiello

23 - D'après Kobayashi Tadashi, l'œuvre date des dernières années de vie de l'artiste : « Itō Jakuchū hitsu Ishidōrō zu byōbu », *Kokka*, nº 1177 (1993), p. 25-26. Sur cette paire de paravents, voir également : *Jakuchū !*, Kyōto Kokuritsu Hakubutsukan, 2000, p. 330 ; Matthew P. McKelway (dir.), *Traditions Unbound: Groundbreaking Painters of Eighteenth-Century Kyoto*, San Francisco, The Asian Art Society, 2005, p. 168-169.

24 - *Encyclopédie de la peinture chinoise*, traduction et commentaires par Raphaël Petrucci, Paris, Librairie You Feng, 2000 [1918], p. 82, 103 et 169.

玄圃瑤華

Les Fleurs précieuses du jardin mystérieux

丹葩耀

绛幘報曉
出泥濯漣

芳菉
雖〻占豊

涼風吹緑葉
落日亂鳴蟬

Table des illustrations

Triade de Śākyamuni
釈迦三尊像

Vers 1755-1763 ; 宝暦5-13 年頃
Rouleau vertical ; 掛幅装
Couleurs sur soie ; 絹本着色
Kyōto, Shōkoku-ji ; 京都, 相国寺

1
Bouddha Śākyamuni
釈迦如来像

212,4 × 111,4 cm
Signature ; 署名 :
Respectueusement copié par Tō Jokin de Heian [Kyōto] ; 平安藤汝鈞㒵宿拝写
Sceaux ; 印章 :
Jokin ; 汝鈞
Tōshi Keiwa ; 藤氏景和

2
Bodhisattva Mañjuśrī
文殊菩薩像

210,4 × 111,4 cm
Signature ; 署名 :
Respectueusement copié par Tō Jokin de Heian [Kyōto] ; 平安藤汝鈞㒵宿拝写
Sceaux ; 印章 :
Jokin ; 汝鈞
Tōshi Keiwa ; 藤氏景和

3
Bodhisattva Samantabhadra
普賢菩薩像

209,4 × 111,1 cm
Signature ; 署名 :
Respectueusement copié par Tō Jokin de Heian [Kyōto] ; 平安藤汝鈞㒵宿拝写
Sceaux ; 印章 :
Jokin ; 汝鈞
Tōshi Keiwa ; 藤氏景和

Le Royaume coloré des êtres vivants
動植綵絵

Tōkyō, Musée des collections impériales, Sannomaru Shōzōkan ; 東京, 宮内庁三の丸尚蔵館

I
Pivoines et papillons
芍薬群蝶図

Vers 1757-1758 ; 宝暦7-8 年頃
Rouleau vertical ; 掛幅装
Couleurs sur soie ; 絹本着色
142 × 79,8 cm
Signature ; 署名 :
Peint par Tō Jokin, ou le pieux laïc Jakuchū de la ville de Heian [Kyōto], dans sa modeste chambre du quartier de Nishiki ; 平安城若冲居士藤汝鈞畫於錦街陋室
Sceaux ; 印章 :
Jokin ; 汝鈞
Tōshi Keiwa ; 藤氏景和
Un concept nouveau dérivé d'un précédent établi ; 出新意於法度之中

II
Prunier en fleur et petits oiseaux
梅花小禽図

1758 ; 宝暦 8 年
Rouleau vertical ; 掛幅装
Couleurs sur soie ; 絹本着色
142,7 × 79,5 cm
Signature ; 署名 :
Peint par le pieux laïc Jakuchū au printemps de la huitième année de l'ère Hōreki ; 寶暦戊寅春居士若冲製
Sceaux ; 印章 :
Jokin ; 汝鈞
Jakuchū koji ; 若冲居士

III
Canards mandarins dans la neige
雪中鴛鴦図

1759 ; 宝暦 9 年
Rouleau vertical ; 掛幅装
Couleurs sur soie ; 絹本着色
142 × 79,8 cm
Signature ; 署名 :
Peint le deuxième mois de la neuvième année de l'ère Hōreki par le pieux laïc Jakuchū ; 寶暦己卯仲春若冲居士製
Sceaux ; 印章 :
Tō Jokin, prénom de courtoisie Keiwa ; 藤汝鈞字景和
Jakuchū koji ; 若冲居士

IV
Millet d'automne et moineaux
秋塘群雀図

1759 ; 宝暦 9 年
Rouleau vertical ; 掛幅装
Couleurs sur soie ; 絹本着色
142,8 × 80,1 cm
Signature ; 署名 :
Peint le huitième mois de la neuvième année de l'ère Hōreki par le pieux laïc Jakuchū ; 寶暦己卯仲秋居士若冲製
Sceaux ; 印章 :
Jokin ; 汝鈞
Jakuchū koji ; 若冲居士

V
Tournesols et coq
向日葵雄鶏図

1759 ; 宝暦 9 年
Rouleau vertical ; 掛幅装
Couleurs sur soie ; 絹本着色
142,3 × 79,7 cm

Signature ; 署名 :
Peint le huitième mois de la neuvième année de l'ère Hōreki par le pieux laïc Jakuchū ; 寶暦己卯仲秋若冲製
Sceaux ; 印章 :
Jokin ; 汝鈞
Jakuchū koji ; 若冲居士

VI

Hortensias, coq et poule
紫陽花双鶏図

1759 ; 宝暦 9 年
Rouleau vertical ; 掛幅装
Couleurs sur soie ; 絹本着色
142,9 × 79,7 cm
Signature ; 署名 :
Créé à l'automne de la neuvième année de l'ère Hōreki par le pieux laïc Jakuchū du quartier de Nishiki de Heian [Kyōto] ; 寶暦己卯秋平安錦街居士若冲造
Sceaux ; 印章 :
Jokin ; 汝鈞
Tōshi Keiwa ; 藤氏景和

VII

Coq et poule
大鶏雌雄図

1759 ; 宝暦 9 年
Rouleau vertical ; 掛幅装
Couleurs sur soie ; 絹本着色
142,3 × 79,1 cm
Signature ; 署名 :
Créé dans la neuvième année de l'ère Hōreki par le pieux laïc Jakuchū du quartier de Nishiki de Heian [Kyōto] ; 寶暦己卯年平安錦街居士若冲造
Sceaux ; 印章 :
Jokin ; 汝鈞
Jakuchū koji ; 若冲居士

VIII

Fleurs de prunier et lune
梅花皓月図

Vers 1757-1760 ; 宝暦 7-10 年頃
Rouleau vertical ; 掛幅装
Couleurs sur soie ; 絹本着色
142,3 × 79,7 cm
Signature ; 署名 :
Fait par le pieux laïc Jakuchū ; 居士若冲製
Sceaux ; 印章 :
Jokin ; 汝鈞
Tōshi Keiwa ; 藤氏景和

IX

Vieux Pin et paon
老松孔雀図

Vers 1757-1760 ; 宝暦 7-10 年頃
Rouleau vertical ; 掛幅装
Couleurs sur soie ; 絹本着色
142,9 × 79,6 cm
Signature ; 署名 :
Fait par le pieux laïc Jakuchū ; 居士若冲製
Sceaux ; 印章 :
Jokin ; 汝鈞
Jakuchū koji ; 若冲居士

X

Hibiscus, coq et poule
芙蓉双鶏図

Vers 1757-1760 ; 宝暦 7-10 年頃
Rouleau vertical ; 掛幅装
Couleurs sur soie ; 絹本着色
143,4 × 79,9 cm
Signature ; 署名 :
Créé par le pieux laïc Jakuchū du Pavillon de l'esprit détaché ; 心遠館若冲居士造
Sceaux ; 印章 :
Jokin ; 汝鈞
Jakuchū koji ; 若冲居士

XI

Vieux Pin, coq et poule blancs
老松白鶏図

Vers 1757-1760 ; 宝暦 7-10 年頃
Rouleau vertical ; 掛幅装
Couleurs sur soie ; 絹本着色
142,6 × 79,7 cm
Signature ; 署名 :
Créé par le pieux laïc Jakuchū ; 若冲居士作
Sceaux ; 印章 :
Jokin ; 汝鈞
Tōshi Keiwa ; 藤氏景和

XII

Vieux Pin et cacatoès
老松鸚鵡図

Vers 1757-1760 ; 宝暦 7-10 年頃
Rouleau vertical ; 掛幅装
Couleurs sur soie ; 絹本着色
142,6 × 79,7 cm
Signature ; 署名 :
Peint par Jakuchū, le maître du Pavillon de l'esprit détaché ; 心遠館主人若冲寫
Sceaux ; 印章 :
Jokin ; 汝鈞
Jakuchū koji ; 若冲居士

XIII

Oie et roseaux
芦鵞図

1761 ; 宝暦 11 年
Rouleau vertical ; 掛幅装
Couleurs sur soie ; 絹本着色
142,6 × 79,5 cm
Signature ; 署名 :
Créé par le pieux laïc Jakuchū au printemps de 1761 ; 寶暦辛巳春居士若冲造
Sceaux ; 印章 :
Jokin ; 汝鈞
Tōshi Keiwa ; 藤氏景和

XIV

Nandina et coq
南天雄鶏図

Vers 1761-1765 ; 宝暦 11-明和 2 年頃
Rouleau vertical ; 掛幅装
Couleurs sur soie ; 絹本着色
142,6 × 79,9 cm
Sceaux ; 印章 :
Jokin ; 汝鈞
Tōshi Keiwa ; 藤氏景和

XV

Prunier en fleur et grues
梅花群鶴図

Vers 1761-1765 ; 宝暦 11-明和 2 年頃
Rouleau vertical ; 掛幅装
Couleurs sur soie ; 絹本着色
141,8 × 79,7 cm
Sceaux ; 印章 :
Jokin ; 汝鈞
Jakuchū koji ; 若冲居士
En haut à droite ; 右上 :
Quand il peint, il ne se préoccupe pas de son vieil âge ; 丹青不 知 咾将 至

XVI

Palmiers de Chine et coqs
棕櫚雄鶏図

Vers 1761-1765 ; 宝暦 11-明和 2 年頃
Rouleau vertical ; 掛幅装
Couleurs sur soie ; 絹本着色
142,7 × 79,7 cm
Sceaux ; 印章 :
Jokin ; 汝鈞
Jakuchū koji ; 若冲居士

XVII

Étang aux lotus et poissons
蓮池遊魚図

Vers 1761-1765 ; 宝暦 11-明和 2 年頃
Rouleau vertical ; 掛幅装
Couleurs sur soie ; 絹本着色
142,6 × 79,7 cm
Signature ; 署名 :
Jakuchū, le maître de l'Ermitage du boisseau de riz ; 斗米菴主若冲
Sceaux ; 印章 :
Jokin ; 汝鈞
Jakuchū koji ; 若冲居士
En haut à droite ; w
La suprême habileté de la main qui compose ces peintures communique avec le divin.
丹青活手妙通神

XVIII

Fleurs de pêcher et petits oiseaux
桃花小禽図

Vers 1761-1765 ; 宝暦 11-明和 2 年頃
Rouleau vertical ; 掛幅装
Couleurs sur soie ; 絹本着色

142,6 × 79,4 cm
Signature ; 署名 :
Jakuchū koji ; 若冲居士
Sceaux ; 印章 :
Tō Jokin'in ; 藤汝鈞印
Jakuchū koji ; 若冲居士

XIX
Faisans dorés dans la neige
雪中錦鶏図

Vers 1761-1765 ; 宝暦11-明和 2 年頃
Rouleau vertical ; 掛幅装
Couleurs sur soie ; 絹本着色
142,3 × 79,5 cm
Signature ; 署名 :
Fait par Jakuchū du quartier de Nishiki ;
錦街若冲製
Sceaux ; 印章 :
Jokin ; 汝鈞
Jakuchū koji ; 若冲居士

XX
Coqs
群鶏図

Vers 1761-1765 ; 宝暦11-明和 2 年頃
Rouleau vertical ; 掛幅装
Couleurs sur soie ; 絹本着色
142,6 × 79,7 cm
Sceaux ; 印章 :
Tō Jokin'in ; 藤汝鈞印
Jakuchū koji ; 若冲居士

XXI
Roses et petit oiseau
薔薇小禽図

Vers 1761-1765 ; 宝暦 11-明和 2 年頃
Rouleau vertical ; 掛幅装
Couleurs sur soie ; 絹本着色
142,6 × 79,7 cm
Signature ; 署名 :
Peint par Jakuchū du Pavillon de l'esprit détaché ; 心遠館若冲畫
Sceaux ; 印章 :
Tō Jokin'in ; 藤汝鈞印
Jakuchū koji ; 若冲居士

XXII
Pivoines et petits oiseaux
牡丹小禽図

Vers 1761-1765 ; 宝暦 11-明和 2 年頃
Rouleau vertical ; 掛幅装
Couleurs sur soie ; 絹本着色
142,7 × 80 cm
Signature ; 署名 :
Jakuchū ; 若冲
Sceaux ; 印章 :
La suprême habileté de la main qui compose ces peintures communique avec le divin.
丹青活手妙通神
Jokin ; 汝鈞

XXIII
Étang aux insectes
池辺群虫図

Vers 1761-1765 ; 宝暦 11-明和 2 年頃
Rouleau vertical ; 掛幅装
Couleurs sur soie ; 絹本着色
142,3 × 79,7 cm
Signature ; 署名 :
Jakuchū de l'Ermitage du boisseau de riz ;
斗米菴若冲
Sceaux ; 印章 :
Tō Jokin'in ; 藤汝鈞印
Jakuchū koji ; 若冲居士
En haut à gauche ; 左上 :
La suprême habileté de la main qui compose ces peintures communique avec le divin.
丹青活手妙通神

XXIV
Coquillages
貝甲図

Vers 1761-1765 ; 宝暦11-明和 2 年頃
Rouleau vertical ; 掛幅装
Couleurs sur soie ; 絹本着色
142,2 × 79,7 cm
Sceaux ; 印章 :
Jokin ; 汝鈞
Jakuchū koji ; 若冲居士

XXV
Vieux Pin et phénix blanc
老松白鳳図

Vers 1765-1766 ; 明和 2-3 年頃
Rouleau vertical ; 掛幅装
Couleurs sur soie ; 絹本着色
141,8 × 79,7 cm
Sceaux ; 印章 :
Tō Jokin'in ; 藤汝鈞印
Jakuchū koji ; 若冲居士

XXVI
Oie sauvage et roseaux
芦雁図

Vers 1765-1766 ; 明和 2-3 年頃
Rouleau vertical ; 掛幅装
Couleurs sur soie ; 絹本着色
142,6 × 79,3 cm
Sceaux ; 印章 :
Tō Jokin'in ; 藤汝鈞印
Jakuchū koji ; 若冲居士

XXVII
Poissons
諸魚図

Vers 1765-1766 ; 明和 2-3 年頃
Rouleau vertical ; 掛幅装
Couleurs sur soie ; 絹本着色
142,6 × 79,4 cm
Sceaux ; 印章 :
Tō Jokin'in ; 藤汝鈞印
Jakuchū koji ; 若冲居士

XXVIII
Poissons
群魚図

Vers 1765-1766 ; 明和 2-3 年頃
Rouleau vertical ; 掛幅装
Couleurs sur soie ; 絹本着色
142,3 × 78,9 cm
Sceaux ; 印章 :
Tō Jokin'in ; 藤汝鈞印
Jakuchū koji ; 若冲居士

XXIX
Chrysanthèmes et ruisseau
菊花流水図

Vers 1765-1766 ; 明和 2-3 年頃
Rouleau vertical ; 掛幅装
Couleurs sur soie ; 絹本着色
142,7 × 79,1 cm
Sceaux ; 印章 :
Tō Jokin'in ; 藤汝鈞印
Jakuchū koji ; 若冲居士

XXX
Érable et petits oiseaux
紅葉小禽図

Vers 1765-1766 ; 明和 2-3 年頃
Rouleau vertical ; 掛幅装
Couleurs sur soie ; 絹本着色
142,3 × 79,7 cm
Sceaux ; 印章 :
Tō Jokin'in ; 藤汝鈞印
Jakuchū koji ; 若冲居士

p. 139-142
Les Fleurs précieuses du jardin mystérieux
玄圃瑤華

1768 ; 明和 5 年
Xylographie de type *takuhanga* ;
紙本拓版
1 vol. ; 一帖
48 images ; 48 図
28,2 × 17,8 cm
Musée national de Tōkyō ; 東京国立博物館
Collection particulière ; 個人蔵
(Six doubles pages extraites du volume)

Chronologie

1716 Naissance de Itō Jakuchū, fils aîné de Itō Genzaemon, marchand grossiste en légumes et propriétaire du magasin Masuya, au marché Nishiki de Kyōto. L'artiste aura deux frères, Sōgon et Sōjaku, et une sœur, Shinjaku.

1738 À la mort de son père, Jakuchū, en tant que fils aîné, doit reprendre l'affaire familiale.

1752 Début de son amitié avec Baisō Kenjō, connu comme Daiten, moine érudit du monastère zen Shōkoku-ji, auteur d'ouvrages en vers et en prose. C'est à lui qu'on doit une grande partie des renseignements sur la biographie de l'artiste. Jakuchū adopte le titre de «pieux laïc» (*koji*).

1755 Jakuchū confie la gestion du commerce familial à son frère Sōgon et peut enfin se consacrer à la peinture.

1757 Il commence à travailler à son œuvre, *Le Royaume coloré des êtres vivants*.

1759 Période de grande activité pour l'artiste qui poursuit la réalisation des rouleaux du *Royaume coloré des êtres vivants* ainsi que le cycle de peintures monochromes sur cloisons coulissantes du temple Rokuon-ji, mieux connu sous le nom de Kinkaku-ji.

1764 Voyage à Shikoku au cours duquel il réalise la décoration des salles de l'Okushoin du sanctuaire Kotohiragū.

1765 Mort de son frère Sōjaku. Peu après, il offre au monastère Shōkoku-ji la *Triade de Śākyamuni* et vingt-quatre rouleaux du *Royaume coloré des êtres vivants*.

1766 L'artiste érige dans le temple un monument funéraire (*juzō*) destiné à accueillir un jour sa dépouille. Y figure une inscription de Daiten (k*etsumei*).

1767 Jakuchū et Daiten font un voyage en barque de Kyōto à Ōsaka pour rendre visite à Kimura Kenkadō, homme de lettres, poète, calligraphe et collectionneur.

1770 Une cérémonie commémorative est donnée en l'honneur du père de Jakuchū qui offre, en cette occasion, les six derniers rouleaux du *Royaume coloré des êtres vivants* au Shōkoku-ji.

Événements historiques

Jakuchū a exercé son art de peintre dans la seconde moitié du XVIIIe siècle. Cette période particulièrement féconde de l'art japonais vit divers mouvements artistiques, comme l'ukiyo-e, l'école réaliste Maruyama-Shijō ou le courant sinisant du Nanga, atteindre des formes d'expression d'une extraordinaire vivacité.

1716 Naissance à Kyōto de Yosa Buson, poète et peintre du courant sinisant bunjinga («peinture de lettrés») ou Nanga («peinture du Sud»). Mort de Ogata Kōrin, représentant majeur du courant décoratif Rinpa (litt. «école de [Kō]rin»). Arrivée au pouvoir du shogun Tokugawa Yoshimune qui renforce la période de paix (*pax Tokugawa*) instaurée dès le début du XVIIe siècle par Tokugawa Ieyasu.

1723 Naissance de Ike no Taiga, qui est, avec Yosa Buson, l'un des deux peintres les plus célèbres de la peinture de lettrés.

1730 Naissance de Soga Shōhaku, considéré avec Jakuchū et Nagasawa Rosetsu (1754-1799) comme l'un des trois peintres excentriques de Kyōto.

1731 Arrivée au Japon du peintre chinois Shen Nanpin (vers 1682 – après 1760) qui s'installe à Nagasaki et fait connaître le style coloré et minutieux de la peinture chinoise de fleurs et oiseaux.

1775 D'après le *Heian Jinbutsushi* (un annuaire des personnalités éminentes de Kyōto), Jakuchū est classé second après le peintre Maruyama Ōkyo.

1776 Jakuchū débute son projet des *Cinq cents arhats* en pierre pour le Sekihō-ji, un temple au sud de Kyōto, qui sera achevé dans les années 1790.

1779 Mort de la mère de l'artiste.

1790 Il termine les peintures sur cloisons coulissantes (*fukusa*) pour le Saifuku-ji près d'Ōsaka et le Kaihō-ji à Fushimi. Peu de temps après, il tombe malade.

1792 Mort de son frère Sōgon.

1793 Le peintre séjourne désormais à Fukakusa, au sud de Kyōto, dans une résidence pas loin du Seikihō-ji, avec sa sœur Shinjaku, restée veuve, et son enfant.

1799 Jakuchū réalise les peintures circulaires pour le plafond à caissons de la chapelle votive dédiée à Kannon, au Sekihō-ji.

1800 Mort de Jakuchū. Il est enterré au temple de Sekihō-ji.

1733 Naissance de Maruyama Ōkyo, le fondateur de l'école de peinture réaliste qui porte son nom. Shen Nanpin rentre en Chine.

1743 Mort du peintre, calligraphe et céramiste Ogata Kenzan, frère cadet du célèbre Kōrin.

1745 Arrivée au pouvoir du shogun Tokugawa Ieshige, fils aîné de Tokugawa Yoshimune, qui dirige jusqu'en 1760.

1746 Le moine érudit Daiten devient responsable du Jiun-in, temple sous l'autorité du Shōkoku-ji.

1760 Arrivée au pouvoir de Tokugawa Ieharu qui gouverne jusqu'en 1786.

1776 Mort de Ike no Taiga.

1779 Daiten est à la tête du Shōkoku-ji.

1781 Mort de Soga Shōhaku.

1783 Mort de Yosa Buson.

1788 Un incendie important se déclenche à Kyōto, détruisant, entre autres, les propriétés du peintre et deux bâtiments du Shōkoku-ji. La série du *Royaume coloré des êtres vivants* est heureusement sauvée.

1795 Mort de Maruyama Ōkyo.

1799 Mort de Nagasawa Rosetsu.

1801 Mort de Daiten.

Bibliographie sélective

Addiss Stephen, *Zenga and Nanga: Paintings by Japanese Monks and Scholars; Selections from the Kurt and Millie Gitter Collection,* cat. exp., Nouvelle-Orléans, New Orleans Museum of Art (20 novembre 1976 – 9 janvier 1977), Nouvelle-Orléans, New Orleans Museum of Art, 1976.

Arima Raitei, *Daiten zenji to Jakuchū,* Kyōto, Shōkokuji Jōtenkaku Bijutsukan, 2001.

Bukkyō bunka jiten, Tōkyō, Kōsei Shuppansha, 1989.

Cahill James, *Scholar painters of Japan: the Nanga School,* New York, The Asia Society, 1972.

Cahill James, *Sakaki Hyakusen and Early Nanga painting,* Berkeley, University of California, Institute of East Asian studies, Center for Japanese studies, 1983.

Doi Tsugiyoshi, **Miyajima Shin.ichi**, *Kokka. n° 1046,* Tōkyō, Kokkasha, 1981.

Dōshoku sai-e: Jakuchū byōsha no myōgi (Doshoku sai-e. Colourful Realm of Living Beings: Jakuchū Exquisite Skill of Depiction), Tōkyō, Sannomaru Shōzōkan, 2006.

Graham, Patricia Jane, *Faith and power in Japanese Buddhist art,* 1600-2005, Honolulu, University of Hawaii Press, 2007.

Goto Kenichirō, «Itō Jakuchū no takuhanga sakuhin ni tsuite Sokenjō, Genpo yōka o chūshin ni», *Bigaku Ronkyū,* Kansai Gakuin Daigaku, 2004, n° 19, 20 mars, p. 21-38.

Hayami Akira, *Rekishi Jinkōgaku de mita Nihon,* Tōkyō, Bungeishunjū, 2001.

He Li, **Knight Michael**, *Power and Glory: Court Arts of China's Ming dynasty,* San Francisco, Asian Art Museum, Chong-Moon Lee Center for Asian Art and Culture, 2008.

Hickman Money L., *Jakuchū, Shōhaku,* Tōkyō, Shūeisha, 1977.

Hickman Money L., **Satō Yasuhiro**, *The Paintings of Jakuchū,* cat. exp., New York, The Asia Society Galleries, (5 octobre – 6 décembre 1989), Tōkyō, The Agency for Cultural Affairs, New York, The Asia Society Galleries, 1989.

Hiraga Gennai, *Butsurui Hinshitsu,* Tōkyō, Nihon Koten Zenshū, 1928.

Hōjō no Nihon bijutsu – Kobayashi Tadashi sensei koki kinen ronbunshū, *Tōkyō,* Geika shoin, 2012.

Homage to All Creatures Great and Small : the Visionary World of Itō Jakuchū (1716-1800), New York - Japan Foundation, 2009.

Itō Jakuchū: anazā wārudo *(Itō Jakuchū: Another world),* cat. exp., Shizuoka Kenritsu Bijutsukan (10 avril - 16 mai 2010), Chibashi Bijutsukan (22 mai - 27 juin 2010).

Itō Jakuchū Dōshoku sai-e zen sanjuppuku, Tōkyō, Shōgakukan, 2010.

Izumi Miho, «Itō Jakuchū no masume-gaki sakhuin o saikō suru – Nishijin-ori shō-e kankei kara», *Geijutsugaku gakuhō,* 1999, p. 3-24.

Jakuchū to Edo kaiga: Puraisu korekushon, Tōkyō, Kokuritsu Hakubutsukan et Nihon Keizai Shinbunsha, 2006.

Jakuchū Dōshoku sai-e shūri jigyō hōkokusho, Agence de la Maison impériale, 2009.

Johnson H., «Ito Jakuchu and his Innovative Approach in Painting», *Oriental Art,* vol. 46, 2000 n° 1, p. 28-34.

Kanō Hiroyuki, *Jakuchū! Tokubetsu tenrankai botsugo 200-nen,* Kyōto, Kokuritsu Hakubutsukan, 2000.

Kanō Hiroyuki, *Me o miharu Itō Jakuchū no Dōshoku sai-e,* Tōkyō, Shōgakukan, 2000.

Kanō Hiroyuki, *Itō Jakuchū taizen,* Tōkyō, Shōgakkan, 2002.

Kanō Hiroyuki, *Jakuchū to Rinpa: kirameku Nihon no bi, Hosomi bijutsukan korekushon yori,* cat. expo., Ōsaka, Namba Takashimaya (27 décembre 2003 - 12 janvier 2004), Tōkyō, Nihonbashi Takashimaya (28 janvier – 9 février 2004), Yokohama, Yokohama Takashimaya (26 février– 15 mars 2004), Tōkyō, Mainichi Shimbunsha, 2003.

Kanō Hiroyuki, *Jōkyōshū (Imperial river voyage),* Kyōto, Kokuritsu Hakubutsukan, 2005.

Kobayashi Tadashi, *Jakuchū Tokubetsu Tenkan Zuroku (Catalogue of the Special Exhibition of Jakuchū's Paintings),* Tōkyō, Tōkyō National Museum, 1971.

Kobayashi Tadashi, **Tsuji, Nobuo**, **Yamakawa Takeshi**, *Jakuchū, Shōhaku, Rosetsu,* Tōkyō, Kōdansha, 1977.

Kobayashi Tadashi, «Itō Jakuchū dokusō no ikkaku byōhō ni tsuite», *Museum,* n° 359, février 1981, p. 31-40.

Kobayashi Tadashi, **Nakamura Tanio**, «Yamagata de mitsukatta Jakuchū», *Geijustsu Shinchō* vol. 35, n° 3, 1984, p. 50-52.

Kobayashi Tadashi, «Itō Jakuchū hitsu Ishidōrō zu byōbu», *Kokka,* n° 1177, 1993.

Kobayashi Tadashi, «Itō Jakuchū: A Man Rejoicing in Painting», *Orientations,* vol.43, n° 3, avril 2012, p. 36-43.

Kobayashi Tadashi, *Jakuchū to Buson: seitan sanbyaku-nen o iwau (Jakuchū & Buson: Celebrating their 300th Birthdays),* Hakone, Okada Museum, 2016.

Kobayashi Tadashi, **Ōta Aya**, *Seitan sanbyaku-nen kinen: Jakuchū ten, The 300th Anniversary of his birth : Jakuchū,* cat. exp., Tōkyō, Tōkyō-to Bijutsukan (22 avril – 24 mai 2016), Tōkyō, Metropolitan Art Museum, 2016.

Kobayashi Tadashi, **Komiya Teruyuki**, **Yuasa Hiroshi**, *Jakuchū no egaita ikimonotachi,* Tōkyō, Kabushiki Kaisha Gakken Purasu, 2016.

Lachaud François, *Le vieil homme qui vendait du thé: excentricité et retrait du monde dans le Japon du* XVIII*e siècle*, Paris, Cerf, 2010.

Lippit Yukio, Ōta Aya, Oka Yasuhiro, Hayakawa Yasuhiro, *Colorful realm: Japanese Bird-and-Fower Paintings by Itō Jakuchū*, cat. exp., Washington, National Gallery of Art (30 mars – 29 avril 2012), Washington, National Gallery of Art, Chicago, University of Chicago Press, 2012.

Ōnishi Hiroshi, *On a Riverboat Journey. A handscroll by Ito Jakuchu with poems by Daiten*, New York, George Braziller, 1989.

Ōta Aya, *Itō Jakuchū Sakuhinshū*, Tōkyō, Tōkyō Bijutsu, 2015.

McKelway Matthew P., **Woodson Yoko**, **Rinne Melissa M.**, *Traditions Unbound : Groundbreaking Painters of Eighteenth-Century Kyōto*, San Francisco, Asian Art Museum-Chong-Moon Lee Center, 2005.

Morel Guillaume, **Bayou Hélène**, *Konpira-san, sanctuaire de la mer : trésors de la peinture japonaise*, cat. expo., Paris, Musée national des arts asiatiques Guimet (15 octobre – 8 décembre 2008), Paris, Société française de promotion artistique, 2008.

Moscatiello Manuela, *Itō Jakuchū – Les Fleurs précieuses du jardin mystérieux*, Arles, Éditions Philippe Picquier, 2015.

Murakami Chizuko, «Itō Jakuchū to iu ikikata sakuhin no bunseki to kyūdō no kōsatsu Dōshoku sai-e o chūshin ni zenshū bunseki shinrigaku no shiten kara» (Analysis of Itō Jakuchū's paintings and his way of life: from the perspective of Zen Buddhism and analytical psychology), *Bulletin de Kaichi International University*, n° 9, 2010, p. 3-19.

Murase Miyeko, *Japanese art: Selections from the Mary and Jackson Burke Collection*, New York, The Metropolitan Museum of Art, 1975.

Petrucci Raphaël, *Encyclopédie de la peinture chinoise*, Paris, Librairie You Feng, 2000.

Sanford James H., **La Fleu William R.**, **Nagatomi Masatoshi**, *Flowing Traces: Buddhism in the Literary and Visual Arts of Japan*, Princeton University Press, 2014.

Satō Yasuhiro, *Motto shiritai Itō Jakuchū: shōgai to sakuhin*, Tōkyō, Tōkyō Bijutsu, 2006.

Shimizu Yoshiaki, **Wheelwright Carolyn**, *Japanese ink paintings from American collections: the Muromachi period, an exhibition in honor of Shujiro Shimada*, Princeton, Princeton University Press, 1976.

Shimizu Yoshiaki, «Multiple Commemorations: The Vegetable Nehan of Ito Jakuchu», *Flowing Traces: Buddhism in the Literary and Visual Arts of Japan*, James H. Sandford (dir.), Princeton, Princeton University Press, 1992, p. 201-233.

Shirane Haruo, *Japan and the Culture of the Four Seasons: Nature, Literature, and the Arts*, New York, Columbia University Press, 2012.

Shōkokuji, pavillon d'Or, pavillon d'Argent: Art et zen à Kyōto, cat. exp., Paris, musée du Petit Palais (16 octobre – 14 décembre 2008), Paris, Paris Musées, 2008.

Takeuchi Melinda, «Birds of a Feather: Jakuchū, Natural Science and the Artistic Imagination», *Orientations*, vol. 43, n° 3, avril 2012, p. 52-61.

Tokuriki Tomikichirō, **Maekawa Fumio**, **Yamanouchi Chōzō**, *Jakuchū no takuhanga*, Tōkyō, Ruri Shobō, 1981.

Tsuji Nobuo, *Edo jidai no bijutsu: kaiga chōkoku kōgei kenchiku sho*, Tōkyō, Yuhikaku, 1984.

Tsuji Nobuo, *Jakuchū*, Tōkyō, Bijutsu Shuppan-Sha, 1974.

Tsuji Nobuo, *Jakuchū to Shōhaku*, Tōkyō, Iwanami Shoten, 2014.

Tsuji Nobuo, «Dōshoku sai-e wo chūshin to shite», *Museum*, n° 245, 1971.

Tsuji Nobuo, *Japanese Masterworks from the Price collection*, Washington, Arthur M. Sackler Gallery, 2007.

Tsuji Nobuo (dir), *Jakuchū wandārando, Jakuchū wonderland*, Shiga, Miho Museum, 2009.

Tsuji Nobuo, Kobayashi Tadashi, Kanō Hiroyuki, Ōta Aya, *Jakuchū wandafuru wârudo (Jakuchu wonderful world)*, Tōkyō, Shinchōsha, 2016.

Tsuji Nobuo, Kobayashi Tadashi, **Ōta Aya**, *Jakuchū ten: Shaka sannon zō to Dōshoku sai-e 120-nen buri no saikai kaiki Ashikaga Yoshimitsu roppyaku-nen ki kinen*, Tōkyō, Nihon Keizai Shinbunsha, 2007.

Twelve Centuries of Japanese art from the Imperial collections, Washington, Freer Gallery of Art and the Arthur M. Sackler Gallery, Smithsonian Institution Press, 1997.

Yonezawa Yoshiho, Yoshizawa Chū, *Japanese painting in the Literati Style*, New York, Weatherhill, Tōkyō, Heibonsha, 1974.

Yoshizawa Chū, *Nihon nanga ronkō*, Tōkyō, Kōdansha, 1977.

Remerciements de la Fondation du Japon, Nikkei Inc. et l'Agence de la Maison impériale du Japon :

Nous voudrions exprimer notre sincère gratitude à l'égard des organismes suivants pour leur coopération et leur généreux concours, ainsi qu'à toutes les personnes dont nous n'avons pas été en mesure de reproduire la liste, pour leur assistance, sous toutes les formes que ce soit, dans la préparation de cette exposition :

Fondation Hiraki Ukiyo-e
Fondation Tokugawa Memorial
Kotohira-gu, Kagawa
Metropolitan Museum of Art, New York
Musée Hosomi, Kyōto
Musée national de Kyōto
Musée national de Tōkyō
Musée de la ville de Kōbe
Musée de Kyōto
Musée Shōkoku-ji Jōtenkaku, Kyōto
Temple Sekihō-ji, Kyōto
Temple Shōkoku-ji, Kyōto
Temple Rokuon-ji, Kyōto

Raitei Arima
Tadashi Kobayashi
Joe et Etsuko Price
Nobuo Tsuji

Remerciements de Manuela Moscatiello :

Catherine Alassimone
Laurène Barbier
Alice Bianchi
Hélène Chollet
Sara Durt Nonaka
Anne Fort
Nathalie Frémaux
Éric Lefebvre
Clémence Le Moign
Yuki Maeki
Élodie Pascal
Michèle Pirazzoli-t'Serstevens
Yumi Kayano
Béatrice Robert-Boissier
Jade Shima Shimizu
Yuki Takehara
Yuki Uematsu

Ouvrage publié à l'occasion de l'exposition «Jakuchū, *Le Royaume coloré des êtres vivants*», présentée au Petit Palais, musée des Beaux-Arts de la Ville de Paris, Paris Musées, du 15 septembre au 14 octobre 2018, dans le cadre de «Japonismes 2018».

Cette exposition a été organisée conjointement par le Petit Palais, musée des Beaux-Arts de la Ville de Paris, Paris Musées, la Fondation du Japon, Nikkei Inc., l'Agence de la Maison impériale du Japon.

Avec le concours de Japan Airlines

Commissariat général :
Aya Ōta, conservateur en chef, musée des collections impériales (Sannomaru Shōzōkan)
Manuela Moscatiello, responsable des collections japonaises, musée Cernuschi – musée des Arts de l'Asie de la Ville de Paris

Comité d'honneur :
Anne Hidalgo
Maire de Paris

Bruno Julliard
Premier adjoint chargé de la Culture, du Patrimoine, des Métiers d'art, des Relations avec les arrondissements et de la Nuit, président de Paris Musées

Japonismes 2018
JAPANFOUNDATION
NIKKEI
Agence de la Maison impériale du Japon
JAPAN AIRLINES

PARIS MUSÉES

Delphine Lévy
Directrice générale

PETIT-PALAIS, MUSÉE DES BEAUX-ARTS DE LA VILLE DE PARIS

Christophe Leribault
Conservateur général, directeur

Simon Cnockaert
Secrétaire général

François Roussy
Secrétaire général adjoint et sécurité-bâtiment

Didier Pothin
Relai technique sécurité-bâtiment

Service des expositions

Susana Gállego Cuesta
Conservatrice, responsable du service

Charlotte Piot
Régisseuse scientifique, chargée de la conservation préventive

Agnès Faure
Assistante d'exposition

Service éducatif et culturel

Fabienne Cousin
Responsable du service

Catherine André
Chargée des projets pédagogiques et accessibilité

Communication et relations presse

Mathilde Beaujard
Responsable communication et presse

Monique Bouscasse
Chargée de communication

Partenariats et auditorium

Sophie Adelle
Responsable

Chloé Decrouy
Chargée de location d'espaces

EXPOSITION ET PUBLICATIONS

Olivier Donat
Directeur

Julie Bertrand
Directrice adjointe, chef du service des expositions

Julie Pierrat
Responsable de projet

Élise Blin
Chargée de production

Isabelle Jendron
Directrice des éditions

Marie-Brigitte Metteau
Responsable éditoriale

Amélie Segonds
Responsable iconographe

Saint-Véron Pompée
Chef de fabrication

Hideo Ikeda
Conception scénographiquc

Alexis Patras
Scénographe exécutif

Tania Hagemeister
Graphiste

Yasuhiro Oka
Restaurateur

Sarah Scouarnec
Éclairagiste

DÉVELOPPEMENT DES PUBLICS, DES PARTENARIATS ET DE LA COMMUNICATION

Josy Carrel-Torlet
Directrice

Philippe Rivière
Chef des services Communication et Numérique

Nina Garnier
Responsable de la communication, Adjointe au chef de service

Blandine Cottet
Responsable de communication, Partenariats et publicité

Andréa Longrais
Chargée des relations presse

Valeria Guerra
Chargée de communication

Ravith Trinh
Chargé de l'éditorialisation Web

Marine Baudry
Chargée de projet numérique

Kristel Fauconnet
Chargée de projet numérique

Scarlett Greco
Chargée de projet numérique

Nathalie Coulon
Chef du service Mécénat et des activités commerciales

Clémence le Mouël
Responsable du mécénat

Laura Mingam
Chargée de mécénat

Virginie Ribadeau-Dumas
Chargée de mécénat

Sophie Demont
Adjointe au chef de service du développement des publics

Anne Stephan
Chargée de projet médiation

ADMINISTRATION ET FINANCES

Solveig Mondy
Directrice

Samuel Taïeb
Responsable juridique et conseiller international

Jérôme Berrier
Chef du service achats/marchés

Christine Marchandise
Acheteur dans le domaine muséal, patrimonial et éditorial

Et l'ensemble des collaborateurs de Paris Musées

Éditions Paris Musées

Olivier Donat
Directeur des expositions et des publications

Julie Bertrand
Directrice adjointe, chef du service des expositions

Isabelle Jendron
Directrice des éditions

Responsable éditoriale
Marie-Brigitte Metteau

Graphisme
Catherine Barluet

Droits iconographiques
Amélie Segonds

Chef de fabrication
Saint-Véron Pompée

Relecture
Laurence Peydro – Livretlibre

Ouvrage composé en Velino

Papier
Symbol Freelife Satin en 170 g,
Arcoset en 140 g,
Stucco Old Mill pour la couverture

Photogravure
Graphium, Paris

Musées de la Ville de Paris
27, rue des Petits-Écuries
75010 Paris
www.parismusees-paris.fr

Diffusion Flammarion
Distribution UD-Union Distribution
ISBN : 978-2-7596-0396-1
Dépôt légal, septembre 2018

Achevé d'imprimer sur les presses
de Technostampa, Italie, septembre 2018